Fernando Pessoa was born in Lisbon in 1888. He spent most of his life there but, after his father's death, he lived in South Africa for nine years when his mother married the Portuguese consul in Durban. In those years he became fluent in English and developed a love for English writers such as Shakespeare and Milton. This influenced him to write his first collections of poems and journals in English, while his first book in Portuguese was published just two years before his death.

On leaving South Africa he returned to Lisbon, where he became involved in the modernist group 'Orpheu' and had a major role in the development of modernism in Portugal. During his life he was virtually unknown, avoiding society and the literary world, and although he wrote a vast amount, most of it was published posthumously. After his death in Lisbon in 1935, a trunk was found containing over 25,000 items – among them were collections of poems, letters and journals, from which *The Book of Disquiet* is a selection.

Praise for *The Book of Disquiet*

'It could not have been written in England: there is too much thought racing hopelessly around. The elegance of the style, well conveyed in what seems to be a more than adequate translation, is an important component and a very ironic one. The diary disturbs from beginning to end... There is a distinguished mind at work beneath the totally acceptable dullness of clerking. The mind is that of Pessoa. We must be given the chance to learn more about him' Anthony Burgess, *Observer*

'Pessoa's near-novel is a complete masterpiece, the sort of book one makes friends with and cannot bear to be parted with. Boredom informs it, but not boringly. Pessoa loved the minutiae of what we care to deem the ordinary life, and that love enriches and deepens his art' Paul Bailey, *Independent*

'The very book to read when you wake at 3am and can't get back to sleep – mysteries, misgivings, fears and dreams and wonderment. Like nothing else' Philip Pullman

'It was a real bonus when Serpent's Tail published *The Book of Disquiet*, a meandering, melancholic series of reveries and meditations. Pessoa's amazing personality is as beguiling and mysterious as his unique poetic output. We cannot learn too much about him' William Boyd, *TLS Books of the Year*

'In a time that celebrates fame, success, stupidity, convenience and noise, here is the perfect antidote' John Lanchester, *Daily Telegraph*

'[A] classic of existential literature' Emma Tennant, *Independent on Sunday*

'Many British reviewers have pegged Pessoa as a great long-lost modernist, but he also calls up echoes of Beckett's exquisite boredom; the dark imaginings of Baudelaire; Melville's evasive confidence man; the dreamscapes of Borges; even the cranky hermeticism of Witold Gombrowicz' *Village Voice*

'This is an astonishing novel, one which batters you, pierces you, awakens and numbs you' *Independent on Sunday*

'This book has moved me more than anything I have read in years. I have rarely encountered such exhilarating lugubriousness' *Daily Telegraph*

'Portugal's greatest poet' *The Times*

'A haunting mosaic of dreams, psychological notations, autobiographical vignettes, shards of literary theory and criticism and maxims' George Steiner, *Observer*

The BOOK of DIS~QUIET

Fernando Pessoa

Edited by Maria José de Lancastre

Translated by Margaret Jull Costa

Introduction by William Boyd

A complete catalogue record for this book can be obtained from the
British Library on request

The right of Fernando Pessoa to be identified as the author of this
work has been asserted in accordance with the Copyright, Designs and
Patents Act 1988

First published as *Livro do desassossego por Bernardo Soares*

This edition follows the selection made by Maria José de Lancastre for
the Italian edition published by Feltrinelli.

First published in 1991 by Serpent's Tail,
an imprint of Profile Books Ltd
3A Exmouth House
Pine Street
London EC1R 0JH
website: www.serpentstail.com

First published in this edition in 2010

ISBN 978 1 84668 735 8

Printed and bound by CPI Group (UK) Ltd, Croydon, CR0 4YY

Introduction

O homem nâo é um animal
É uma carne inteligente
Embora às vezes doente.

[*Man is not an animal*
Is intelligent flesh
Although sometimes ill.]

Something of the baffling, beguiling, disturbing appeal of Fernando Pessoa is contained in these three lines of poetry taken from a short poem he wrote in 1935, the year of his death, called 'Love is the Essential'. Pessoa was obsessed by the schism between our 'concrete' and our 'abstract' natures – summed up here in the concept of *carne inteligente*. Sometimes he wished he were a simple unreflecting animal, untroubled by self-consciousness, but he saw in our uniquely human ability to reflect on and analyse ourselves the source of all our pleasures in life (he described sunsets as 'an intellectual experience') – and its pain. Hence the wry rejoinder – 'although sometimes ill' – a very Pessoa-esque note to strike. The comedic aspects of our short, troubled existences also entertained him. The hilarious absurdity of the human predicament was as obvious to him as its inherent, melancholy pointlessness.

Fernando Pessoa (1888–1935) is one of the great figures of 20th-century European modernism. The most exotic portion of his life occurred in his youth. At the age of seven he left Lisbon for Durban, South Africa, where he lived with his mother and step-father until he was seventeen. This sojourn provoked in him an enduring anglophilia (his first poems were in English) and a sense of being a permanent outsider. It is perhaps helpful to see him as a Portuguese cross between Franz Kafka and TS Eliot – a maverick, unclassifiable spirit wrapped up in a carapace of petit-bourgeois conformity. Like Kafka (insurance) and Eliot (banking), Pessoa earned his living on his return from South Africa in a humdrum professional world. He became a commercial translator, writing business letters in English and French for Portuguese companies. In the many photographs we have of him in his adult life he looks the perfect dry functionary: moustachioed, dapper, always with a hat and a tie – *l'homme moyen sensual* – as if the rectitude and tedium of his daily job were in some way necessary to curb the teeming, abundant life of the mind within.

Intriguingly, Pessoa's literary fame is entirely posthumous. During his life he was a very minor figure on the fringes of the Lisbon artistic and intellectual scene, an obscure footnote in the annals of 20th-century Portuguese poetry. He published hardly anything and it was only the discovery of a vast trunk of manuscripts after his death that has provided us with the copious poetry and other prose writings – of which *The Book of Disquiet* is by far the major element.

What makes Pessoa extraordinary in a modernist–literary sense is his invention of what he called 'heteronyms'. Pessoa published poems under his own name but also under the names of other identities. Possessing a disguise far more complex than mere pseudonyms, these heteronym-poets had styles, biographies and personalities of their own, as if they really were distinct individuals who were born, lived and died apart from their creator. There are seventy-two distinct heteronyms in the Pessoa oeuvre but four predominate: the poets Alberto Caiero, Ricardo Reis, and Alvaro de Campos and the author of *The Book of Disquiet*, Bernardo Soares.

Pessoa regarded Soares as the closest to himself – a minor clerk whiling away his life in rented rooms – describing him as a 'mutilation of my personality'. The Soares heteronym evolved earlier and lasted far longer than any of the others and his life's work – the fragmented journal and collection of philosophical musings that make up *The Book of Disquiet* – was both incomplete and unorganised when Pessoa died in 1935 (of hepatitis, in fact:

Pessoa was also a dedicated but discreet alcoholic). Indeed, the form that the published book takes is something of an estimation – so random and confused were Pessoa's plans for the finished volume. But, fittingly, the mystery and disorder of the jottings and pages somehow suit the book's tone and atmosphere. Pessoa has been described by Octavio Paz as a 'solemn investigator of futile things', the epitome of an empty man who, in his helplessness, creates a world in order to discover his true identity. It's in this spirit that we should read *The Book of Disquiet*, not only to locate the echo of our own disquiet about our life and the world we occupy, but also to go on a mesmerizing journey with one of the most fascinating minds in European literature.

Translator's note

The *Book of Disquiet* (*Livro do desassossego*) is the most extensive prose work written by Portugal's greatest poet, Fernando Pessoa. He was engaged in writing it, always in fragmentary form, from 1912 until his death in 1935, although the first complete Portuguese edition only appeared in 1982. As well as writing under his own name, Pessoa created a number of 'heteronyms', imaginary authors to whom he gave complete biographies and who wrote in styles and expressed philosophies and attitudes different from his own. Pessoa attributed the authorship of *The Book of Disquiet* to Bernardo Soares, who was, he said only 'a semi-heteronym because, although his personality is not mine, it is not different from but rather a simple mutilation of my personality. It's me minus reason and affectivity.'

Very little of this 'intimate diary' was published in his lifetime. The book itself was handwritten in notebooks or typed on frequently undated and undatable sheets of paper. The work of deciphering and collating all this material was carried out by Maria Aliete Galhoz, Teresa Sobral Cunha and Jacinto do Prado Coelho. This translation is based on the thematic selection edited by Maria José de Lancastre, a leading Pessoa scholar. The numbers given in parentheses at the beginning of each text refer to the numbering of the original 1982 edition published in Lisbon by Ática. [. . .] indicates that words or phrases in the original are either illegible or missing.

The translator would like to thank Pete Ayrton, Annella McDermott, Faye Carney and Martin Jenkins for all their help and advice.

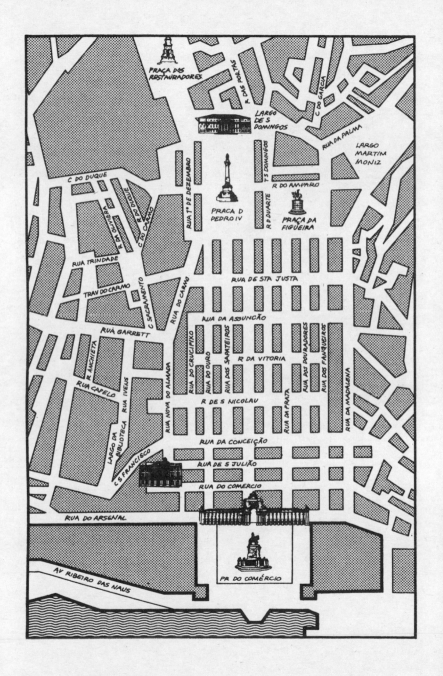

Introduction

Bernardo Soares

Installed on the upper floors of certain respectable taverns in Lisbon can be found a small number of restaurants or eating places, which have the stolid, homely look of those restaurants you see in towns that lack even a train station. Amongst the clientele of such places, which are rarely busy except on Sundays, one is as likely to encounter the eccentric as the nondescript, to find people who are but a series of parentheses in the book of life.

There was a period in my life when a combination of economic necessity and a desire for peace and quiet led me to frequent just such a restaurant. I would dine at around seven each night and, as chance would have it, I was almost always there at the same time as one particular man. At first I took little notice of him but as time passed he came to interest me.

He was a man in his thirties, thin, fairly tall, very hunched when sitting though less so when standing, and dressed with a not entirely unselfconscious negligence. Not even the suffering apparent in his pale, unremarkable features added any interest to them nor was it easy to pinpoint the origin of that suffering. It could have been any number of things: hardship, grief or simply the suffering born of the indifference that comes from having suffered too much.

He always ate sparingly and afterwards would smoke a cigarette rolled from cheap tobacco. He would watch the other customers, not suspiciously, but as if genuinely interested in them. He did not scrutinize them as though wanting to fix their faces or any outward evidence of their personalities in his memory, rather he was simply intrigued by them. And it was this odd trait of his that first aroused my curiosity.

I began to observe him more closely. I noticed that a certain hesitant intelligence illuminated his features, but his face was so often clouded by exhaustion, by the inertia of cold fear, that it was usually hard to see beyond this.

I learned from a waiter at the restaurant that he worked as a clerk in a company that had its office nearby.

One day there was a scuffle in the street immediately outside the restaurant – a fight between two men. The customers all rushed to the windows, as did I and the man I've been describing. I made some banal comment to him and he replied in kind. His voice was dull and tremulous, the voice of one who hopes for nothing because all hope is vain. But perhaps it was foolish of me to attribute so much to my evening companion at the restaurant.

I don't quite know why but after that we always used to greet each other. And then one day; prompted perhaps by the foolish coincidence of us both turning up for supper later than usual, at half past nine, we struck up a casual conversation. At one point he asked me if I was a writer. I said I was. I mentioned the magazine *Orpheu**, which had recently come out. To my surprise he praised it, indeed praised it highly. When I voiced my surprise, saying that the art of those who wrote for *Orpheu* tended to appeal only to a small minority, he replied that maybe he was one of that minority. Anyway, he added, he was not entirely unfamiliar with that art for, he remarked timidly, since he had nowhere to go and nothing to do, no friends to visit and no interest in reading books, after supper he usually returned to his rented room and passed the night writing.

Fernanda Pessoa

---

* The literary magazine *Orpheu* was formed in 1915 by Femando Pessoa, Mário Sá de Carneiro and Luis de Montalvor. Although only two issues were produced the magazine had a considerable impact on the evolution of modern Portuguese literature.

1 [90]

Sometimes I think I will never leave Rua dos Douradores. Once written down, that seems to me like eternity.

2 [124]

The journey in my head

In the plausible intimacy of approaching evening, as I stand waiting for the stars to begin at the window of this fourth floor room that looks out on the infinite, my dreams move to the rhythm required by long journeys to countries as yet unknown, or to countries that are simply hypothetical or impossible.

3 [81]

Today, during one of those periods of daydreaming which, though devoid of either purpose or dignity, still constitute the greater part of the spiritual substance of my life, I imagined myself free forever of Rua dos Douradores, of my boss Vasques, of Moreira the book-keeper, of all the other employees, the errand boy, the post boy, even the cat. In dreams, that freedom felt to me as if the South Seas had proffered up a gift of marvellous islands as yet undiscovered. Freedom would mean rest, artistic achievement, the intellectual fulfilment of my being.

But suddenly, even as I imagined this (during the brief holiday afforded by my lunch break), a feeling of displeasure erupted into the dream: I would be sad. Yes, I say it quite seriously: I would be sad. For my boss Vasques, Moreira the book-keeper, Borges the cashier, all the lads, the cheery boy who takes the letters to the post office, the errand boy, the friendly cat – they have all become part of my life. I could never leave all that behind without weeping, without realizing, however displeasing the thought, that part of me would remain with them and that losing them would be akin to death.

Moreover, if I left them all tomorrow and discarded this Rua dos Douradores suit of clothes I wear, what else would I do? Because I would have to do something. And what suit would I wear? Because I would have to wear another suit.

We all have a Senhor Vasques; sometimes he's a tangible human being, sometimes not. In my case he really is called Vasques and he's a pleasant, healthy chap, a bit brusque at times but he's no doubledealer. He's selfish but basically fair, much fairer than many of the great geniuses and many of the human marvels of civilization on both left and right. For many people Vasques takes the form of vanity, a desire for greater wealth, for glory or immortality . . . Personally I prefer to have Vasques as my real life boss since, in times of difficulty, he's easier to deal with than any abstraction the world has to offer.

The other day a friend, who's a partner in a prosperous company that does business throughout the country and who considers my salary to be distinctly on the low side, said to me: 'You're being exploited, Soares.' This made me realize that indeed I am; but since it's the fate of everyone in this life to be exploited, my question would be: is it any worse being exploited by Senhor Vasques and his textile company than by vanity, glory, resentment, envy or the impossible?

Some, the prophets and saints who walk this vacuous world, are exploited by God himself.

And I return to an other's house, to the spacious office in the Rua dos Douradores, the way some return to their homes. I approach my desk as if it were a bulwark against life. I feel such an overwhelming sense of tenderness that my eyes fill with tears for my books that are in reality the books of other people whose accounts I keep, for the inkwell I use, for Sergio's stooped shoulders as, not far from me, he sits writing out bills of lading. I feel love for all this, perhaps because I have nothing else to love or perhaps too, because even though nothing truly merits the love of any soul, if, out of sentiment, we must give it, I might just as well lavish it on the smallness of an inkwell as on the grand indifference of the stars.

4 [114]

With the soul's equivalent of a wry smile, I calmly confront the prospect that my life will consist of nothing more than being shut up for ever in Rua dos Douradores, in this office, surrounded by these people. I have enough money to buy food and drink, I have somewhere to live and enough free time in which to dream, write – and sleep – what more can I ask of the gods or hope for from Fate?

I had great ambitions and extravagant dreams, but so did the errand boy and the seamstress, for everyone has dreams; the only difference is whether or not we have the strength to fulfil them or a destiny that will fulfil them through us.

When it comes to dreams, I'm no different from the errand boy and the seamstress. The only thing that distinguishes me from them is that I can write. Yes, that's an activity, a real fact about myself that distinguishes me from them. But in my soul I'm just the same.

I know that there are islands in the South and grand cosmopolitan passions and [...]. I'm sure that even if I held the world in my hand, I'd exchange it all for a tram ticket back to Rua dos Douradores.

Perhaps it's my destiny to remain a book-keeper for ever and for poetry and literature to remain simply butterflies that alight on my head and merely underline my own ridiculousness by their very beauty.

I'll miss Moreira, but what does missing someone matter compared with a chance for real promotion?

I know that the day I'm made chief book-keeper to Vasques & Co. will be one of the greatest days of my life. I know it with a prescient bitterness and irony but I know it with all the finality that certainty can bring.

5 [91]

Senhor Vasques. I often find myself mesmerized by Senhor Vasques. What does this man represent to me beyond the chance inconvenience of his being master of my time, of the daylight hours of my life? He treats me well, he always talks to me in a friendly enough manner except on the odd occasion when he's been offhand because of some private worry, but then he was offhand with everyone. So why do I think about him so much? Is he a symbol? A motive force? What is he to me?

Senhor Vasques. I remember him now as I will in the future with the nostalgia I know I will feel for him then. I'll be living quietly in a little house somewhere in the suburbs, enjoying a peaceful existence not writing the book I'm not writing now and, so as to continue not doing so, I will come up with different excuses from the ones I use now to avoid actually confronting myself. Or else I'll be interned in a poorhouse, content with my utter failure, mingling with the riffraff who believed they were geniuses when in fact they were just beggars with dreams, mixing with the anonymous mass of people who had neither the strength to triumph nor the power to turn their defeats into victories. Wherever I am, I will think nostalgically of my boss Senhor Vasques and the office in Rua dos Douradores, and for me the monotony of my daily life will be like the memory of loves that never came my way and of triumphs that were never to be mine.

Senhor Vasques. I see him from that future perspective as clearly as I see him here today: medium height, thickset, coarse, with his particular limitations and affections, frank and astute, brusque and affable. It isn't only money that marks him out as a boss, you can see it in his slow, hairy hands marked by plump veins like coloured

4

muscles, his neck, strong but not too thick, and his firm, rosy cheeks above the dark, neatly trimmed beard. I see him, see the deliberate but energetic gestures, his eyes reflecting from within his thoughts about the world without. I'm troubled if I displease him and my soul is gladdened by his smile, a broad, human smile, warm as the applause of a large crowd.

Perhaps the reason the ordinary, almost vulgar figure of Senhor Vasques so often tangles with my intelligence and distracts me from myself is simply because there's no one else in my life of greater stature. I think there's some symbolism in all this. I believe, or almost believe, that somewhere in a distant life this man was something more to me than he is today.

6 [155]

Ah, now I understand! Senhor Vasques is Life; Life, monotonous and necessary, commanding and unknowable. This banal man represents the banality of life. On the surface he is everything to me, just as, on the surface, Life is everything to me.

And if the office in the Rua dos Douradores represents Life for me, the second floor room I live in on that same street represents Art. Yes, Art, living on the same street as Life but in a different room; Art, which offers relief from life without actually relieving one of living, and which is as monotonous as life itself but in a different way. Yes, for me Rua dos Douradores embraces the meaning of all things, the resolution of all mysteries, except the existence of mysteries themselves which is something beyond resolution.

7 [63]

I went into the barber's as I usually do, experiencing the pleasure I always get from being able to enter places known to me without suffering the least distress. My sensitivity to all things new is a

5

constant affliction to me; I only feel safe in places I have been in before.

When I sat down in the chair and the young barber placed a clean, cold linen towel around my neck, it occurred to me to ask after his colleague, a vigorous, older man, who had been ill but who usually worked at the chair to my right. The question arose spontaneously, simply because the place reminded me of him. As fingers busied themselves tucking in the last bit of towel between my neck and my collar, the voice behind the towel and me answered flatly: 'He died yesterday.' My irrational good humour died as suddenly as the now eternally absent barber from the chair beside me. My every thought froze. I said nothing.

Nostalgia! I feel it even for someone who meant nothing to me, out of anxiety for the flight of time and a sickness bred of the mystery of life. If one of the faces I pass daily on the streets disappears, I feel sad; yet they meant nothing to me, other than being a symbol of all life.

The dull old man with dirty gaiters I often used to pass at half past nine in the morning. The lame lottery salesman who pestered me without success. The plump, rosy old gentleman with the cigar, who used to stand at the door of the tobacconist's. The pale-cheeked tobacconist himself. What has become of those people who, just because I saw them day after day, became part of my life? Tomorrow I too will disappear from Rua da Prata, Rua dos Douradores, Rua dos Fanqueiros. Tomorrow I too – this feeling and thinking soul, the universe I am to myself – yes, tomorrow I too will be someone who no longer walks these streets, someone others will evoke with a vague: 'I wonder what's become of him?' And everything I do, everything I feel, everything I experience, will be just one less passer-by on the daily streets of some city or other.

8 [153]   *25.4.1930*

The sleeping partner of the company, a man much troubled by obscure ailments, was suddenly taken with the notion (a caprice that came on him, it seems, between afflictions) that he wanted to have a group photograph taken of the office staff. So, the day before yesterday, following the instructions of the jolly photographer, we all lined up against the grubby white partition that serves as a rickety wooden division between the general office and Senhor Vasques's office. In the centre stood Vasques himself; on either side of him, according to a hierarchy that began logically enough but rapidly broke down, stood the other men who gather here each day, in body, to perform the small tasks, the ultimate aim of which is a secret known only to the gods.

Today, when I arrived at the office, a little late and having in fact completely forgotten about the frozen moment captured twice by the photographer, I found Moreira, an unexpectedly early bird, and one of the clerks poring over some blackish objects that I recognized with a start as being the first prints of the photographs. They were, in fact, two copies of the same photograph, the one that had come out best.

I experienced the pain of truth when I saw myself there, because, inevitably, it was my face I looked for first. I have never had a very high opinion of my physical appearance but never before have I felt such a nonentity as I did then, comparing myself with the other faces, so familiar to me, in that line-up of my daily companions. I look like a rather dull Jesuit. My thin, inexpressive face betrays no intelligence, no intensity, nothing whatever to make it stand out from the stagnant tide of the other faces. But they're not a stagnant tide. There are some really expressive faces there. Senhor Vasques is exactly as he is in real life – the firm, likable face, the steady gaze, all set off by the stiff moustache. The energy and intelligence of the man – qualities which are after all utterly banal and to be found in thousands of other men all over the world – are stamped on that photograph as if it were a psychological passport. The two travelling salesmen look superb; the clerk has come out well but he's half hidden behind Moreira. And Moreira! My immediate superior Moreira, the embodiment of monotony and routine, looks much more human than I do! Even the errand boy – I detect in myself, without being able to suppress it, a feeling that I hope is not envy — has a directness in his smile that far outshines the insignificant dullness of my face, of me, the sphinx of the stationery cupboard.

What does all this mean? Is it true that the camera never lies? What is this truth documented by a cold lens? Who am I that I possess such a face? Honestly... And then to add insult to injury... Moreira suddenly said to me: 'It's a really good one of you.' And then, turning to the clerk, 'It's the absolute image of him, isn't it?' The clerk's happy and companionable agreement signalled my final relegation to the rubbish heap.

9 [27]

My soul is a hidden orchestra; I know not what instruments, what fiddlestrings and harps, drums and tambours I sound and clash inside myself. All I hear is the symphony.

10 [28]   *1.12.1931*

Today, suddenly, I reached an absurd but unerring conclusion. In a moment of enlightenment, I realized that I'm nobody, absolutely nobody. When the lightning flashed, I saw that what I had thought to be a city was in fact a deserted plain and, in the same sinister light that revealed me to myself, there seemed to be no sky above it. I was robbed of any possibility of having existed before the world. If I was ever reincarnated, I must have done so without myself, without a self to reincarnate.

I am the outskirts of some non-existent town, the long-winded prologue to an unwritten book. I'm nobody, nobody. I don't know how to feel or think or love. I'm a character in a novel as yet unwritten, hovering in the air and undone before I've even existed, amongst the dreams of someone who never quite managed to breathe life into me.

I'm always thinking, always feeling, but my thoughts lack all reason, my emotions all feeling. I'm falling through a trapdoor, through infinite, infinitous* space, in a directionless, empty fall. My soul is a black maelstrom, a great madness spinning about a vacuum, the swirling of a vast ocean around a hole in the void, and in the waters, more like whirlwinds than waters, float images of all I ever saw or heard in the world: houses, faces, books, boxes, snatches of music and fragments of voices, all caught up in a sinister, bottomless whirlpool.

And I, I myself, am the centre that exists only because the geometry of the abyss demands it; I am the nothing around which all this spins, I exist so that it can spin, I am a centre that exists only because every circle has one. I, I myself, am the well in which the walls have fallen away to leave only viscous slime. I am the centre of everything surrounded by the great nothing.

And it is as if hell itself were laughing within me but, instead of the human touch of diabolical laughter, there's the mad croak of the dead universe, the circling cadaver of physical space, the end of all worlds drifting blackly in the wind, misshapen, anachronistic, without the God who created it, without God himself who spins in the dark of darks, impossible, unique, everything.

If only I could think! If only I could feel!

My mother died very young; I never knew her...

11 [29]

Give to each emotion a personality, to each state of mind a soul.

12 [67]   *20.6.1931*

Today is one of those days when the monotony of everything closes about me as if I had just entered a prison. That monotony,

---

*Pessoa uses a neologism 'infinitupla'.

however, is just the monotony of being me. Each face, even if it belongs to someone we saw only yesterday, is different today simply because today is not yesterday. Each day is the day it is, and there will never be another like it in the world. Only in the soul is there the absolute identity (albeit a false identity) in which everything resembles everything else and everything is simplified. The world is made up of promontories and peaks but all our myopic vision allows us to see is a thin all-pervading mist.

I'd like to run away, to flee from what I know, from what is mine, from what I love. I want to set off, not for some impossible Indies or for the great islands that lie far to the south of all other lands, but for anywhere, be it village or desert, that has the virtue of not being here. What I want is not to see these faces, this daily round of days. I want a rest from, to be other than, my habitual pretending. I want to feel the approach of sleep as if it were a promise of life, not rest. A hut by the sea, even a cave on a rugged mountain ledge, would be enough. Unfortunately, my will alone cannot give me that.

Slavery is the only law of life, there is no other, because this law must be obeyed; there is no possible rebellion against it or refuge from it. Some are born slaves, some become slaves, some have slavery thrust upon them. The cowardly love we all have of freedom – which if it were given to us we would all repudiate as being too new and strange — is the irrefutable proof of how our slavery weighs upon us. Even I, who have just expressed my desire to have a hut or a cave where I could be free from the monotony of everything, that is to say from the monotony of being myself, would I really dare to go off to this hut or cave, knowing and understanding that, since the monotony exists in me alone, I would never be free of it? Suffocating where I am and because I am where I am, would I breathe any better there when it is my lungs that are diseased and not the air about me? Who is to say that I, longing out loud for the pure sun and the open fields, for the bright sea and the wide horizon, would not miss my bed, or my meals, or having to go down eight flights of stairs to the street, or dropping in at the tobacconist's on the corner, or saying good morning to the barber standing idly by?

Everything that surrounds us becomes part of us, it seeps into us with every experience of the flesh and of life and, like the web of the great Spider, binds us subtly to what is near, ensnares us in a fragile cradle of slow death, where we lie rocking in the wind. Everything is us and we are everything, but what is the point if everything is nothing? A ray of sun, a cloud whose own sudden shadow warns of its coming, a breeze getting up, the silence that follows when it drops, certain faces, some voices, the easy smiles as they talk, and then the night into which emerge, meaningless, the broken hieroglyphs of the stars.

13 [133]

I often wonder what kind of person I would be if I had been protected from the cold wind of fate by the screen of wealth, and my uncle's moral hand had never led me to an office in Lisbon, and I had never moved on from there to other offices to reach the tawdry heights of being a good assistant book-keeper in a job that is about as demanding as an afternoon nap and offers a salary that gives me just enough to live on.

I know that had that non-existent past existed, I would not now be capable of writing these pages, which, though few, are at least better than all the pages I would undoubtedly have only day-dreamed about given more comfortable circumstances. For banality is a form of intelligence, and reality, especially if it is brutish and rough, forms a natural complement to the soul.

Much of what I feel and think I owe to my work as a book-keeper since the former exists as a negation of and flight from the latter.

If I had to fill in the space provided on a questionnaire to list one's formative literary influences, on the first dotted line I would write the name of Cesário Verde*, but the list would be

---

*Cesário Verde (1855–1886) was one of the forerunners of modern Portuguese poetry who worked most of his life as a clerk. Pessoa felt a deep affinity with his poetry and shared his love of Lisbon.

incomplete without the names of Senhor Vasques, Moreira the book-keeper, Vieira the cashier and Antonio the office boy. And after each of them I would write in capital letters the key word: LISBON.

In fact, they were all as important as Cesário Verde in providing corrective coefficients for my vision of the world. I think 'corrective coefficients' is the term (though, of course, I'm unsure of its exact meaning) that engineers use of a methodology that applies mathematics to life. If it is the term, that's what they were to me. If it isn't, let it stand for what might have been, and my intention serve in place of a failed metaphor.

When I consider, with all the clarity I can muster, what my life has apparently been, I imagine it as some brightly coloured scrap of litter – a chocolate wrapper or a cigar ring – that the eavesdropping waitress brushes lightly from the soiled tablecloth into the dustpan, amongst the crumbs and crusts of reality itself. It stands out from those things whose fate it shares by virtue of a privilege that is also destined for the dustpan. The gods continue their conversations above the sweeping, indifferent to these incidents in the world below.

Yes, if I had been rich, cosseted, carefully groomed and ornamental, I would never have known that brief moment as a pretty piece of paper amongst the breadcrumbs; I would have been left on one of fortune's trays – 'Not for me, thank you' – and returned to the sideboard to grow old and stale. Discarded once I have served my purpose, I am thus relegated to the rubbish bin, along with the crumbs of what remains of Christ's body, unable even to imagine what will come after, under what stars; but I know there will be an 'after'.

14 [118]

I've come to the realization that I'm always thinking and listening to two things at once. I expect everyone does that a little. Some impressions are so vague that only when we remember them afterwards are we aware of them at all. I think these impressions form a part (the internal part, perhaps) of this double attention we all pay to things. In my case the two realities I attend to have equal weight. In that lies my originality. In that, perhaps, lie both my tragedy and the comedy of my tragedy.

I write carefully, bent over the book in which I measure out in balance sheets the futile history of an obscure company and, at the same time and with equal attention, my thoughts follow the route of an imaginary ship through oriental landscapes that have never existed. The two things are equally clear, equally visible to me: the ruled page on which I meticulously write the lines of the epic commercial poem that is Vasques & Co. and the deck where, a little to one side of the lines made by the tarred spaces between the planks, I watch intently the rows of deckchairs and the stretched-out legs of people relaxing on the voyage.

(If I were knocked down by a child's bicycle, that bicycle would become part of my story.)

The smoking room protrudes on to the deck, preventing me from seeing anything more than their legs.

I reach for the inkwell with my pen and from the door of the smoking room – [. . .] right where I feel myself to be standing – emerges the figure of the stranger. He turns his back on me and goes over to the others. He walks slowly and I can deduce nothing from his back [. . .]. I begin another entry in the accounts book. I try to see where I went wrong. Marques's accounts should be debited not credited (I imagine him: plump, amiable, full of jokes and, in an instant, the ship has vanished).

15 [20]   *30.12.1932*

After the last of the rain had fallen from the sky and come to earth – leaving the sky clear and the earth damp and gleaming – the world below grew joyful in the cool left by the rain, and the greater clarity of life that returned with the blue of the heavens furnished each soul with its own sky, each heart with a new freshness.

Whether we like it or not, we are slaves to the hour in all its forms and colours, we are the subjects of heaven and earth. The part of us that despises its surroundings and plunges deepest into the forests within us does not take the same paths when it rains as when the sky is clear. Simply because it's raining or has stopped raining, obscure transmutations take place, felt only perhaps in the very heart of our most abstract feelings; we feel these transmutations without knowing it because we feel the weather even when we are unaware that we do.

Each of us is more than one person, many people, a proliferation of our one self. That's why the same person who scorns his surroundings is different from the person who is gladdened or made to suffer by them. In the vast colony of our being there are many different kinds of people, all thinking and feeling differently. Today, as I note down these few impressions in a legitimate break brought about by a shortage of work, I am the person carefully transcribing them, the person who is pleased not to have to work just now, the person who looks at the sky even though he can't actually see it from here, the person who is thinking all this, and the person feeling physically at ease and noticing that his hands are still slightly cold. And, like a diverse but compact multitude, this whole world of mine, composed as it is of different people, projects but a single shadow, that of this calm figure who writes, leaning against Borges's high desk where I have come to find the blotter he borrowed from me.

16 [74]

[...] ships that pass in the night and neither acknowledge nor recognize one another [...]

17 [96]

As with all tragedies, the real tragedy of my life is just an irony of

Fate. I reject life because it is a prison sentence, I reject dreams as being a vulgar form of escape. Yet I live the most sordid and ordinary of real lives and the most intense and constant of dream lives. I'm like a slave who gets drunk during his rest hour – two miseries inhabiting one body.

With the clarity afforded by the lightning flashes of reason that pick out from the thick blackness of life the immediate objects it is composed of, I see with utter lucidity all that is base, flaccid, neglected and factitious in this Rua dos Douradores that makes up my entire life: the squalid office whose squalor seeps into the very marrow of its inhabitants' bones, the room, rented by the month, in which nothing happens except the living death of its occupant, the grocer's shop on the corner whose owner I know only in the casual way people do know each other, the boys standing at the door of the old tavern, the laborious futility of each identical day, the same characters constantly rehearsing their roles, like a drama consisting only of scenery and in which even that scenery is facing the wrong way . . .

But I also see that in order to flee from all this I must either master it or repudiate it. I do not master it because I cannot rise above reality and I do not repudiate it because, whatever I may dream, I always remain exactly where I am.

And what of my dreams? That shameful flight into myself, the cowardice of mistaking for life the rubbish tip of a soul that others only visit in their sleep, in that semblance of death through which they snore, in that calm state in which, more than anything, they look like highly evolved vegetables! Unable to make a single noble gesture other than to myself, or to have one vain desire that was not utterly vain!

Caesar gave the ultimate definition of ambition when he said: 'Better to be the chief of a village than a subaltern in Rome'. I enjoy no such position either in a village or in Rome. At least the grocer merits some respect on the block between Rua da Assumpção and Rua da Victoria; he's the Caesar of the whole block. Am I superior to him? In what respect when nothingness confers no superiority, no inferiority, and permits no comparisons?

The grocer is the Caesar of a whole block and the women, quite rightly, adore him.

And so I drag myself along, doing things I don't want to do and dreaming of what I cannot have [. . .] as pointless as a public clock that's stopped. . .

18 [107]

In the first few days of this sudden autumn, when the darkness seems in some way premature, it feels as if we have lingered too long over our daily tasks and, even in the midst of the daily round, I savour in advance the pleasure of not working that the darkness brings with it, for darkness means night and night means sleep, home, freedom. When the lights go on in the big office, banishing the darkness, and we move seamlessly from day to evening shift, I am assailed by an absurd sense of comfort, like the memory of another, and I feel as contented with what I write as if I were sitting reading myself to sleep in bed.

We are all of us the slaves of external circumstance: even at a table in some backstreet café, a sunny day can open up before us visions of wide fields; a shadow over the countryside can cause us to shrink inside ourselves, seeking uneasy shelter in the doorless house that is our self; and, even in the midst of daytime things, the arrival of darkness can open out, like a slowly spreading fan, a deep awareness of our need for rest.

But we don't get behind in our work because of this, rather it cheers us on. We're not working any more; we're enjoying ourselves performing the task to which we are condemned. And suddenly, there on the vast ruled sheet of my book-keeper's destiny, stands my old aunts' house, quite shut off from the world, where the tea is still brought in at the sleepy hour of ten o'clock, and the oil lamp of my lost childhood, its pool of light illuminating only the tablecloth, plunges into darkness my vision of Moreira, infinitely far from me, lit now by a black electricity. Tea is served – by the maid who's even older than my aunts and who brings it in with the slightly sleepy demeanour and the tetchily patient tenderness of very old servants – and across the whole of my dead past I faultlessly write a number or a sum. I am reabsorbed into myself again, I lose myself in me, I forget myself in those far-off nights, unpolluted by duty and the world, virginally pure of mystery and future.

And so gentle is this feeling distracting me from my debit and credit columns that if someone asks me a question, I reply with equal gentleness, as if my very being were hollow, as if I were nothing but a typewriter that I carry with me, a portable version of my own open self. Such an interruption of my dreams does not jar; so gentle are they that I continue to dream them even while I speak, write, answer, carry on a conversation. At last the lost teatime draws to an end and it's time for the office to close. I slowly shut the book and raise my eyes, weary with unshed tears, and of all the mingled feelings this arouses, I feel more than anything a sense of sadness that the closing of the office may mean the ending of my dream; that the gesture of my hand closing the book may mean covering up my own irreparable past; that I will go to the bed of life not in the least tired, but companionless and troubled, caught in the ebb and flow of my confused consciousness, twin tides flowing in the black night, at the outer limits of nostalgia and desolation.

19 [115]

Today my body felt afflicted by the old anguish that occasionally wells up inside me and at the restaurant or eating house, whose upstairs room provides some basis of continuity to my existence, I neither ate properly nor drank as much as I would normally drink. When I left, the waiter, noticing that the bottle of wine was still half-full, turned to me and said: 'Goodnight, Senhor Soares. Hope you feel better tomorrow.'

Just as if the wind had suddenly dispersed the clouds obscuring the sky, the clarion call of that simple phrase eased my soul. And then I realized something I have never fully recognized before: that

I have a spontaneous, natural sympathy with these waiters in cafés and restaurants, with barbers and street corner errand boys, which I cannot honestly say I feel for those with whom I have more intimate relations, if 'intimate' is the right word. . .

Fraternity is a very subtle thing.

Some govern the world, others are the world. Between an American millionaire with property in England and Switzerland and the Socialist boss of a village there is no qualitative difference, only quantitative. Below [. . .] them come us, the amorphous ones, the unruly dramatist William Shakespeare, the school teacher John Milton, that vagabond Dante Alighieri, the boy who ran an errand for me yesterday, the barber who always tells me stories, and the waiter who, simply because I drank only half my bottle of wine, proffered the fraternal hope that I would feel better tomorrow.

20 [56]

Only one thing surprises me more than the stupidity with which most men live their lives and that is the intelligence inherent in that stupidity.

To all appearances, the monotony of ordinary lives is horrific. I'm having lunch in this ordinary restaurant and I look over at the cook behind the counter and at the old waiter right next to me, serving me as he has served others here for, I believe, the past thirty years. What are these men's lives like? For forty years the cook has spent nearly all of every day in a kitchen; he has a few breaks; he sleeps relatively little; sometimes he goes back to his village whence he returns unhesitatingly and without regret; he slowly accumulates his slowly earned money, which he does not propose spending; he would fall ill if he had to abandon (for ever) his kitchen for the land he bought in Galicia; he's lived in Lisbon for forty years and he's never even been to the Rotunda*, or to the theatre, and only once

---

*The Rotunda was the name given by *lisboetas* (natives of Lisbon) to the Praça Marquês de Pombal.

to the Coliseu (whose clowns still inhabit the inner interstices of his life). He got married, how or why I don't know, has four sons and one daughter and, as he leans out over the counter towards my table, his smile conveys a great, solemn, contented happiness. He isn't pretending, nor does he have any reason to. If he seems happy it's because he really is.

And what about the old waiter who serves me and who, for what must be the millionth time in his career, has just placed a coffee on the table before me? His life is the same as the cook's, the only difference being the four or five yards that separate the kitchen where one works from the restaurant dining room where the other works. Apart from minor differences like having two rather than five children, paying more frequent visits to Galicia, and knowing Lisbon better than the cook (as well as Oporto where he lived for four years), he is equally contented.

I look again, with real terror, at the panorama of those lives and, just as I'm about to feel horror, sorrow and revulsion for them, discover that the people who feel no horror or sorrow or revulsion are the very people who have the most right to, the people living those lives. That is the central error of the literary imagination: the idea that other people are like us and must therefore feel like us. Fortunately for humanity, each man is only himself and only the genius is given the ability to be others as well.

In the end, everything is relative. A tiny incident in the street, which draws the restaurant cook to the door, affords him more entertainment than any I might get from the contemplation of the most original idea, from reading the best book or from the most pleasant of useless dreams. And, if life is essentially monotonous, the truth is that he has escaped from that monotony better and more easily than I. He is no more the possessor of the truth than I am, because the truth doesn't belong to anyone; but what he does possess is happiness.

The wise man makes his life monotonous, for then even the tiniest incident becomes imbued with great significance. After his third lion the lionhunter loses interest in the adventure of the hunt. For my monotonous cook there is something modestly apocalyptic about every streetfight he witnesses. To someone who has never been out of Lisbon the tram ride to Benfica is like a trip to the infinite and if one day he were to visit Sintra, he would feel as if he had journeyed to Mars. On the other hand, the traveller who has covered the globe can find nothing new for 5,000 miles around, because he's always seeing new things; there's novelty and there's the boredom of the eternally new and the latter brings about the death of the former.

The truly wise man could enjoy the whole spectacle of the world from his armchair; he wouldn't need to talk to anyone or to know how to read, just how to make use of his five senses and a soul innocent of sadness.

One must monotonize existence in order to rid it of monotony. One must make the everyday so anodyne that the slightest incident proves entertaining. In the midst of my day-to-day work, dull, repetitive and pointless, visions of escape surface in me, vestiges of dreams of far-off islands, parties held in the avenues of gardens in some other age, different landscapes, different feelings, a different me. But, between balance sheets, I realize that if I had all that, none of it would be mine. The truth is that Senhor Vasques is worth more than any Dream King; the office in Rua dos Douradores is worth more than all those broad avenues in impossible gardens. Because I have Senhor Vasques I can enjoy the dreams of the Dream Kings; because I have the office in Rua dos Douradores I can enjoy my inner visions of non-existent landscapes. But if the Dream Kings were mine, what would I have to dream about? If I possessed the impossible landscapes, what would remain of the impossible?

May I always be blessed with the monotony, the dull sameness of identical days, my indistinguishable todays and yesterdays, so that I may enjoy with an open heart the fly that distracts me, drifting randomly past my eyes, the gust of laughter that wafts volubly up from the street somewhere down below, the sense of vast freedom when the office closes for the night, and the infinite rest of my days off.

Because I am nothing, I can imagine myself to be anything. If I were somebody, I wouldn't be able to. An assistant book-keeper can imagine himself to be a Roman emperor; the King of England can't do that, because the King of England has lost the ability in his dreams to be any other king than the one he is. His reality limits what he can feel.

21 [119]

The morning unfurls itself upon the city, interleaving light and shade (or rather degrees of intensity of light) amongst the houses. It does not seem to come from the sun but from the city itself, for the light issues forth from the city's walls and roofs (not from them physically but from the simple fact of their being there).

As I feel that, I feel full of hope, at the same time recognizing that hope is a purely literary feeling. Tomorrow, spring and hope are all words connected poetically with one emotion and in the soul with the memory of that emotion. No, if I observe myself as closely as I observe the city, I realize that all I have to hope for is that today, like every other day, will come to an end. The eyes of reason also look at the dawn and I see that the hope I placed in it, if it ever existed, was not mine. It belonged to those men who live for the passing hour and whose way of thinking I, for a moment, unwittingly embodied.

Hope? What have I got to hope for? The only promise the day holds for me is that it will be just another day with a fixed course to run and a conclusion. The light cheers but does not change me for I will leave here as I came – older by a few hours, gladdened by a new feeling but saddened by thought. Whenever something is being born one can as easily concentrate on the fact of its birth as imagine its inevitable death. Now, in the strong, generous sunlight, the city landscape looks like a field of houses – broad, natural and orderly. But, even as I see all this, can I really forget my own existence? Deep down my consciousness of the city is my consciousness of myself.

I suddenly remember as a child seeing, as I can no longer see it, day breaking over the city. The sun did not rise for me then, it rose for all of life, because I (still an unconscious being) was life. I saw the morning and I was happy; today I see the morning and I am first happy, then sad. The child in me is still there but has fallen silent. I see as I used to see but from behind my eyes I see myself seeing and that one fact darkens the sun, dulls the green of the trees and withers the flowers before they even appear. Yes, once I belonged here; today, however new a landscape might be to me, I return from my first sight of it a foreigner, a guest and a wanderer, a stranger to all I see and hear, old man that I am.

I've seen everything before, even what I have never seen and never will see. Even the least significant of future landscapes flows already in my blood and the anguish of knowing that I will have to see again landscapes seen before fills me in advance with boredom.

Leaning over the balcony, enjoying the day, looking out at the diverse shapes of the whole city, just one thought fills my soul – the deep-seated will to die, to finish, no more to see light falling on a city, not to think or feel, to leave behind me, like discarded wrapping paper, the course of the sun and all its days, and to peel off the involuntary effort of being as one would discard one's heavy clothing at the foot of the great bed.

22 [123]

With an enormous effort I rise from my seat only to find that I still seem to be carrying it around with me, only now it's even heavier because it's become the seat of my own subjectivity.

23 (65)

In these lingering summer evenings, I love the quiet of this the commercial part of town, all the more because it's such a contrast with the noisy bustle that fills it during the day. Rua do Arsenal, Rua da Alfândega, the sad roads that reach out to the east where the Alfândega ends, and the long, solitary line of quiet quays: they comfort me with sadness on those evenings when I choose to share their solitude. I'm transported back to a time long before the one I actually live in. I like to imagine myself a contemporary of Cesário Verde* and feel within myself, not more verses like the ones he wrote, but the substance of his verses.

The life I drag around with me until night falls is not dissimilar to that of the streets themselves. By day they are full of meaningless bustle and by night full of an equally meaningless lack of bustle. By day I am nothing, by night I am myself. There is no difference between me and the streets around the Alfândega, except that they are streets and I am a human soul, and this, when weighed against the essence of all things, might also count for little. Men and objects share a common abstract destiny: to be of equally insignificant value in the algebra of life's mystery.

But there is something else . . . In those slow, empty hours a sense of the sadness of all existence rises from my soul to my mind, the bitter sense that everything is at once both felt by me and external to me, and that I am powerless to change it. How often have I seen my own dreams take physical shape – assailing me from without in the form of a tram turning the corner at the end of the street, or the voice of a streetseller at night (selling who knows what) singing an Arab melody, a sudden gush of sound breaking the monotony of the evening – not in order to provide me with a substitute reality but to declare themselves equal in their independence from my will.

24 [68]

I'm writing late on a Sunday morning, on a day full of soft light in which the blue of the still new sky above the ragged rooftops of the

---

* Cesário Verde (1855-1886) was one of the forerunners of modern Portuguese poetry who worked most of his life as a clerk. Pessoa felt a deep affinity with his poetry and shared his love of Lisbon.

city locks up in oblivion the mysterious existence of the stars. . .

It's Sunday inside me as well. . .

And my heart dons a child's velvet suit to go to a church it does not know; its face, above a wide, white collar, is flushed with the excitement of first impressions, and smiles with not a trace of sadness in its eyes.

25 [12]

I envy – though I'm not sure if envy is the right word – those people about whom one could write a biography, or who could write their autobiography. Through these deliberately unconnected impressions I am the indifferent narrator of my autobiography without events, of my history without a life. These are my Confessions and if I say nothing in them it's because I have nothing to say.

What could anyone confess that would be worth anything or serve any useful purpose? What has happened to us has either happened to everyone or to us alone; if the former it has no novelty value and if the latter it will be incomprehensible. I write down what I feel in order to lower the fever of feeling. What I confess is of no importance because nothing is of any importance. I make landscapes out of what I feel. I make a holiday of sensation. I understand women who embroider out of grief and those who crochet because life is what it is. My old aunt passed the infinite evenings playing patience. These confessions of my feelings are my game of patience. I don't interpret them, the way some read cards to know the future. I don't scrutinize them because in games of patience the cards have no value in themselves. I unwind myself like a length of multicoloured yarn, or make cat's cradles out of myself, like the ones children weave around stiff fingers and pass from one to the other. Taking care that my thumb doesn't miss the vital loop I turn it over to reveal a different pattern. Then I start again.

Living is like crocheting patterns to someone else's design. But while one works, one's thoughts are free and, as the ivory hook dives in and out amongst the wool, all the enchanted princes that ever existed are free to stroll through their parks. The crochet of things ... A pause ... Nothing...

For the rest, what qualities can I count on in myself? A horribly keen awareness of sensation and an all too deep consciousness of feeling... A sharp self-destructive intelligence and an extraordinary talent for dreams to entertain myself with ... A defunct will and a reflective spirit in which to cradle it like a living child ... In short, crochet ...

26 [24]

At the end of this day there remains what remained yesterday and what will remain tomorrow: the insatiable, unquantifiable longing to be both the same and other.

27 [59]

Thunderstorm

A low sky of unmoving clouds. The blue of the sky was sullied with transparent white.

The post boy at the other end of the office pauses for a moment in his eternal tying up of parcels ... 'Listen to that [...],' he remarks appreciatively.

A cold silence. The sounds from the street stop as if cut with a knife. For what seemed an age one sensed a malaise in everything, a cosmic holding of breath. The whole universe stopped. Minutes and minutes passed. The darkness grew black with silence.

Then, suddenly, the flash of bright steel [...].

How human the metallic clanking of the trams seemed! How joyful the landscape of simple rain falling in streets dragged back from the abyss!

Oh, Lisbon, my home!

28 [40]

In the gentlest of voices, he was singing a song from some far-off land. The music made the strange words seem familiar. It sounded like a *fado* composed for the soul, though it was nothing like a *fado* really.

Through its veiled words and its human melody, the song spoke of things that exist in every soul and yet are unknown to all of us. He was singing as if in a trance, standing in the street wrapped in a sort of ecstasy, not even aware he had an audience.

The people who had gathered there to listen to him did so without a trace of mockery. The song belonged to us all and sometimes the words spoke to us directly of the oriental secret of some lost race. The noise of the city, if we noticed it at all, went unheard and the cars passed so close to us that one brushed my jacket. But I only felt it, I didn't hear it. There was an intensity in the stranger's singing that nourished the dreamer in us, or the part that cannot dream. For us, though, it was just something to look at in the street and we all noticed the policeman coming slowly round the corner. He came towards us at the same slow pace then paused for a moment behind the boy selling umbrellas, like someone who has just spotted something. At that point the singer stopped. No one said a word. Then the policeman stepped in.

29 [87]

In the light morning mist of mid spring the Baixa* comes sluggishly awake and even the sun seems to rise only slowly. A quiet joy fills the chilly air and, in the gentle breath of a barely existent breeze, life shivers slightly in the cold that is already past, shivers at the memory of the cold rather than at the cold itself, at the contrast with the coming summer rather than at the present weather.

---

*The Baixa is Lisbon's lower town, containing the main shopping streets and offices, where Pessoa (and Bernardo Soares) worked.

Apart from cafés and dairies nothing is open yet, but the quietness is not the indolent quiet of Sunday mornings, it is simply quiet. The air has a blonde edge to it and the blue sky reddens through the thinning mist. A few passers-by signal the first hesitant stirrings of life in the streets and high up at a rare open window the occasional early morning face appears. As the trams pass, they trace a yellow, numbered furrow through the air, and minute by minute the streets begin to people themselves once more.

I drift, without thoughts or emotions, attending only to my senses. I woke up early and came out to wander aimlessly through the streets. I observe them meditatively. I see them with my thoughts. And, absurdly, a light mist of emotion rises within me; the fog that is lifting from the outside world seems slowly to be seeping into me.

I realize with a jolt that I have been thinking about my life. I didn't know I had been, but it's true. I thought I was just seeing and listening, that in my idle wanderings I was nothing but a reflector of received images, a white screen onto which reality projected colours and light instead of shadows. But, though I was unaware of it, I was more than that. I was still my self-denying soul, and my own abstract observation of the street was in itself a denial.

As the mist lifts, the air covers itself in pale light in which the mist is somehow mingled. I notice suddenly that there is much more noise, that there are many more people about. The footsteps of this larger number of passers-by seem less hurried. Making a reappearance on the street, in sharp contrast to the leisurely pace of everyone else, come the brisk step of the women selling fish and the swaying stride of the bakers with their monstrous baskets. The diverse monotony of the sellers of other produce is broken only by what's in their baskets, varying more in colour than in content. The milkmen rattle the miscellaneous metal cans of their meandering trade as if they were a bunch of absurd hollow keys. The policemen stand stolidly at the crossroads, civilization's uniformed denial of the imperceptibly rising day.

If only, I feel now, if only I could be someone able to see all this as if he had no other relation with it than that of seeing it, someone able to observe everything as if he were an adult traveller newly arrived today on the surface of life! If only one had not learned, from birth onwards, to give certain accepted meanings to everything, but instead was able to see the meaning inherent in each thing rather than that imposed on it from without. If only one could know the human reality of the woman selling fish and go beyond just labelling her a fishwife and the known fact that she exists and sells fish. If only one could see the policeman as God sees him. If only one could notice everything for the first time, not apocalyptically, as if they were revelations of the Mystery, but directly as the flowerings of Reality.

I hear the hour struck by some bell or clocktower – it must be eight o'clock though I don't count. The banal fact of the existence of time, the confines that social life imposes on continuous time – a frontier around the abstract, a limit on the unknown – brings me back to myself. I come to, look around at everything, full of life and ordinary humanity now, and I see that, apart from the patches of imperfect blue where it still lingers, the mist has cleared completely from the sky and seeped instead into my soul and into all things, into that part of them that touches my soul. I've lost the vision of what I saw. I'm blinded by sight. My feelings belong now to the banal realm of knowledge. This is no longer Reality: it is simply Life.

. . .Yes, Life to which I belong and which belongs to me; not Reality which belongs only to God or to itself, contains neither mystery nor truth and, given that it is real or pretends to be, exists somewhere in some fixed form, free from the need to be either transient or eternal, an absolute image, the ideal form of a soul made visible.

Slowly (though not as slowly as I imagine) I make my way back to my own door in order to go up to my room again. But I don't go in, I hesitate then continue on. The Praça da Figueira, replete with goods of various colours, fills with customers and peoples my horizon with vendors of all kinds. I advance slowly, a dead man, and my vision, no longer my own, is nothing now: it is merely that of a human animal who unwittingly inherited Greek culture,

Roman order, Christian morality and all the other illusions that . make up the civilization in which I live and feel.

What's become of the living?

30 [142]   *26.1.1932*

One of my constant preoccupations is trying to understand how it is that other people exist, how it is that there are souls other than mine and consciousnesses not my own, which, because it is a consciousness, seems to me unique. I understand perfectly that the man before me uttering words similar to mine and making the same gestures I make, or could make, is in some way my fellow creature. However, I feel just the same about the people in illustrations I dream up, about the characters I see in novels or the dramatis personae on the stage who speak through the actors representing them.

I suppose no one truly admits the existence of another person. One might concede that the other person is alive and feels and thinks like oneself, but there will always be an element of difference, a perceptible discrepancy, that one cannot quite put one's finger on. There are figures from times past, fantasy-images in books that seem more real to us than these specimens of indifference-made-flesh who speak to us across the counters of bars, or catch our eye in trams, or brush past us in the empty randomness of the streets. The others are just part of the landscape for us, usually the invisible landscape of a familiar street.

I feel closer ties and more intimate bonds with certain characters in books, with certain images I've seen in engravings, than with many supposedly real people, with that metaphysical absurdity known as 'flesh and blood'. In fact 'flesh and blood' describes them very well: they resemble cuts of meat laid out on the butcher's marble slab, dead creatures bleeding as though still alive, the sirloin steaks and cutlets of Fate.

I'm not ashamed to feel this way because I know it's how everyone feels. The lack of respect between men, the indifference that allows them to kill others without compunction (as murderers do) or without thinking that they are killing (as soldiers do), comes from the fact that no one pays due attention to the apparently abstruse idea that other people have souls too.

On certain days, at certain times, with an awareness wafted to me on some unknown breeze, revealed to me by the opening of some secret door, I am suddenly conscious that the grocer on the corner is a spiritual being, that his assistant at the door, bending down over a sack of potatoes, truly is a soul capable of suffering.

Yesterday, when they told me that the assistant in the tobacconist's had committed suicide, I couldn't believe it. Poor lad, so he existed too! We had all forgotten that, all of us; we who knew him only about as well as those who didn't know him at all. We'll forget him more easily tomorrow. But what is certain is that he had a soul, enough soul to kill himself. Passions? Worries? Of course. But for me, and for the rest of humanity, all that remains is the memory of a foolish smile above a grubby woollen jacket that didn't fit properly at the shoulders. That is all that remains to me of someone who felt deeply enough to kill himself, because, after all there's no other reason to kill oneself . . . I remember thinking once, when I was buying some cigarettes from him, that he would probably go prematurely bald. In the event, he didn't have time to go bald. But that's just a memory I have of him. But what other memory is likely to remain of him, if my memory is not in fact of him but of a thought I had?

I have a sudden vision of the corpse, of the coffin they placed him in, of the alien grave to which they must have carried him. And I see that in a way, badly cut jacket and all, the tobacconist's assistant represents all humanity.

The vision lasted only a moment. Today, of course, being merely human, I think only that he died. Nothing more.

No, other people don't exist . . . It is for me alone that the setting sun holds out its heavy wings of harsh, misty colours. It is for me alone, even though I cannot see its waters flowing, that the wide river glitters beneath the sunset. It is for me alone that this open square was built looking out over the river and its turning tide. Was it today that the tobacconist's assistant was buried in a common grave? Today's nset is not for him. But, even as I'm thinking that, quite against my will I suddenly understand that it's not for me either ...

31 [150]   *25.2.1929*

The two large pages of the heavy book lie before me on the writing desk; from the sloping pages I raise my weary eyes and a soul wearier still. Beyond the nothingness that all this represents, the warehouse stretches as far as Rua dos Douradores, displaying its regular ranks of shelves and employees, the human order and peace afforded by the ordinary. Against the windowpane beats the noise of the diverse world, and that noise is as ordinary as the peace that prevails near the shelves.

I lower refreshed eyes to the two white pages on which my careful numbers transcribe the company balance sheet. And, smiling to myself, I remember that life, which contains these pages, some blank, others ruled or written on, with their names of textiles and sums of money, also includes the great navigators, the great saints, poets from every era, none of whom appear on any balance sheet, being the vast offspring cast out by those who decide what is and isn't valuable in this world.

On the same page that contains the names of unfamiliar textiles, the doors to the Indus and to Samarkand swing open, and the poetry of Persia, which is nothing to do with either of those two places, lends distant support to my disquiet in quatrains whose every third line is left unrhymed. Yet I make no mistakes, I write and add up and so the keeping of the accounts by a clerk of this establishment continues uninterrupted.

32 [151]   *10 and 11.9.1931*

Contrary to the sunny custom of this bright city, the successive rows of houses, the empty lots, the ragged outline of roads and buildings have, since early morning, been wrapped in a light blanket of mist that the sun has slowly turned to gold. Towards midmorning the soft fog began to unravel and, tenuously, in shadowy gusts like the lifting of veils, to vanish. By ten o'clock, the only remaining evidence of the vanished mist was a slight hesitancy in the blue of the sky.

As the mask of veils fell away, the features of the city were reborn. The day, which had already dawned, dawned anew, as if a window had been suddenly flung open. The noises in the streets took on a slightly different quality, as if they too had only just appeared. A blueness insinuated itself even into the cobblestones and the impersonal auras of passers-by. The sun was hot but gave off a humid heat as if infiltrated by the now non-existent mist.

I've always found the awakening of a city, whether wreathed in mists or not, more moving than sunrise in the country. There is a stronger sense of rebirth, more to look forward to; the sun, instead of merely illuminating the fields, the silhouettes of trees and the open palms of leaves with first dark then liquid light and finally with pure luminous gold, multiplies its every effect in windows, on walls, on roofs [. . .]. Seeing dawn in the countryside does me good, seeing dawn in the city affects me for both good and ill and therefore does me even more good. For the greater hope it brings me contains, as does all hope, the far-off, nostalgic aftertaste of unreality. Dawn in the countryside just exists; dawn in the city overflows with promise. One makes you live, the other makes you think. And, along with all the other great unfortunates, I've always believed it better to think than to live.

33 [154]   *15.9.1931*

Clouds . . . I'm very conscious of the sky today, though there are days when, though I feel it, I don't see it, living as I do in the city and not out in the country where the sky is always so present. Clouds . . . They are the principal reality of the day and I'm as preoccupied with them as if the clouding over of the sky were one of the great dangers that fate has in store for me. Clouds . . . From the river up to the castle, from west to east, they drift along, a disparate, naked tumult. Some are white, the tattered vanguard of some unknown army; others, more ponderous and almost black, are swept slowly along by the audible wind; besmirched with white, they seem inclined to linger and plunge into darkness the illusion of space afforded to the serried ranks of houses by the narrow streets, a darkness provoked more by their approach than by any actual shadow they cast.

Clouds . . . I exist unconsciously and I'll die unwillingly. I am the interval between what I am and what I am not, between what I dream and what life has made of me, the abstract, carnal halfway-house between things, like myself, that are nothing. Clouds . . . How disquieting it is to feel, how troubling to think, how vain to want! Clouds . . . They continue to pass, some so large (though just how large it's hard to judge because of the houses) they seem about to take over the whole sky; others, of uncertain size, which could be two clouds together or one about to split into two, drift, directionless, through the high air across the weary sky; to one side, in grand and chilly isolation, are other smaller clouds that look like the playthings of powerful creatures, irregularly shaped balls to be used in some absurd game.

Clouds . . . I question myself but do not know myself. I've done nothing nor will I ever do anything useful to justify my existence. The part of my life not wasted in thinking up confused inter-pretations of nothing at all, has been spent making prose poems out of the incommunicable feelings I use to make the unknown universe my own. Both objectively and subjectively speaking, I'm sick of myself. I'm sick of everything, and of everything about everything. Clouds . . . Today they are everything, dismantled fragments of heaven, the only real things between the empty earth and the non-existent sky, indescribable scraps of a tedium I impose on them, mist condensed into bland threats, soiled tufts of cotton wool in a hospital without walls. Clouds . . . They are, like me, a ruined road between sky and earth, at the mercy of some invisible impulse, they may or may not thunder, they gladden the earth with their whiteness, sadden it with their darkness, fictions born of empty intervals and aimless meanderings, remote from earthly noises, but lacking the silence of the sky. Clouds ... They continue to drift past, on and on, as they always will, like a constantly interrupted winding and unwinding of dull yarns, the diffuse prolongation of a false, fragmented sky.

34 [158]   *16.12.1931*

Today, the man we call the office boy left for his village, for good they say; today, the same man whom I've come to consider part of this human company and, therefore part of me and my world, left. When we met by chance in the corridor for the inevitable surprise of our farewells, he shyly reciprocated my embrace and I mustered enough self-control not to cry even though, against my will, my heart and burning eyes longed to.

Everything that was ours, simply because it was once ours, even those things we merely chanced to live with or see on a daily basis, becomes part of us. It was not the office boy who left today for some place in Galicia unknown to me, it was a part, vital because both visual and human, of the very substance of my life. Today I am diminished, no longer quite the same. The office boy left today.

Everything that happens in the world we live in, happens in us. Anything that ceases to exist in the world we see around us, ceases to exist in us. Everything that was, assuming we noticed it when it was there, is torn from us when it leaves. The office boy left today.

As I sit down at the high desk and return to yesterday's accounts, I feel heavier, older, my will weaker. But today's vague tragedy interrupts what should be the automatic process of drawing up accounts with meditations that I have to struggle to suppress. The only way I can find the heart to work is by turning myself, through active inertia, into my own slave. The office boy left today.

Yes, tomorrow or another day or whenever the silent bell of death or departure tolls for me, it will be me who is no longer here, an old copybook to be tidied away into a cupboard under the stairs. Yes, tomorrow, or whenever Fate decrees, what was supposedly me will die. Will I go back to my native village? Who knows where I'll go. Today tragedy is made visible by an absence and tangible because it barely deserves to be felt. Ah, but the office boy left today.

35 [159]   21.4.1930

Some feelings are like dreams that pervade every corner of one's spirit like a mist, that do not let one think or act or even be. Some trace of our dreams persists in us as if we had not slept properly, and a daytime torpor warms the stagnant surface of the senses. It is the intoxication of being nothing, when one's will is a bucket of water kicked over in the yard by some clumsy passing foot.

One looks but does not see. The long street crowded with human creatures is like a fallen inn sign on which the jumbled letters no longer make sense. The houses are merely houses. Although one sees things clearly, it's impossible to give meaning to what one sees.

The ringing hammer blows coming from the boxmaker's shop have a familiar strangeness. Each blow is separated in time, each with its echo and each utterly vain. The passing carts sound the way they do on days when thunder threatens. Voices emerge not from people's throats but from the air itself. In the background, even the river seems weary.

It is not tedium that one feels. It is not grief. It is the desire to go to sleep clothed in a different personality, to forget, dulled by an increase in salary. You feel nothing except the mechanical rise and fall of your legs as they walk involuntarily forwards on feet conscious of the shoes they're wearing. Perhaps you don't even feel that much. Something tightens inside your head, blinding you and stopping up your ears.

It's like having a cold in the soul. And with that literary image of illness comes a longing for life to be like a long period of convalescence, confined to bed; and the idea of convalescence evokes the image of large villas on the outskirts of the city, but deep in the heart of them, by the hearth, far from the streets and the traffic. No, you can't hear anything. You consciously pass through the door you must enter, you go through it as if asleep, unable to make your body go in any other direction. You pass through everything. Where's your tambourine now, sleeping bear?

Fragile as something just begun, the evil sea smell carried on the breeze hovered over the Tagus and grubbily infiltrated the fringes of the Baixa. It blew cool and rank over the torpor of the warm sea. Life became something lodged in my stomach and my sense of smell inhabited some space behind my eyes. High up, perching on nothing at all, thin skeins of cloud dissolved from grey into false white. The atmosphere was like a threat made by a cowardly sky, like inaudible thunder, full of nothing but air.

Even the gulls as they flew seemed static, lighter than the air itself, as if someone had simply left them hanging there. But it wasn't oppressive. Evening fell on our disquiet; the air grew intermittently cool.

My poor hopes, born of the life I've been forced to lead! They are like this hour and this air, vanished mists, inept attempts at stirring up a false storm. I feel like shouting out, to put an end to this landscape and this meditation. But the salt smell of the sea fills all my good intentions, and the low tide has laid bare in me the muddy gloom which only my sense of smell tells me is there.

What a lot of nonsense just to satisfy myself! What cynical insights into purely hypothetical emotions! All this mixing up of soul and feelings, of my thoughts with the air and the river, just to say that life wounds my sense of smell and my consciousness, just because I do not have the wit to use the simple, all-embracing words of the Book of Job: 'My soul is weary of my life!'

36 [170]

Oh, night, in which the stars masquerade as light, oh night, equal only to the Universe in magnitude, make me, body and soul, part of your body, and let me lose myself in mere darkness, make me night too, with no dreams to be as stars to me, nor longed-for sun to light the future.

37 [130]   *4.11.1931*

Anyone wanting to make a catalogue of monsters would need only to photograph in words the things that night brings to somnolent souls who cannot sleep. These things have all the incoherence of dreams without the unacknowledged excuse of sleep. They hover like bats over the passivity of the soul, or like vampires that suck the blood of our submissiveness.

They are the larvae of decline and waste, shadows filling the valley, the last vestiges of fate. Sometimes they are worms, repellent to the very soul that cossets and nourishes them; sometimes they are ghosts sinisterly haunting nothing at all; sometimes they emerge like cobras from the bizarre grottoes of lost emotions.

They are the ballast of falsehood, their only purpose is to render us useless. They are doubts from the deep that settle in cold, sleepy folds upon the soul. They are as ephemeral as smoke, as tracks on the ground, and all that remains of them is the fact of their once having existed in the sterile soil of our awareness of them. Some are like fireworks of the mind that glitter for a moment between dreams, the rest are just the unconsciousness of the consciousness with which we saw them.

Like a bow that's come undone, the soul does not in itself exist. The great landscapes all belong to a tomorrow we have already lived. The interrupted conversation was a failure. Who would have guessed life would be like this?

The moment I find myself, I am lost; if I believe, I doubt; I grasp hold of something but hold nothing in my hand. I go to sleep as if I were going for a walk, but I'm awake. I wake as if I slept, and I am not myself. Life, after all, is but one great insomnia and there is a lucid half-awakeness about everything we think or do.

I would be happy if only I could sleep. At least that's what I think now when I can't sleep. The night is an immense weight pressing down on my dream of suffocating myself beneath the silent blanket. I have indigestion of the soul.

Always, after everything, day will come, but it will be late, as usual. Everything, except me, sleeps and is contented. I rest a little without daring to sleep. And, confusedly, from the depths of my being the enormous heads of imaginary monsters emerge. They are Oriental dragons from the abyss, with illogically scarlet tongues and lifeless eyes that stare at my dead life which does not look back.

Someone, please, close the lid on all this! Let me be done with consciousness and life! Then, fortunately, through the cold window with the shutters thrown back, I see a wan thread of pallid light beginning to disperse the shadows on the horizon. Fortunately, what is about to break upon me is the day bringing rest, almost, from the weariness of this unrest. Absurdly, right in the city centre, a cock crows. The pale day begins as I drift into vague sleep. At some point I will sleep. The noise of wheels evokes a cart passing by. My eyelids sleep but I do not. In the end, there is only Fate.

38 [152]   *2.7.1931*

No one likes us when we've slept badly. The sleep we missed carried off with it whatever it was that made us human. There is, it seems, a latent irritation in us, in the empty air that surrounds us. Ultimately it is we who are in dispute with ourselves, it is within ourselves that diplomacy in the secret war breaks down.

All day I've dragged my feet and this great weariness around the streets. My soul has shrunk to the size of a tangled ball of wool and what I am and was, what is me, has forgotten its name. Will there be a tomorrow? I don't know. I only know that I didn't sleep and the jumble of half-slept interludes fills with long silences the conversation I hold with myself.

Ah, the great parks enjoyed by others, the gardens taken for granted by so many, the marvellous avenues belonging to people who will never know me! Between sleepless nights I stagnate like someone who never dared to be superfluous and what I meditate upon wakes up, startled, with one closing dream.

I am a widowed house, cloistered in upon itself, darkened by timid, furtive spectres. I am always in the room next door, or they are, and all around me great trees rustle. I wander around and I find things and I find things because I wander. My childhood days stand before me dressed in a pinafore!

And in the midst of all this, made drowsy by my wanderings, I drift out into the street, like a leaf. The gentlest of winds has swept me up from the ground and I wander, like the very close of twilight, through whatever the landscape presents to me. My eyelids grow heavy, my feet drag. Because I'm walking I would like to sleep. I keep my mouth pressed tight shut as if to seal my lips. I am the shipwreck of my own wanderings.

No, I didn't sleep, but I'm better when I haven't slept and can't sleep. I am more truly myself in this random eternity, symbolic of the half-souled state in which I live deluding myself. Someone looks at me as if they knew me or thought they knew me. With painful eyes beneath sore eyelids I feel myself look back at them; I don't want to know about the world out there.

All I feel is tired, tired, utterly tired!

39 [61]

It starts as a noise that sets off another noise in the dark pit of things. Then it becomes a vague howling joined in turn by the rasp of swaying shop signs in the street. Then the clear voice of space falls suddenly silent. Everything trembles then stops and there is quietness amidst all this fear, a suppressed fear that only [...] when it is gone.

Afterwards there is only the wind, just the wind, and I notice sleepily how the doors strain at their hinges and the glass in the windows moans resistance.

I do not sleep. I half-exist.

Scraps of consciousness float to the surface. I am heavy with sleep but unconsciousness eludes me. I am not. The wind ... I wake and drift back to sleep without as yet having slept. There is a landscape of loud and terrible noise beyond which I do not know myself. Modestly I enjoy the possibility of sleeping. I do in fact sleep, but without knowing that I do. In everything we judge to be a noise there is always another noise heralding the end of everything, the wind in the dark and, if I listen harder, the sound of my own lungs and heart.

40 [49]

If I have no other virtue at least there exists in me the unending novelty of liberated sensation.

Today, walking down Rua Nova do Almada, I suddenly noticed the back of the man walking ahead of me: the ordinary back of an ordinary man, the jacket of a modest suit on the back of a chance passer-by. He was carrying an old briefcase under his left arm and, with each step he took, he tapped the pavement with the point of the rolled umbrella he carried in his right hand.

Suddenly I felt something approaching tenderness for that man. I felt in him the tenderness one feels for human ordinariness, for the banal daily life of the head of a family on his way to work, for his humble, happy home, for the sad and joyous pleasures that no doubt make up his life, for the innocence of living unreflectively, for the animal naturalness of that clothed back.

I looked again at the man's back, the window through which I saw these thoughts.

It was exactly the same feeling that comes over you in the presence of someone sleeping. When someone sleeps they become a child again, perhaps because in sleep one can do no evil and one is unaware even of one's own existence. By some natural magic, the worst criminal, the most inveterate egotist is made sacred by sleep.

I can see no perceptible difference between killing a child and killing someone while they sleep.

That man's back sleeps. Every part of the man walking ahead of me, at the same speed as me, is asleep. He moves unconsciously. He lives unconsciously. He sleeps just as we all sleep. All of life is a dream. No one knows what he does, no one knows what he wants, no one knows what he knows. We sleep our lives away, the eternal children of Fate. That's why, if I think with that feeling, I experience an immense, boundless tenderness for all of infantile humanity, for the somnambulist lives people lead, for everyone, for everything.

What sweeps over me in such moments is a pure humanitarianism that draws no conclusions and knows no ulterior motives. I'm overwhelmed by tenderness as if I saw all this with the eyes of a god. I see everyone with the compassion of the only conscious being alive: poor men, poor humanity. What is it all doing here?

From the simple rise and fall of our lungs to the building of cities and the drawing up of imperial frontiers, I consider every movement, every motivating force in life to be a form of sleep, to be dreams or intervals that occur involuntarily in the pauses between one reality and the next, between one day of the Absolute and the next. And at night, like some abstractly maternal figure, I bend over the beds of both good and bad children, made equal in the sleep that makes them mine. My tenderness for them has the generosity of some infinite being.

I shift my gaze away from the back of the man immediately in front of me to look at everyone else, at everyone walking down this street, and I consciously include them all in the same absurd, cold tenderness provoked in me by the back of the unconscious being in whose steps I follow. They are all like him: the girls chatting on their way to the workshop, the young clerks laughing en route to the office, the maids returning home laden with shopping, the boys out running their first errands of the day – all of this is just one unconsciousness wearing different faces and bodies, puppets moved by strings pulled by the fingers of the same invisible being. They give every appearance of consciousness but, because they are not conscious of being conscious, they are conscious of nothing. Whether intelligent or stupid, they are all in fact equally stupid. Whether young or old, they all share the same age. Whether men or women, they all belong to the same non-existent sex.

41 [50]

There are days when each person I meet, especially the people I have to mix with on a daily basis, take on the significance of symbols, either isolated or connected, which come together to form occult or prophetic writings, shadowy descriptions of my life. The office becomes a page on which the people are the words; the street is a book; words exchanged with acquaintances, encounters with strangers are sayings that appear in no dictionary but which my understanding can almost decipher. They speak, they communicate but it is not of themselves that they speak, nor themselves that they communicate; as I said, they are words that reveal nothing directly but rather allow meaning to be revealed through them. But, with my poor crepuscular vision, I can only vaguely make out whatever it is that those windowpanes suddenly appearing on the surface of things choose to show of the interiors they both guard and reveal. I understand without knowledge, like a blind man to whom people speak of colours.

Sometimes, walking down the street, I hear snatches of private conversations and they are almost all about another woman, another man, the son of some third party or someone else's lover [...].

Just hearing these shadowy fragments of human discourse, which are after all what most conscious lives are taken up with, I carry away with me a tedium born of disgust, a terror of being exiled amongst illusions and the sudden realization of how bruised I am by other people; I am condemned by the landlord and by the other tenants, to being just one more tenant among many, peering disgustedly through the bars on the window at the back of the storeroom at other people's rubbish piling up in the rain in the inner courtyard that is my life.

42 (165)   *16.3.1932*

Months have gone by since I last wrote anything. My understanding has lain dormant and I have lived as if I were someone else. I've often had a sense of vicarious happiness. I haven't existed, I have been someone else and lived unthinkingly.

Today, suddenly, I returned to what I am or what I dream I am. It was in a moment of great weariness that came upon me after completing some fairly meaningless task. I rested my head on my hands, with my elbows on the high, sloping desk. Then, closing my eyes, I found myself again.

In the remoteness of that false sleep I remembered everything I had been; suddenly, with all the clarity of a real landscape, there rose before me the long wall of the old farm and then, in the midst of that vision, I saw the empty threshing-floor.

I had an immediate sense of the meaninglessness of life. Seeing, feeling, remembering, forgetting were all one, all mixed up with a slight ache in my elbows, the fragmented murmurings from the street below and the faint sounds of steady work going on in the quiet office.

When I rested my hands on the desk again and glanced round with what must have been the terrible weariness of worlds long dead, the first thing my eyes saw was a bluebottle perched on my inkwell (so that was where the vague buzzing extraneous to the other office noises came from!). Anonymous and watchful, I regarded it from the pit of the abyss. Its lustrous green and blue-black tones were oddly repellent but not ugly. It was a life!

Perhaps there are supreme forces, the gods or devils of the Truth in whose shadows we wander, for whom I am just a lustrous fly resting for a moment before their gaze. A facile observation? A clichéd remark? Unconsidered philosophy? Perhaps, except that I did not just think it: I felt it. It was directly, with my own flesh, and with a sense of utter horror [. . .] that I made this laughable comparison. When I compared myself to the fly I *was* a fly. I felt myself to be a fly when I imagined I felt it. And I felt I had a fly's soul, I went to sleep as a fly, I felt myself trapped in a fly's body. And the most horrific part was that at the same time I was myself. Involuntarily I looked up at the ceiling to check there was no supreme being wielding a ruler to squash me as I could squash that fly. Fortunately, when I looked again, the fly, noiselessly it seemed, had disappeared. Quite against its will the office was once more bereft of all philosophy.

43 [168]   *11.6.1932*

Once the heat had passed and the first light spots of rain began to fall heavily enough to make themselves heard, there was a quietness in the air that had been absent from the earlier heat, a new peace into which the rain introduced a breeze all its own. Such was the bright, sheer joy of that soft rain, with no storms or dark skies, that even those who had come out without umbrellas or waterproof clothing, almost everyone in fact, laughed as they hurried, chattering, down the shining street.

In an idle moment I went over to the open window in the office – it had been opened because of the heat and left open when the rain came – and looking out at the scene with my usual mixture of intense and indifferent attentiveness, I saw exactly the scene I had described even before I had seen it. Sure enough, there was joy walking down the street in the guise of two ordinary men, talking and smiling in the fine rain, not hurrying, just strolling briskly through the clean clarity of the darkening day.

However, a surprise was waiting just around the corner: suddenly, a miserable old man, poor but not humble, came making his ill-tempered way through the slackening rain. This man, while clearly without any urgent goal, was possessed at least of a keen impatience. I studied him intently, not with the distracted eye with which one usually looks at things, but with the analytical eye reserved for deciphering symbols. He symbolized nobody; that was why he was in such a hurry. He symbolized those who have never been anybody; that was at the root of his suffering. He did not belong with those who smiled beneath the inconvenient joy of the rain, he belonged to the rain itself – an unconscious being, so unconscious that he could feel reality.

But that isn't what I wanted to say. A mysterious distraction, a crisis of the soul that rendered me incapable of continuing insinuated itself between my observation of that passer-by (whom in fact I immediately lost sight of because I stopped looking at him) and the nexus of these observations. And at the back of my distractedness, I hear without hearing the sound of the post-room boys at the other end of the office where the warehouse begins and, on the table by the window that looks out onto the yard, amongst the joking voices and the click of scissors, I see without seeing the twine for the parcels wound twice around the packages wrapped in strong brown paper and fastened with double knots.

One can see only what one has already seen.

44 [167]   2.11.1933

There are some deepseated griefs so subtle and pervasive that it is difficult to grasp whether they belong to our soul or to our body, whether they come from a malaise brought on by pondering on the futility of life, or whether they are caused rather by an indisposition in some chasm within ourselves – the stomach, liver or brain. How often my ordinary consciousness of myself is obscured by the dark sediment stirred up in some stagnant part of me. How often existence wounds me to the point that I feel a nausea so indefinable that I can't tell if it's just tedium or an indication that I'm actually about to be sick! How often . . .

. My soul today is sad to the very marrow of its bones. Everything hurts me – memory, eyes, arms. It's like having rheumatism in every part of my being. The limpid brightness of the day, the great pure blue sky, the steady tide of diffuse light, none of this touches my being. I remain unmoved by the light autumnal breeze, that still bears a trace of unforgotten summer and lends colour to the air. Nothing means anything to me. I'm sad, but not with a definite or even an indefinite sadness. My sadness is out there, in the street strewn with boxes.

These words do not convey exactly what I feel because doubtless nothing can convey exactly what someone feels. But I'm trying in some way to give an idea of what I feel, a mixture of various aspects of me and the street below which, because I also see it, belongs to me, is part of me, in some intimate way that defies analysis.

I would like to live different lives in distant lands. I would like to die another person beneath unknown flags. I would like to be acclaimed emperor in another time (a time better simply because it is not today), that appears to me in shimmering colours, amongst unknown sphinxes. I want anything that makes the person I am seem ridiculous just because it does make what I am seem ridiculous. I want, I want ... But there is always the sun when the sun shines and the night when night falls. There's always grief when grief afflicts us and dreams when dreams cradle us. There is always what there is and never what there should be, not because it's better or worse, but because it's other. There's always ...

The dustmen are working down below, clearing the street of boxes of rubbish. Laughing and talking they put the boxes one by one onto the carts. From high up at my office window I watch them with indolent eyes beneath drooping lids. And something subtle and incomprehensible links what I'm feeling to the boxes I watch being loaded up; some unknown feeling puts all my tedium, anguish, nausea or whatever into a box, lifts it up on the shoulders of a man making loud jokes and places it on a cart that is not here. And the light of day, serene as ever, falls obliquely along the narrow street, onto the place where they're loading up the boxes, not on the boxes themselves, which are in the shade, but on the corner down there where the errand boys are busy randomly doing nothing.

45 [99]

The clock in the depths of the deserted house, deserted because everyone's asleep, slowly lets fall the clear quadruple sound of four o'clock in the morning. I haven't yet slept, nor do I expect to. With nothing to distract me and keep me from sleeping, or weigh on my body and prevent my resting, I lay down the dull silence of my strange body in the shadow that the vague moonlight of the streetlamps makes even more solitary. I'm too tired even to think, too tired even to feel.

All around me is the abstract, naked universe, composed of nothing but the negation of night. I am split between tiredness and restlessness and reach a point where I physically touch a metaphysical knowledge of the mystery of things. Sometimes my soul softens and then the formless details of everyday life float up to the surface of my consciousness and I draw up a balance sheet on the back of my insomnia. At other times I wake within the half-sleep in which I lie stagnating, and vague images in random poetic colours let their silent spectacle slide by my inattentive mind. My eyes are not quite closed. My weak sight is fringed with distant light from the streetlamps still lit below, in the abandoned regions of the street.

To cease, to sleep, to replace this intermittent consciousness with better, more melancholy things uttered in secret to a stranger! ... To cease, to flow, fluid as a river, as the ebb and flow of a vast sea along coasts seen in a night in which one could really sleep! ... To cease, to be unknown and external, the stirring of branches in remote avenues, the tenuous falling of leaves that one senses without hearing them fall, the subtle sea of distant fountains, and the whole indistinct world of gardens at night, lost in endless complexities, the natural labyrinths of the dark! ... To cease, to end once and for all, but yet to survive in another form, as the page of a book, a loose lock of hair, a swaying creeper outside a half-open window, insignificant footsteps on the fine gravel on the curve of a path, the last twist of smoke high above a village as it falls asleep, the idle whip of the waggoner stopped by the road in the morning ... Absurdity, confusion, extinction – anything but life ...

And I do sleep in this vegetative life of conjecture, after a fashion, that is, without sleeping or resting, and over my unquiet eyelids there hovers, like the silent foam of a grubby sea, the far-off gleam of the dumb streetlamps down below.

I sleep and half-sleep.

Beyond me, beyond where I lie, the silence of the house touches the infinite. I hear time falling, drop by drop, but do not hear the drops themselves fall. My own heart physically oppresses my memory, reduced to nothing, of everything that was and that I was. I feel my head resting on the pillow in which I've made a hollow. The contact of the pillowcase is like skin touching skin in the shadows. The ear on which I lie stamps itself mathematically on my brain. My eyelids droop with weariness and my eyelashes make a tiny, almost inaudible sound on the sensitive whiteness of the plump pillow. I breathe out, sighing, and my breath just happens, it is not mine. I suffer without feeling or thinking. In the house, the clock, occupying a precise place in the heart of things, strikes the half hour, sharp, futile. It is all too much, too deep, black and cold!

I pass through time, through silences, as formless worlds pass through me.

Suddenly, like a child of the Mystery, innocent of the existence of night, a cock crows. I can sleep now because it is morning in me. And I feel my lips smile, pressing lightly into the soft folds of the pillow that cradles my face. I can abandon myself to life, I can sleep, I can forget about me . . . And through the new sleep washing darkly over me I remember the cock that crowed, either that or it really is him, crowing a second time.

46 [101]   *18.5.1930*

To live is to be other. Even feeling is impossible if one feels today what one felt yesterday, for that is not to feel, it is only to remember today what one felt yesterday, to be the living corpse of yesterday's lost life.

To wipe everything off the slate from one day to the next, to be new with each new dawn, in a state of perpetually restored virginity of emotion – that and only that is worth being or having, if we are to be or to have what we imperfectly are.

This dawn is the first the world has seen. Never before has this pink light dwindling into yellow then hot white fallen in quite this way on the faces that the window-paned eyes of the houses in the west turn to the silence that comes with the growing light. Never before have this hour, this light, my being existed. What comes tomorrow will be different, and what I see will be seen through different eyes, full of a new vision.

Tall mountains of the city! Great buildings, rooted in, raised up upon steep slopes, an avalanche of houses heaped indiscriminately together, woven together by the light out of shadows and fire – you are today, you are me, because I see you, you are what [...] and, leaning as if against the rail on a ship, I love you as ships passing one another must love, feeling an unaccountable nostalgia in their passing.

47 [102]

From the terrace of this café I look tremulously out at life. I can't see much of it, just the bustle of people concentrated in this small bright square of mine. Like the beginnings of drunkenness, a profound weariness illuminates the souls of things. Life, obvious and unanimous, flows past outside me in the footsteps of the passers-by.

In this moment my feelings all stagnate and everything seems other than it is, my feelings a confused yet lucid mistake. Like an imaginary condor, I spread my wings but do not fly.

As a man of ideals, perhaps my greatest aspiration really does not go beyond occupying this chair at this table in this café.

Everything is as utterly vain as stirring up cold ashes, as insubstantial as the moment just before dawn.

And the light bursts serenely and perfectly forth from things, gilds them with a smiling, sad reality. The whole mystery of the world appears before my eyes sculpted from this banality, this street.

Ah, how mysteriously the everyday things of life brush by us! On the surface, touched by light, of this complex human life, Time, a hesitant smile, blooms on the lips of the Mystery! How modern all this sounds, yet deep down it is so ancient, so hidden, so different from the meaning that shines out from all of this.

48 [103]

Knowing how easily even the smallest things torture me, I deliberately avoid contact with them. A cloud passing in front of the sun is enough to make me suffer, how then should I not suffer in the darkness of the endlessly overcast sky of my own life?

My isolation is not a search for happiness, which I do not have the heart to win, nor for peace, which one finds only when it will never more be lost; what I seek is sleep, extinction, a small surrender.

To me the four walls of my miserable room are both prison cell and far horizon, both bed and coffin. My happiest hours are those in which I think nothing, want nothing, when I do not even dream, but lose myself in some spurious vegetable torpor, moss growing on the surface of life. Without a trace of bitterness I savour my absurd awareness of being nothing, a mere foretaste of death and extinction.

I never had anyone I could call 'Master'. No Christ died for me. No Buddha showed me the right path. In the depths of my dreams no Apollo or Athena appeared to me to enlighten my soul.

49 [104]

Everything has become unbearable to me, except life – the office, my house, the streets – even their contrary, if such a thing existed – everything overwhelms and oppresses me. Only the totality affords me relief. Yes, any part of it is enough to console me. A ray of sunlight falling endlessly into the dead office; a street cry that soars up to the window of my room; the existence of people, of climates and changes in the weather; the terrifying objectivity of the world...

Suddenly the ray of sun entered into me, by which I mean that I suddenly saw it ... It was a bright stripe of almost colourless light cutting like a naked blade across the dark, wooden floor, enlivening everything around it, the old nails and the grooves between the floorboards, black ruled sheets of non-whiteness.

For minutes on end I observed the imperceptible effect of the sun penetrating into the still office ... Prison pastimes! Only the imprisoned, with the fascination of someone watching ants, would pay such attention to one shifting ray of sunlight.

50 [105]

In flickering intervals a firefly pursues itself. All around, in the darkness, the countryside is a great absence of sound that almost smells good. The peace of it all hurts me and weighs on me. A formless tedium suffocates me.

I don't often go to the country, I hardly ever spend a day there or stay overnight. But today, because the friend in whose house I'm staying would not hear of me declining his invitation, I came, full of misgivings, like the shy man on his way to a big party. But I felt glad when I arrived; I enjoyed the fresh air and the open spaces; I lunched and dined well but now, at dead of night, sitting in my lampless room, the uncertainty of the place fills me with anxiety.

The window of the room where I'll sleep gives onto the open countryside, onto an indefinite countryside, which is all country-sides, onto the great, vaguely starry night where I can feel a silent breeze stirring. Sitting at the window I contemplate with my senses the nothingness of the universal life out there. The hour settles into an uneasy harmony that reigns over all, from the visible invisibility of everything to the wood (on the bleached windowledge on which I rest my left hand) that is slightly rough to the touch where the old paint has blistered.

How often, though, have my eyes longed for this peace from which now, were it easy or polite, I would flee! How often, down there amongst the narrow streets of tall houses, have I thought I believed that peace, prose and certainty could be found here, amongst natural things, rather than where the tablecloth of civilization makes one forget the varnished pine it rests on! And now, here, feeling healthy and healthily tired, I am ill at ease, trapped and homesick.

I don't know if it's only to me that this happens or to everyone for whom civilization has meant being reborn. But it seems that for me, or for people who feel as I do, the artificial has come to seem natural and the natural strange. No, that's not quite it: the artificial has not become natural; the natural has simply become different. I detest and could happily do without cars and the other products of science – telephones and telegrams – that make life easy, or the by-products of fantasy – gramophones and radios – which, to those who like them, make it fun.

I'm not interested in any of that; I want none of it. But I love the Tagus because of the great city on its banks. I enjoy the sky because I see it from a fourth floor window in a street in the Baixa. Nothing in the countryside or in nature can give me anything to equal the ragged majesty of the calm moonlit city seen from Graça or São Pedro de Alcântara. For me no flowers can match the endlessly varied colours of Lisbon in the sunlight.

Only people who wear clothes find the naked body beautiful. The overriding value of modesty for sensuality is that it acts as a brake on energy. Artificiality is a way of enjoying naturalness. What I enjoyed about these vast fields I enjoyed because I don't live here. Someone who has never known constraint can have no concept of freedom. Civilization is an education of nature. The artificial provides an approach to the natural. What we must never do, however, is mistake the artificial for the natural. In the harmony between the natural and the artificial lies the essence of the superior human soul.

51 [106]   *15.5.1930*

A glimpse of countryside over a suburban wall gives me a more intense sense of freedom than a whole journey might to another person. The point at which we stand to view something forms the apex of an inverted pyramid whose base is indeterminable.

52 [39]

A shrug of the shoulders

We generally give to our ideas about the unknown the colour of our notions about what we do know: if we call death a sleep it's because it has the appearance of sleep; if we call death a new life, it's because it seems different from life. We build our beliefs and hopes out of these small misunderstandings with reality and live off husks of bread that we call cakes, the way poor children play at being happy.

But that's how all of life is; at least that's how the particular way of life generally known as civilization is. Civilization consists in giving an inappropriate name to something and then dreaming what results from that. And in fact the false name and the true dream do create a new reality. The object really does become other, because we have made it so. We manufacture realities. We use the raw materials we always used but the form lent it by art effectively prevents it from remaining the same. A table made out of pinewood is a pinetree but it is also a table. We sit down at the table not at the pinetree. Although love is a sexual instinct, we do not love with that instinct, rather we presuppose the existence of another feeling, and that presupposition is, effectively, another feeling.

These meandering thoughts that I calmly record in the café I chanced to sit down in were evoked by something as I was walking down the street, what I don't know, a sudden subtle trick of the light, a vague noise, the memory of a perfume or a snatch of music, each strummed into being by some unknown influence from without. I don't know where those thoughts were leading or where I would choose to lead them. There's a light mist today, damp and warm, unthreateningly sad, oddly monotonous. Some feeling I don't recognize aches in me; I feel as if I had lost the thread of some discussion; the words I write are utterly will-less. Sadness lurks beneath consciousness. I write, or rather scribble, these lines not in order to say anything in particular but to give my distraction something to do. With the soft marks made by a blunt pencil I haven't the heart to sharpen, I slowly fill the white paper the café uses to wrap up sandwiches (and which they provided me with because I required nothing better and anything would have done, as long as it was white). And I feel content. I lean back. Evening falls, monotonous and rainless, in a discouraged, uncertain sort of light . . . And I stop writing just because I stop writing.

53 [124]

The trivialities natural to life, the insignificancies of the normal and despicable, lie like a layer of dust, tracing a blurred, grotesque line beneath the squalor and meanness of my human existence.

The cashbook lying open before eyes whose life dreams of all the worlds of the Orient; the office manager's inoffensive joke that offends against the whole universe; the boss being told it's the phone, his girlfriend, Mrs so-and-so [. . .] in the middle of my meditation on the most least sexual part of a theory that is purely aesthetic and intellectual.

Everyone has a boss always ready with some inappropriate joke and a soul out of touch with the universe. Everyone has a boss and a boss's girlfriend and a telephone call that always comes at an inopportune moment just on the edge of the splendid fall of evening and mistresses [. . .] risk speaking ill of their lover who, as we all know, is that very minute having a pee.

But all dreamers, even if they don't do their dreaming in an office in the Baixa, or in front of a balance sheet for a textile company, each one of them has an account book open before them — whatever it may be, whether it's the woman they married or [...] a future they've inherited, whatever it might be as long as it clearly is.

And then there are the friends, great lads all of them, it's fun talking to them, having lunch with them, having supper with them and yet also, somehow or other, so sordid, so despicable, so small, still so tied to the workplace even when you're out in the street, still with your nose in the account book even when you venture abroad, still with the boss standing over you even in the infinite.

All of us, we who dream and think, are book-keepers and assistant book-keepers in a textile company or dealing in some other merchandise in some other Baixa. We draw up the accounts and make a loss; we add up the figures and pass on; we close the account and the invisible balance is never in our favour.

Though I smile as I write these words, my heart feels as if it would break, would break the way things break, into fragments, into shards, into so much rubbish to be dumped in the dustbin and carried shoulder high to the eternal dustcart of all municipal councils.

Open and adorned, everything awaits the King who will come, who is about to arrive, for the dust from his retinue forms a new mist in the slowly dawning east and in the distance the lances shine out their own dawn.

54 [43]

The most contemptible thing about dreams is that everyone has them. In the dark, the errand boy dozes away the day as he leans against the lamp post in the intervals between chores, immersed in thoughts about something or other. I know what he's daydreaming about: the same dreams I plunge into between entries in the summer tedium of the utterly still, silent office.

55 [85]

Sometimes when I raise my heavy head from the books in which I keep track of other people's accounts and of the absence of a life of my own, I feel a physical nausea. It may come from sitting so bent over but it goes beyond a mere question of numbers and disillusion. Life sickens me like a dose of bad medicine. And it's then, with immense clarity of vision, that I see how easy it would be to remove myself from this tedium if I just had the strength truly to want to do so.

We live through action, that is, through the will. Those of us – be we geniuses or beggars – who do not know how to want are brothers in our shared impotence. What's the point of calling myself a genius when in fact I'm just an assistant book-keeper? When Cesário Verde had himself announced to the doctor not as Senhor Verde, commercial clerk, but Cesário Verde, poet, he was using one of those expressions of futile pride that stink of vanity. Poor man, he was never anything but Senhor Verde, commercial clerk. The poet was born only after he died, because it was only after his death that his poetry came to be appreciated.

To act, that is true intelligence. I will be what I want to be. But I have to want whatever that is. Success means being successful, not just having the potential for success. Any large area of land has the potential to be a palace, but where's the palace if no one builds there?

56 [113]

I daydream the journey between Cascais and Lisbon. I went to Cascais in order to pay the tax on a house my boss Vasques owns in Estoril. I looked forward eagerly to the trip, an hour there and an hour back, a chance to watch the ever-changing face of the great river and its Atlantic estuary. In the event, on the way there I lost myself in abstract thoughts, watching, without actually seeing, the waterscapes I was so looking forward to, and on the way back I lost myself in the analysis of those feelings. I would be unable to describe the smallest detail of the trip, the least fragment of what I saw. I've wrested these pages from oblivion and contradiction. I don't know if that's better or worse than whatever its contrary might be.

The train slows, we're at Cais de Sodre*. I've arrived in Lisbon but not at any conclusion.

57 [230]   3.12.1931

When I first came to Lisbon the sound of someone playing scales on a piano used to drift down from the flat above, the monotonous piano practice of a little girl I never saw. Today, through processes of assimilation I fail to comprehend, I discover that if I open up the door to the cellars of my soul, those repetitive scales are still audible, played by the little girl who is now Mrs Someone-or-other, or else dead and shut up in a white place overgrown by black cypresses.

I was a child then, now I am not. In my memory, though, the sound is the same as it was in reality and, when it raises itself up from the place where it lies feigning sleep, there it is, perennially present, the same slow scales, the same monotonous rhythm. Whenever I feel it or think of it, I am invaded by a diffuse, anguished sadness that is mine alone.

I do not weep for the loss of my childhood; I weep because everything, and with it my childhood, will be lost. What makes my mind ache with the repeated, involuntary recurrence of the piano scales from upstairs, so horribly distant and anonymous, is the abstract flight of time, not the concrete flight of time that affects me directly. It is the whole mysterious fact of nothing lasting which again and again hammers out the notes, notes that are not quite music, but rather a mixture of nostalgia and longing that lurks in the absurd depths of my memory.

---

*Cais de Sodre is the train station for the Estoril–Cascais line.

Slowly, there rises before me the sitting room I never saw, where the pupil I never knew is even today playing, finger by careful finger, the same repetitive scales of something already dead. I look and see and, seeing, reconstruct the scene. And, full of a poignancy it lacked then, a vision of family life in the upstairs flat emerges from my perplexed contemplation.

I suppose, though, that I am merely a vehicle for all this and that the longing I feel is neither truly mine nor truly abstract, but the intercepted emotion of some unknown third party for whom these emotions, which in me are literary, would be – as Vieira* would say – literal. My hurt and anguish come from my imagined feelings and it is only in my imagination and my sense of otherness that I think and feel this nostalgia, which nevertheless leaves my own eyes awash with tears.

And still, with a constancy born in the depths of the world, with a studied metaphysical persistence, the sound of someone practising piano scales echoes and re-echoes up and down the physical spine of my memory. It evokes ancient streets thronged by other people, the same streets as today only different; they are the dead speaking to me through the transparent walls of their absence; they are feelings of remorse for what I did or didn't do, the rushing of streams in the night, noises downstairs in the still house.

In my head I feel like screaming. I want to stop, smash, break in two that intangible torturer, that impossible record playing inside my head, in someone else's house. I want to order my soul to stop and let me out, then drive on without me. I grow mad with hearing it. But then at last I'm myself again, with my horribly sensitive mind, my paper-thin skin stretched over nerves too near the surface, notes playing scales on the awful, inner piano of memory.

As if in some part of my brain that had declared itself independent, the scales still play, drifting up to me from below, from above, from what was my first home in Lisbon.

*António Vieira (1608–1697) was a Jesuit priest, who worked as a diplomat in Europe and as a missionary in Brazil where he died. He was a great orator and one of Portugal's major baroque prose writers.

58 [55]   *20.7.1930*

Whenever I've dreamt a lot, I go out into the street with my eyes open but I'm still wrapped in the safety of those dreams. And I'm amazed how many people fail to recognize my automatism. For I walk through daily life still holding the hand of my astral mistress, and my footsteps in the street are concordant and consonant with the obscure designs of my sleeping imagination. And yet I walk straight down the street; I don't stumble; I react as I should; I exist.

But whenever there's an interval in which I don't have to watch where I'm going in order to avoid cars or passers-by, when I don't have to talk to anyone or dodge into some nearby doorway, I let myself drift off once more like a paper boat on the waters of the dream and I revisit the dying illusion that warmed my vague awareness of the morning stirring into life amidst the sounds of carts carrying vegetables to market.

It is there, in the midst of life, that the dream becomes like a vast cinema screen. I go down a dream street in the Baixa and the reality of the dream lives inhabiting it gently binds a white blindfold of false memories about my eyes. I become a navigator through an unknown me. I conquer all in places I have never even visited. And it's like a fresh breeze this somnolent state in which I walk, leaning forwards, in my march on the impossible.

Each of us is intoxicated by different things. There's intoxication enough for me in just living. Drunk on feeling I drift but never stray. If it's time to go back to work, I go to the office just like everyone else. If not, I go down to the river to stare at the waters, again just like everyone else. I'm just the same. But behind this sameness, I secretly scatter my personal firmament with stars and therein create my own infinity.

59 [368]

Phrases I will never write and landscapes I will never be able to describe: with what clarity I dictate them to my inertia and describe them in my meditations when, reclining in a chair, I have only the remotest ties with life. I carve out whole sentences, word perfect, complete dramas plot themselves in my mind, in every word I sense the verbal and metric movement of great poems and a great [. . .] like an invisible slave follows behind me in the shadows. But if I move one step away from the chair in which I sit nurturing these almost finished feelings, and make a move towards the table in order to write them down, the words flee, the dramas die, and all that remains of the vital nexus that drew together these rhythmic murmurings is a distant longing, a trace of sunlight on far-off mountains, a wind stirring the leaves on the edge of the desert, a never-to-be-revealed relationship, an orgy enjoyed by others, the woman whom our intuition tells us will look back, and who never actually existed.

I've undertaken every conceivable project. An inspirational logic lay behind *The Iliad* I composed, and its epodes had an organic coherence that Homer never managed to achieve. The studied perfection of these verses never put into words makes Virgil's precision seem laxity and Milton's strength weakness. The symbolic exactness of every apposite detail of my allegorical satires exceeded anything Swift produced. And the number of Verlaines I have been!

And each time I rise from my chair, where these things have an existence beyond mere dreams, I suffer the double tragedy of knowing them to be worthless but at the same time knowing that indeed they were not entirely dreamed and that some trace of them lingers on in the abstract threshold of my thinking them and their existing.

I was more of a genius in dreams than in life. That is my tragedy. I was the runner who fell just before the finishing line having led the field all the way until then.

60 [186]   *13.6.1930*

I live always in the present. I know nothing of the future and no longer have a past. The former weighs me down with a thousand possibilities, the latter with the reality of nothingness. I have neither hopes for the future nor longings for what was. Knowing what my life has been up till now – so often so contrary to the way I wished it to be – what assumptions can I make about my life except that it will be neither what I presume nor what I want it to be, that it will be something that happens to me from outside, even against my own will? Nothing in my past life fills me with the vain desire to repeat it. I have never been anything more than a mere vestige, a simulacrum of myself. My past is everything I never managed to become. Not even the feelings associated with past moments make me nostalgic; what one feels is of the moment; once that is past the page turns and the story continues but not the text.

Brief, dark shadow of a city tree, the light sound of water falling into a sad pool, the green of smooth grass – a public garden on the edge of dusk – in this moment you are the whole universe to me, because you entirely fill my every conscious feeling. I want nothing more from life than to feel it ebbing away into these unexpected evenings, to the sound of other people's children playing in gardens fenced in by the melancholy of the surrounding streets, and above, the high branches of the trees, vaulted by the ancient sky in which the stars are just beginning to reappear.

61 [33]

By thought alone I made myself both echo and abyss. By going ever deeper into myself I became many. The tiniest episode – a change in the light, the tumbling fall of a dry leaf, the petal that withers and drops from the flower, the voice on the other side of the wall or the footsteps of the person who speaks, together with those of the person I presume to be listening, the half-open gate to the old farm, the inner courtyard that opens through an archway onto the houses huddled in the moonlight – all these things, none of which belongs to me, bind up my sensitive thoughts with knots of plangent longing. I am someone else in each of these moments; I painfully renew myself in each ill-defined impression.

I live off impressions that are not mine, prodigal in renunciations, always other in the way I am myself.

62 [34]

I created various personalities within myself. I create them constantly. Every dream, as soon as it is dreamed, is immediately embodied by another person who dreams it instead of me.

In order to create, I destroyed myself; I have externalized so much of my inner life that even inside I now exist only externally. I am the living stage across which various actors pass acting out different plays.

63 [36]

Amiel* said that a landscape is a state of mind, but the phrase is the feebly felicitous one of a feeble dreamer. A landscape is a landscape and therefore cannot be a state of mind. To objectify is to create and no one says of a finished poem that it is a state of thinking about writing a poem. To see is perhaps to dream but if we use the word 'see' rather than the word 'dream', it's because we distinguish between seeing and dreaming.

Anyway, what's the point of these speculations on the psychology of words? Quite independently of me the grass grows, the rain waters the grass as it grows and the sun turns to gold the whole field of grass that has grown or will grow; the mountains have been there since ancient times and the wind that blows sounds just as it did to Homer (even if he never existed). It would be more correct

---

*Henri-Frédéric Amiel (1821–1881) was a Swiss diarist and critic whose *Fragments d'un journal intime* was published between 1883 and 1887.

to say that a state of mind is a landscape; that would have the advantage of containing not the lie of a theory but the truth of a metaphor.

These random words were dictated to me by the great expanse of city I saw lit by the universal light of the sun, from high up on São Pedro de Alcântara. Every time I look out like this on a vast landscape and free myself of the 1 metre 70 and 61 kilos of which I am physically constituted, I smile a great metaphysical smile at those who dream that a dream is just a dream and, with a noble virtue born of understanding, I love the truth of the absolute exterior world.

The Tagus in the background is a blue lake and the hills on the far shore a squat Switzerland. A small boat – a black cargo steamer – leaves the shores of Poço do Bispo for the estuary mouth that I cannot see from here. Until the day when this outward aspect of my self should cease, may the gods preserve in me this clear, sunny notion of external reality, this sense of my own unimportance, this comforting feeling of being small and capable of imagining being happy.

64 [38]   *29.1.1932*

Once the last heat of summer had relented and given way to a mellower sun, the autumn started – even before it was properly upon us – with a slight, long undefined sadness as if the sky had lost the will to smile. It was sometimes pale blue, sometimes almost green, but always tenuous even where the colour was at its most intense; there was a kind of sluggishness about the clouds in their different shades of faded purples; now, filling the whole still desolation across which the clouds drifted, there was a feeling of tedium, not torpor.

The start of autumn was signalled by a genuine chill in the not-yet-cold air, by a fading of whatever colours had remained unfaded, by the appearance of a hint of shadow and absence that had not been there before in the tone of landscapes and the blurred aspect of things. Nothing was dying yet but everything, as if with a smile as yet unsmiled, looked longingly back at life.

Then at last the real autumn arrived: the air was cooled by winds; the leaves spoke in dry tones even before they had withered and died; the whole earth took on the colour and impalpable form of a treacherous marshland. What had been a last faint smile faded with a weary drooping of eyelids, in gestures of indifference. And so everything that feels, or that we imagine as having feelings, clasped its own farewell close to its breast. The sound of a gust of wind in a hallway floated across our awareness of something else. One longed, in order truly to feel life, to be a patient convalescing from an illness.

But, coming as they did in the midst of this clear autumn, the first winter rains almost disrespectfully washed away these half-tints. Amidst the occasional exclamatory bursts of rain, high winds unleashed distracted words of anonymous protest, sad, almost angry sounds of soulless despair, whistling around whatever was motionless, tugging at whatever was fixed and dragging with them anything movable.

And at last, in cold and greyness, autumn ended. It was a wintry autumn that came now, a dust finally become mud, but it brought with it what is good about the winter cold, with the harsh summer over, the spring to come and the autumn finally giving way to winter. And in the sky above, where the dull colours had lost all memory of heat or sadness, everything was set for night and an indefinite period of meditation.

That was how I saw it without recourse to thinking. I write it down today because I remember it. The autumn I have is the autumn I lost.

65 [434]   14.9.1931

The coming of autumn was announced in the aimless evenings by a certain softening of colour in the ample sky, by the buffetings of a cold breeze that arose in the wake of the first cooler days of the dying summer. The trees had not yet lost their green or their leaves nor was there yet that vague anguish which accompanies our awareness of any death in the external world simply because it reflects our own future death. It was as if what energy remained had grown weary so that a kind of slumber crept over any last attempts at action. Ah, these evenings are full of such painful indifference it is as if the autumn were beginning in us rather than in the world.

Each autumn that comes brings us closer to what will be our last autumn; the same could be said of late spring or summer but autumn, by its very nature, reminds us of the ending of everything, so easy to forget in kinder seasons. It is still not yet quite autumn and the air is not yet filled with the yellow of fallen leaves or the damp sad weather that will eventually turn to winter. But there is an anticipation of sadness, some intimate grief dressed and ready for the journey, in one's sense of being aware, however vaguely, of the diffuse colours of things, of a different tone in the wind, of an ancient quiet which, as night falls, slowly invades the unavoidable presence of the universe.

Yes, we will all pass, everything will pass. Nothing will remain of the person who put on feelings and gloves, who talked about death and local politics. The same light falls on the faces of saints and the gaiters of passers-by, and the dying of that same light will leave in darkness the utter nothingness that will be all that remains of the fact that some were saints and others wearers of gaiters. In the vast vortex, in which the whole world indolently wallows as if in a whirl of dry leaves, the dresses run up by seamstresses have as much value as whole kingdoms; the blonde plaits of children are swept up in the same mortal jig as sceptres that once symbolized empires. All is nothing and in the atrium of the Invisible, whose door swings open only to reveal another closed door beyond, every single thing, large or small, which formed for us and in us the system we understood to be the universe, everything dances in thrall to the wind that stirs all but touches nothing. It is nothing but lightly mixed shadow and dust, there is not even a voice, only the sound the wind makes as it scoops up and sweeps along, there is not even silence except when the wind allows it. Some are whirled up through the atrium like light leaves, less bound to the earth because of their lightness, and they fall outside the circle of heavier objects. Others, indistinguishable unless seen close to, form a single layer within the vortex, almost invisible, like dust. Others again, tree trunks in miniature, are dragged into the circle only to be abandoned in different corners of the floor. One day, when all knowledge ceases, the door beyond will open and everything that we were – a mere detritus of stars and souls – will be swept from the house in order that whatever remains may begin again.

My heart aches as if it were not mine. My brain lulls to sleep everything I feel. Yes, it is the beginning of autumn that touches both the air and my soul with the same unsmiling light that edges with dull yellow the hazy contours of the few clouds at sunset. Yes, it is the beginning of autumn and, in this limpid hour, the beginning of a clear understanding of the anonymous inadequacy of all things. The autumn, yes, the autumn, as it is and always will be: an anticipation of weariness in every gesture, of disillusionment with every dream. What possible hopes can I have? In my thoughts, I already walk amongst the leaves and dust of the atrium, caught up in this senseless orbit around nothing, my footsteps the only human sound on the clean flagstones that an angular sun – from where I know not – burnishes with death.

The autumn will take everything, everything I ever thought or dreamed, everything I did or did not do, spent matches scattered at random on the floor, discarded scraps of paper, great empires, all the religions and philosophies that the drowsy children of the abyss played at making. The autumn will take everything, everything, that is, that made up my soul, from my noblest aspirations to the ordinary house in which I live, from the gods I once worshipped to my boss Vasques. The autumn will take everything, will sweep everything up with tender indifference. The autumn will take everything.

66 [144]

Outside, slowly in the moonlight of the slow night, the wind is shaking things that make shadows as they move. It may be nothing but the clothes hung out to dry on the floor above, but the shadow itself knows nothing of shirts and floats, impalpable, in mute accord with everything around it.

I left the shutters open so that I would wake early, but until now (and it is now so late that not a sound can be heard), I have managed neither to go to sleep nor to remain properly awake. Beyond the shadows in my room lies the moonlight but it does not enter my window. It is just there, like a day of hollow silver, and the roofs of the building opposite, which I can see from my bed, are liquid with inky whiteness. The hard light of the moon contains a sad peace, something resembling words of congratulation spoken from on high to someone unable to hear them.

And without looking, without thinking, my eyes closed now to absent sleep, I consider which words would best describe moonlight. The ancients would say that the moon is white or silver. But the false whiteness of the moon is of many colours. If I were to get up out of bed and look through the cold window panes I know that, high up in the lonely air, the moonlight would be grey-white with a bluish tinge of faded yellow; that on the various rooftops, in diverse degrees of blackness, it polishes the submissive buildings with dark white and floods with transparent colour the chestnut red of the rooftiles. Down below in the quiet chasm of the street, on the irregular roundnesses of the bare cobblestones, its only colour is a blue that emanates perhaps from the grey of the stones themselves. It will be almost dark blue on the distant horizon, but quite different from the blue-black depths of the sky, and dark yellow where it touches the glass of window panes.

From here, from my bed, if I open my eyes filled with a sleep I do not as yet enjoy, the air is like snow made colour in which float filaments of warm mother-of-pearl. And if I think the moonlight with my feelings, it is a tedium made white shadow that grows gradually darker as if my eyes were slowly closing on its vague whiteness.

67 [66]   10.12.1930

I go through periods of great stagnation. By this I don't mean that, like most people, it takes me days and days to reply on a postcard to an urgent letter someone wrote me. I don't mean that, again like other people, I put off indefinitely something easy that might prove useful to me, or something useful that might give me pleasure. My misunderstanding with myself is more subtle than that. I stagnate in my very soul. I suffer a suspension of will, emotion and thought that lasts for days at a time; I can only express myself to others and, through them, express myself to me in the purely vegetative life of the soul, through words, gestures, habits.

In these shadowy times, I am incapable of thinking, feeling or wanting. The only things I manage to write are numbers or mere strokes of the pen. I feel nothing and even the death of someone I love would seem as far removed from me as if it had taken place in a foreign language. I can do nothing; it is as if I slept and my gestures, words and actions were just a surface breathing, the rhythmical instinct of some organism.

Thus days and days pass, how much of my life, were I to add up those days, I couldn't say. Sometimes I think that when I finally slough off these stagnant clothes, I may not stand as naked as I suppose and some intangible vestments may still clothe the eternal absence of my true soul; it occurs to me that to think, feel or want may also be stagnant forms of a more personal way of thinking, of feelings more intimately mine, of a will lost somewhere in the labyrinth of who I really am.

Whatever the truth, I let it be. And to whatever gods or goddesses may exist, I hand over what I am, resigned to whatever fate may send and whatever chance may offer, faithful to some forgotten promise.

68 [148]   *9.6.1934*

With the beginning of summer I grow sad. One would think that the brilliance of summer hours, however harsh, would seem sweet to someone ignorant of his own identity. But that's not the case with me. There is too sharp a contrast between all that exuberant outer life and what I feel and think, without knowing how to feel or think – the perennially unburied corpse of my feelings. I have the impression that, in this formless homeland called the universe, I live beneath a political tyranny which, although it does not oppress me directly, still offends some hidden principle of my soul. And then slowly, secretly, there grows within me the anticipated nostalgia of an impossible exile.

What I most want is to sleep. But the sleep I desire, unlike other varieties, even those induced by sickness, does not include the physical reward of rest. Nor does it help one to forget about life, or even bring with it the promise of dreams, balancing on the tray it carries as it approaches our soul the calm gift of a final abdication. No, this is a sleep that never actually sleeps, it weighs on one's eyelids but never closes them and puckers the corners of unbelieving lips in a gesture one feels to be a combination of repugnance and stupidity. This is the sleep that weighs on one's body during periods of great insomnia of the soul.

Only when night comes do I feel, if not happiness, at least some kind of repose which I experience as contentment by analogy with other states of repose that do bring contentment. Then the drowsiness passes, the confused mental twilight of that state fades and grows clearer, almost light. For a moment a hope for other things arises. But such hopes are short-lived, overridden by a sleepless, hopeless tedium, the comfortless waking of one who has not slept. And, a poor soul weary of body, I stare out from the window of my room at the multitudes of stars; at multitudes of stars and nothing, nothingness, but oh so many stars . . .

69 [132]   *27.6.1930*

Life for us is whatever we imagine it to be. To the peasant with his one field, that field is everything, it is an empire. To Caesar with his vast empire which still feels cramped, that empire is a field. The poor man has an empire; the great man only a field. The truth is that we possess nothing but our own senses; it is on them, then, and not on what they perceive, that we must base the reality of our life.

But all this is apropos of nothing.

I've dreamed a lot. I'm tired now from dreaming but not tired of dreaming. No one tires of dreaming, because to dream is to forget, and forgetting does not weigh on us, it is a dreamless sleep throughout which we remain awake. In dreams I have achieved everything. I've also woken up, but what does that matter? How many countless Caesars I have been! And yet how mean-spirited are the glorious! Saved from death by the generosity of a pirate, Caesar subsequently searched long and hard for that same man, arrested him and ordered him to be crucified. When Napoleon drew up his last will and testament in St Helena, he left a legacy to a criminal who had tried to assassinate Wellington. Such greatness of soul is about on a par with that of their squint-eyed neighbour! . . . How many countless Caesars have I been and still dream of being!

How many countless Caesars have I been, yet I was never like the real Caesars. I was truly imperial in my dreams and for that reason came to nothing. My armies were defeated but it was a thing of no importance and no one died. No flags were taken. I never dreamed the army to the point where those flags might hove into view around the corner of my dreaming gaze. How many countless Caesars have I been right here in Rua dos Douradores. The Caesars I was still live in my imagination, but the real Caesars are all long dead, and the Rua dos Douradores, that is, Reality, would not now recognize them.

I throw an empty matchbox out into the abyss that is the street beyond the sill of my high window. I sit up in my chair and listen.

As if the fact were significant, the fallen matchbox sends back a clear echo telling me the street is deserted. There is no sound apart from the sounds made by the entire city. Yes, the sounds of the entire Sunday city – so many indecipherable sounds and each in its way right.

How little of the real world one needs as a starting point for the best meditations: arriving late for lunch, running out of matches and throwing the empty box out into the street, feeling slightly indisposed after eating lunch too late, it being Sunday with nothing in the air but the promise of a poor sunset, my being no one in this world, and other such metaphysical matters.

But oh how many Caesars I have been!

70 [145]

I woke very early this morning in a sudden tangle of confusion and sat up in bed feeling suffocated by an incomprehensible sense of tedium. It was provoked neither by a dream nor by any reality. It was a feeling of absolute, utter tedium that had its roots in something unknowable. In the dark depths of my soul, invisible unknown forces engaged in a battle in which my being was the battleground, and the whole of me was shaken by this secret struggle. With my waking was born a physical nausea for all of life. A horror at having to live awoke and sat up with me in bed. Everything rang hollow to me and I was filled with the cold realization that every problem, whatever it might be, would prove insoluble.

A terrible anxiety gripped and shook my smallest gesture. I felt afraid I might go mad, not from madness, but just from being there. My whole body was a suppressed scream. My heart beat as if it would speak.

In my bare feet, in long, faltering strides that I vainly tried to make other than they were, I walked the short length of my room and traced an empty diagonal across the room beside mine, which has a door in the corner that opens onto the corridor. As my movements became more uncontrolled and imprecise, I accidentally knocked the brushes on the dressing table, bumped against a chair and, once, my swinging hand struck the harsh iron of the bedstead. I lit a cigarette that I smoked without thinking and only when I saw that ash had fallen on the pillow – but how could it when I hadn't even lain down there? – did I realize that I was possessed (or at least in some state analogous in effect if not in name) and that the consciousness I would normally have had of myself had become fused with the void.

I received the coming of morning, the tenuous cold light that lends a vague bluish whiteness to the emergent horizon, like a sweet kiss from the world. For that light, that true day, freed me, freed me from something, offered a supportive arm to my as yet unvisited old age, patted my false childhood on the head, gave shelter to the beggarly repose of my overflowing sensibility. What a morning this is that wakes me both to the brutishness of life and to its overwhelming tenderness! I could almost cry to see the light growing before and beneath me in the old narrow street, and when the shutters on the grocer's shop on the corner turn dirty brown in the almost glaring light, my heart feels a fairy-tale sense of relief, and the security of not feeling begins to seep back into me.

What a morning this pain brings with it! And what shadows retreat before it? What mysteries were unfolded? None: just the sound of the first tram like a match illuminating the darkness of my soul, and the firm steps of the first passer-by, the friendly voice of physical reality telling me not to upset myself so.

71 [181]   *16 and 17.10.1931*

Yes, it's sunset. I walk, leisurely and distracted, down Rua da Alfândega towards the Tagus and as Terreiro do Paço opens out before me, I can clearly see the sunless western sky. To the left, above the hills on the far shore of the river, a bank of brownish, dull pink mist crouches in the sky and there the colours shade from greenish blue to greyish white. A great sense of peace that I do not possess is scattered in the cold, abstract autumn air. Not having it, I let myself suffer the vague pleasure of imagining its existence. But in reality there is neither peace nor a lack of it, there is only sky, a sky made up of every fading colour – blue-white, blue-green, a pale grey that is neither green nor blue, the faded remote colours of clouds that are not clouds, yellows darkened with blanched reds. And all of this is just a vision that dies the instant it is conceived, a fleeting interval between nothing and nothing, placed on high, prolix and undefined, painted in the colours of heaven and of grief.

I feel and I forget. A sense of nostalgia invades me, like an opiate borne on the cold air, the nostalgia that everyone feels for everything. I am filled with an intimate, illusory ecstasy of seeing.

At the estuary mouth where the last moments of the sun linger to an end, the light finally ebbs away in a livid white that turns blue as it mixes with the cold green. There is a torpor in the air of things unfulfilled. Above, the landscape of the sky falls silent.

At this moment, when I almost overflow with feeling, I would like to have the wit simply to speak out and have as my destiny the capricious freedom of a style. But no, there is only the vast, remote sky slowly cancelling itself, and the emotion I feel – a mixture of many confused emotions – is nothing but the reflection of that empty sky in a lake within myself, silent as a dead man's gaze, a hidden lake amidst tall rocks, in which the oblivious sky contemplates itself.

Now, as many times before, I am troubled by my own experience of my feelings, by my anguish simply to be feeling something, my disquiet simply at being here, my nostalgia for something never known, the setting of the sun on all emotions, this fading, in my external consciousness of myself, from yellow into grey sadness.

Who will save me from existence? It isn't death I want, or life: it's the other thing that shines at the bottom of all longing like a possible diamond in a cave one cannot reach. It's the whole weight and pain of this real and impossible universe, of this sky, of this standard borne by some unknown army, of these colours that grow pale in the fictitious air, out of which there emerges in still, electric whiteness the imaginary crescent of the moon, silhouetted by distance and indifference.

The absence of a true God is become the empty corpse of the vast sky and the closed soul. Infinite prison, because you are infinite no one can escape you!

72 [381]

Down the steps of my dreams and my weariness, descend from your unreality, descend and be my substitute for the world.

73 [384]

Life is an experimental journey undertaken involuntarily. It is a journey of the spirit through the material world and, since it is the spirit that travels, it is in the spirit that it is experienced. That is why there exist contemplative souls who have lived more intensely, more widely, more tumultuously than others who have lived their lives purely externally. The end result is what matters. What one felt was what one experienced. One retires to bed as wearily from having dreamed as from having done hard physical labour. One never lives so intensely as when one has been thinking hard.

The person standing apart in the corner of the room dances with all the dancers. He sees everything and because he sees, he experiences everything. When it comes down to it, it is just another feeling, and seeing or even remembering someone's body is just as good as any actual contact. Thus when I see others dance, I dance too. I agree with the English poet who, describing how he lay far off in the grass watching three reapers at work, wrote: 'A fourth man is there reaping too, and that fourth man is me.'

All this, which I speak just as I feel it, has to do with the great weariness, apparently without cause, that came on me suddenly today. I feel not only tired but embittered and yet the cause of that bitterness is also unknown. I feel such anguish I'm on the verge of tears, tears to be suppressed not cried, tears born of a sickness of the soul not of any physical ill.

I have lived so much without ever having lived. I have thought so much without ever having thought. I feel weighed down by worlds of unenacted violence, of stillborn adventures. I am sick of what I never had nor will have, weary of gods always just about to exist. I bear on my body the wounds of all the battles I did not fight. My muscles are weary from efforts I never even considered making.

Dull, dumb, empty . . . The sky above belongs to a dead, imperfect summer. I look at it as if it were not there. I sleep what I think, I lie down even as I walk, I suffer and feel nothing. My great nostalgia is for nothing at all, is itself nothing, like the sky above, which I do not see and which I gaze at impersonally.

74 [387]

You want to travel? To travel you simply need to exist. In the train of my body or of my destiny I travel from day to day, as from station to station, leaning out to look at the streets and the squares, at gestures and faces, always the same and always different as, ultimately, is the way with all landscapes.

If I imagine something, I see it. What more would I do if I travelled? Only extreme feebleness of imagination can justify anyone needing to travel in order to feel.

'Any road, this simple road to Entepfuhl, will take you to the end of the world.'* But the end of the world, once you've exhausted the world by going round it, is the same Entepfuhl from which you set out. In fact the end of the world, and its beginning, is merely our concept of the world. It is only within us that landscapes become landscapes. That's why if I imagine them, I create them; if I create them, they exist; if they exist, I see them just as I do other

---

*Thomas Carlyle, *Sartor Resartus* (1833–1834), Book II, chapter 2. Carlyle was in turn paraphrasing Schiller: 'Denn jede Strasse führt ans End' der Welt' (*Wilhelm Tell*, IV, iii).

landscapes. So why travel? In Madrid, in Berlin, in Persia, in China, at the North and South Poles, where would I be other than inside myself, feeling my particular kind of feelings?

Life is whatever we make it. The traveller is the journey. What we see is not what we see but who we are.

75 [388]

The only traveller with real soul I've ever met was an office boy who worked in a company where I was at one time employed. This young lad collected brochures on different cities, countries and travel companies; he had maps, some torn out of newspapers, others begged from one place or another; he cut out pictures of landscapes, engravings of exotic costumes, paintings of boats and ships from various journals and magazines. He would visit travel agencies on behalf of some real or hypothetical company, possibly the actual one in which he worked, and ask for brochures on Italy or India, brochures giving details of sailings between Portugal and Australia.

He was not only the greatest traveller I've ever known (because he was the truest), he was also one of the happiest people I have had the good fortune to meet. I'm sorry not to know what has become of him, though, to be honest, I'm not really sorry, I only feel that I should be. I'm not really sorry because today, ten or more years on from that brief period in which I knew him, he must be a grown man, stolid, reliably fulfilling his duties, married perhaps, someone's breadwinner – in other words, one of the living dead. By now he may even have travelled in body, he who knew so well how to travel in his soul.

A sudden memory assails me: he knew exactly which trains one had to catch to go from Paris to Bucharest; which trains one took to cross England; and in his garbled pronunciation of the strange names hung the bright certainty of the greatness of his soul. Now he probably lives like a dead man, but perhaps one day, when he's old, he'll remember that to dream of Bordeaux is not only better, but truer, than actually to arrive in Bordeaux.

And then again perhaps all this has some other explanation, perhaps he was just imitating someone else. Or perhaps . . . Yes, sometimes, when I consider the huge gulf that exists between the intelligence of children and the stupidity of adults, I think that as children we must have a guardian angel who lends us his own astral intelligence and then, perhaps with sadness, but in accordance with a higher law, abandons us, the way female animals abandon their grown-up offspring, to become the fattened pigs it's our destiny to be.

76 [389]

There is an erudition of knowledge, which is what we usually mean by 'erudition', and there is an erudition of understanding, which is what we call 'culture'. But there is also an erudition of sensibility.

This has nothing to do with one's experience of life. Like history, experience of life teaches us nothing. True experience consists in reducing one's contact with reality whilst at the same time intensifying one's analysis of that contact. In that way one's sensibility can widen and deepen since everything lies within us anyway; it is enough that we seek it out and know how to do so.

What is travel and what use is it? One sunset is much like another; you don't have to go to Constantinople in order to see one. And what of the sense of freedom that travel brings? I can enjoy that just going from Lisbon to Benfica and I can feel it more intensely than someone journeying from Lisbon to China because, in my opinion, if that sense of freedom is not in me, then it's nowhere. 'Any road,' said Carlyle, 'this simple road to Entepfuhl, will lead you to the end of world.' But the road to Entepfuhl, if followed right to the end, would lead straight back to Entepfuhl, which means that Entepfuhl, where we started, is that 'end of the world' we set out to find in the beginning.

Condillac begins his famous book* with the words: 'However high we climb and however low we fall we never escape our own feelings.' We can never disembark from ourselves. We can never become another person, except by making ourselves other through the sensitive application of our imaginations to our selves. The true landscapes are those that we ourselves create, because, since we are their gods, we see them as they really are, that is, exactly as they were created. I'm not interested in nor can I truly see any of the seven zones of the world; I travel the eighth zone, which is my own.

Someone who has sailed every sea has merely sailed through the monotony of himself. I have sailed more seas than anyone. I have seen more mountains than exist on earth. I have passed through more cities than were ever built and the great rivers of impossible worlds have flowed, absolute, beneath my contemplative gaze. If I were to travel, I would find only a feeble copy of what I have already seen without travelling.

When other travellers visit countries, they do so as anonymous pilgrims. In the countries I have visited I have been not only the secret pleasure felt by the unknown traveller but the majesty of the king who rules there, I have been the people who live there and their customs, and the whole history of that and other nations. I saw those landscapes and those houses because I *was* them, created in God from the substance of my imagination.

77 [400]

I find the idea of travelling only vicariously seductive as if it were an idea more likely to seduce someone other than myself. The whole vast spectacle of the world fills my awakened imagination with a wave of brilliant tedium; like someone grown weary of all gestures,

---

*Pessoa is paraphrasing Etienne de Condillac (1715–1780), *Essai sur l'origine des connaissances humaines* (1746): 'Soit que nous nous élevions, pour parler métaphoriquement, jusques dans les cieux; soit que nous descendions dans les abîmes, nous ne sortons point de nous-mêmes.'

I sketch out a desire and the anticipated monotony of possible land-scapes disturbs the surface of my stagnant heart like a rough wind.

And as with journeys so with books, and as with books so with everything else ... I dream of an erudite life in the silent company of ancients and moderns, renewing my emotions through other people's, filling myself with contradictory thoughts that spring from the contradictions of real thinkers and those who have only half-thought, in other words, the majority of those who write. But the minute I pick up a book from the table even my interest in reading vanishes; the physical fact of having to read it negates the desire to read ... In the same way the idea of travelling atrophies if I happen to go anywhere near a place whence I could in fact embark. And, being myself a nonentity, I return to the two negatives of which I am certain – my daily life as an anonymous passer-by and the waking insomnia of my dreams.

And as with books so with everything else . . . Given that anything can be dreamed up to serve as a real interruption in the silent flow of my days, I raise eyes of weary protest to the sylph who is mine alone, to the poor girl who, had she only learned to sing, could perhaps have been a siren.

78 [422]

Some people have one great dream in life which they fail to fulfil. Others have no dream at all and fail to fulfil even that.

79 [51]

The storm that was constantly threatening the uneasy calm has finally passed over and three consecutive days of unending heat have brought to the lucid surface of things a tepid but delicious coolness. Much the same thing happens when in the course of living, the soul, weighed down by life, feels the burden suddenly and inexplicably lift.

I think of us as climates constantly threatened by storms that always break somewhere else.

The empty immensity of things, the great forgetting that fills sky and earth ...

80 [60]

I was already feeling uneasy. All at once, the silence stopped breathing.

The infinite day suddenly splintered like steel. I crouched like an animal on the table, my hands useless claws gripping the smooth table top. A cruel light had entered every corner and every soul, and a voice from a nearby mountain fell from on high, a shout ripping the silken walls of the abyss. My heart stopped. My throat pounded. The only thing my mind was aware of was an inkblot on a piece of paper.

81 [64]

Any change in one's usual timetable fills the spirit with a cold novelty, a slightly discomforting pleasure. Someone who normally leaves the office at six but one day happens to leave at five, immediately experiences a kind of mental holiday followed almost at once by a feeling bordering on distress because he does not quite know what to do with himself.

Yesterday because I had some business out of the office, I left at four o'clock and by five had completed my errand. I'm not used to being out in the streets at that time and so I found myself in a different city. The slow light on the familiar shopfronts had a sterile sweetness and the usual passers-by walked in a city parallel to mine, like sailors given shore leave the night before.

Since the office was still open at that hour, I hurried back there to the evident surprise of the other employees whom I had already said goodbye to for the day. Back already? Yes, back already. I was free to feel again, alone with those people who accompanied me in all but spirit ... It was in a way like being at home, that is, in the one place where one does not have feelings.

82 [75]

In the east rises the blonde light of the golden moon. The swathe it cuts across the wide river makes serpents on the sea.

83 [80]

Landscape in the rain[I]

With each drop of rain my failed life weeps with nature. There is something of my own disquiet in the steady drip and patter by which the day vainly empties out its sadness upon the earth.

It rains and rains. My soul grows damp just listening to it. So much rain . . . My flesh turns liquid and watery around my consciousness of it.

An uneasy cold closes icy hands about my poor heart. The hours, grey and [...] stretch out, flatten out in time; the moments drag.

How it rains!

The gutters spout tiny torrents of sudden water. Into my mind percolates the troubling sound of water rushing down pipes. The rain beats indolently, mournfully, against the windowpanes; in the [...]

A cold hand grips my throat and will not let me breathe in life.

Everything is dying in me, even the knowledge that I can dream! I do not feel well, not in any physical sense. My soul finds hard edges to all the soft comforts on which I lean for support. Every gaze I look on has grown dark, defeated by the impoverished light of this day now set to die a painless death.

84 [110]

A blade of languid lightning fluttered darkly in the big room. Before the imminent sound of thunder there was a pause, as if for a gulp of air, followed by a deep migratory rumble. The rain moaned, like professional mourners during breaks in the conversation. Indoors the least sound seemed inordinately loud and restless.

85 [111]   *2.11.1932*

Mist or smoke? Was it rising from the earth or falling from the sky? It was impossible to tell: it was more like a contagion of the air than an emanation from the earth or a precipitation from the sky. At times it seemed more like an affliction of the eyes than a reality of nature.

Whatever it was, the whole landscape was pervaded by a muddy disquiet, composed of forgetting and unreality. It was as if the silence of the sick sun had mistaken some imperfect body for its own. It was as if something, which could be sensed in everything, was about to happen and for that reason the visible world drew a veil about itself.

It was difficult to make out what it was covering the sky – clouds or mist. It was more like a dull torpor touched here and there by a little colour, an odd yellowish grey except where this fragmented into a false pink or blue, but even then you could not tell if it was the sky showing through or merely a layer of blue.

Nothing was definite, not even the indefinite. That's why one felt inclined to call the mist 'smoke', because it did not look like mist, or to wonder which it was, mist or smoke, because it was impossible to tell. The very warmth of the air was accomplice to this doubt. It was neither warm, nor cold, nor cool; it seemed to derive its temperature from something other than heat. In fact it seemed that the mist was cold to the eyes but warm to the touch, as if sight and touch were two different ways of feeling of the same sense.

There was not the shading-off of edges and sharp angles that lingering mists usually lend to the outlines of trees or to the corners of buildings, nor were they half-revealed and half-obscured as one would have expected had it been real smoke. It was as if each thing projected all around it a vague diurnal shadow but without there being any source of light that could produce such a shadow, nor any surface onto which it could be projected and which would account for its visibility.

Not that it really was visible, it was more a suggestion (apparent in equal measure everywhere) of something about to be seen, as if what was about to be revealed hesitated to appear.

And what kind of feeling did it create? The impossibility of there being any, a confusion of heart and mind, a perplexity of feelings, a torpor of awakened existence, a sharpening of some sense in the soul equivalent to that of straining to catch a definitive but vain revelation, always just about to be revealed, like the truth, and, like the truth, the twin of concealment.

I've dismissed the desire to sleep which thoughts bring on, because even the first yawn seemed too much effort. Even not seeing hurts my eyes. And beyond this blank abdication of the whole soul, all that remains of the impossible world are the distant sounds beyond.

Oh, to have another world, full of other things, another soul with which to feel them and other thoughts with which to know that soul! Anything else, even tedium, but not this melding together of soul and world, not the bluish desolation of this all-pervading lack of definition.

86 [141]   *4.4.1930*

In contrast to the vivid white wings of the seagulls' restless flight, the dark sky to the south of the Tagus was a sinister black. There was, however, no storm as yet. The heavy threat of rain had passed over to the opposite shore and the Baixa, still damp from the brief rainfall, smiled up from the earth at a sky that was slowly, palely, turning blue again to the north. There was a chill in the cool spring air.

At such empty and fathomless moments, I like to guide my thoughts into a meditation. It is nothing in itself but it retains in its empty lucidity something of the solitary cold of the brightening day with its backdrop of distant black clouds and certain intuitive feelings which, like the seagulls, evoke by way of contrast the mystery of everything in the gloom.

Suddenly, contrary to my personal literary aims, the black sky in the south evokes, whether a real or imagined memory I cannot tell, another sky, seen perhaps in another life, over a small river in the north, full of sad reeds and far from any city. Without understanding how or why, a landscape of wild ducks gradually spreads through my imagination and with the clarity of a strange dream I feel very close to that imagined scene.

In this land of reeds and rushes by the banks of rivers, a land made for hunters and for fear, the ragged banks push out like small grubby promontories into the leaden yellow waters and retreat to form muddy bays for boats as small as toys, and shores where the water shines on the surface of the concealed mud amongst the greenish-black stems of rushes too dense to walk through.

The desolation is that of a dead grey sky which here and there crumples up into clouds even blacker than itself. Though I cannot feel it, a wind is blowing and I see that what I thought was the other bank is in fact a long island behind which one can make out, in the flat distance, across the great, desolate river, the other bank, the real one.

No one goes there, no one ever will. Even though, via a contradictory flight through time and space, I can escape from this world into that landscape, no one else will ever go there. I would wait in vain for something I did not even know I was waiting for and in the end there would be nothing but the slow fall of night in which everything would slowly take on the colour of the blackest clouds and lose itself little by little in the negation of the sky.

And here, suddenly, I feel the cold. It seeps into my body from my bones. I take a deep breath and wake up. The man who passes me beneath the Arcade by the Stock Exchange looks at me with uncomprehending distrust. The black sky, now even darker, hangs still lower over the southern shore . . .

87 [160]

(rain)

And at last, over the darkness of the shining roofs, the cold light of the warm morning breaks like a torment out of the Apocalypse. Once more the immense night of the growing brightness. Once more the same horror – another day, life and its fictitious usefulness and vain activity; my physical personality, visible, social, communicable through words that mean nothing, usable by other people's thoughts and gestures. I am me again, exactly as I am not. With the coming of the dark light that fills with grey doubts the chinks of the shutters (so very far from being hermetic), I begin to feel that I will be unable to remain much longer in my refuge, lying on my bed, not asleep but with a sense of the continuing possibility of sleep, of drifting off into dreams, not knowing if truth or reality exist, lying between the cool warmth of clean sheets unaware, apart from the sense of comfort, of the existence of my own body. I feel ebbing away from me the happy lack of consciousness with which I enjoy my consciousness, the lazy, animal way I watch, from between half-closed eyes, like a cat in the sun, the logical movements of my unchained imagination. I feel slipping away from me the privileges of the penumbra, the slow rivers that flow beneath the trees of my half-glimpsed eyelashes, and the whisper of waterfalls lost amongst the sound of the slow blood pounding in my ears and the faint persistent rain. I slowly lose myself into life.

I don't know if I'm asleep or if I just feel as if I were. I don't dream this precise interval, but I notice, as if I were beginning to wake from a waking dream, the first stirrings of life in the city, rising like a tide from that indefinite place down below, from the streets that God made. They are joyous sounds, filtered by the sad rain that falls, or was falling, for I can't hear it now . . . I can tell from the excess of grey in the splintered light in the far distance, in the shadows cast by a hesitant brightness, that it is unusually dark for this time in the morning, whatever time that is. The sounds I hear are joyful, scattered, and they make my heart ache as if they had come to call me to go with them to an examination or an execution. Each day that I hear the dawn, from the bed on which I lie empty of knowledge, seems to me the day of some great event in my life that I will lack the courage to confront. Each day I feel it rise from its bed of shadows, scattering bedclothes along the streets and lanes below, in order to summon me to some trial. Each day that dawns I will be judged. And the eternal condemned man in me clings to the bed as if to the lost mother, and strokes the pillow as if my nanny could defend it from strangers.

The great beast's untroubled siesta in the shade of trees, the weariness of the street urchin amidst the cool of tall grasses, the heavy drowsiness of the negro in some warm, far-off afternoon, the pleasure of the yawn that closes languid eyes, the quiet comfort of our resting heads: everything that rocks us from forgetting into sleep slowly closes the windows of the soul in the anonymous caress of sleep.

To sleep, to be far off without even realizing it, to lay oneself down, to forget one's own body, to enjoy the freedom of unconsciousness, that refuge by a forgotten lake stagnating amongst the leafy trees of vast, remote forests.

A nothing that only seems to breathe, a little death from which one wakes feeling fresh and revived, a yielding of the fibres of the soul to fit the raiments of oblivion.

But, like the renewed cries of protest of an unconvinced listener, I hear again the sudden clamour of rain drenching the slowly brightening universe. I feel cold to my hypothetical bones, as if I were afraid. Crouching, desolate and human, all alone in the little dark that remains to me, I weep, yes, I weep for my solitude and for life and for my pain that lies abandoned by the roadside of reality, amongst the dung, useless as a cart without wheels. I cry for everything, for the loss of that lap I used to sit on, the death of the hand held out to me, the arms that could not hold me, the shoulder to weep on that was never there ... And the day that finally breaks, the pain that dawns in me like the crude truth of day, everything that I dreamed, thought and forgot in me – all this, in an amalgam of shadows, fictions and remorse, is tumbled together in the wake of passing worlds and falls amongst the detritus of life like the skeleton of a bunch of grapes, eaten on the corner by the young lads who stole it.

Like the sound of a bell calling people to prayer, the noise of the human day grows suddenly louder. Indoors, like an explosion, I hear the sound of someone softly closing the first door to open onto the universe today. I hear the sound of slippers walking down an absurd corridor that leads straight to my heart. And with an abrupt gesture, like someone at last finding the resolve to kill himself, I throw off the heavy bedclothes that shelter my stiff body. I'm awake. Somewhere outside, the sound of the rain diminishes. I feel happier. I have fulfilled some unknown duty. With sudden bold decisiveness I get up, go to the window and open the shutters to a day of clear rain that drowns my eyes in dull light. I open the windows. The cool air is damp on my hot skin. Yes, it's raining, but even if everything remains just the same, in the end what does it matter! I want to feel refreshed, I want to live and I bow my neck to life as if to bear the weight of a huge yoke.

88 [112]   *1.2.1931*

After endless rainy days the sky restores the blue, hidden until now, to the great spaces up above. There's a contrast between the streets, where puddles doze like country pools, and the bright, cold joy above them, which makes the dirty streets seem pleasant and the dull winter sky spring-like. It's Sunday and I have nothing to do. It's such a lovely day, I don't even feel like dreaming. I enjoy it with a sincerity of feeling to which my intelligence abandons itself. I walk around like a clerk let off work. I feel old merely in order to have the pleasure of feeling myself grow young again.

Another type of day stirs solemnly in the great Sunday square. At the church of São Domingos people are coming out from one mass and another is about to begin. I watch those who are leaving and those who have not yet gone in and who, waiting for others to arrive, do not even notice the other people coming out.

None of these things is of any importance. Like all ordinary things in life, they are a dream of mysteries and castle battlements from which I look out upon the plain of my meditations like a herald newly arrived.

Years ago, when I was a child, I used to go to mass here (at least I think it was here, though it may have been somewhere else). Conscious of the importance of the occasion, I would put on my best suit and simply enjoy it all, even those things there was no reason to enjoy. I lived outwardly then and the suit I had on was brand new and spotless. What more could be wished for by someone who one day must die but who, holding tight to his mother's hand, as yet knows nothing of death?

Years ago I used to enjoy all this, perhaps that's why only now do I realize how much I did enjoy it. For me going to mass was like penetrating a great mystery and leaving it like stepping out into a clearing in the woods. And that is how it really was, and how it still is. Only the unbelieving adult, whose soul still remembers and weeps, only he is but fiction and turmoil, confusion and the cold grave.

Yes, what I am would be unbearable if I could not remember the person I was. And this crowd of strangers still filing out of mass and the people gathering for the next mass, they are like ships that pass me by, a slow river flowing beneath the open windows of my home built on its banks.

Memories, Sundays, mass, the pleasure of having been, the miracle of time still present because it is past and which, because it was mine, never forgets . . . By some maternal paradox of time, somehow surviving into the present along the absurd diagonal of possible sensations, beyond the noisy silences of the cars, the sound of cab wheels rattles into this precise moment, between what I am and what I lost, in the anterior gaze of the me that I call I . . .

What do I know? What do I want? What do I feel? What would I ask for if I had the chance?

89 [93]   *31.5.1932*

It's not in broad fields or large gardens that I first notice the spring arrive. It's in the few pathetic trees growing in a small city square. There the bright green seems like a gift and is as joyful as a good bout of sadness.

I love these solitary squares that are dotted amongst quiet streets and are themselves just as quiet and free of traffic. They are things that wait, useless clearings amidst distant tumults. They are remnants of village life surviving in the heart of the city.

I walk on, go up one of the streets that flows into the square, then walk back down just to see it again. Seen from the other side it is different but the same peace bathes in unexpected nostalgia the side I did not see before. Everything is as useless as I feel. Everything I've lived through I've forgotten as if it were something I had only vaguely overheard. And of what I will be there is no trace in my memory, as if I had already lived through and forgotten it.

A sunset full of subtle griefs hovers vaguely about me. Everything grows cold, not because it really is colder, but simply because I've walked up a narrow street and can no longer see the square.

90 [54]

After the last rains had passed over and gone south and only the wind that swept them away remained, the joy of the certain sun returned to the city's disorderly piles of houses, and white sheets suddenly appeared, hanging and dancing on the lines stretched between poles fixed outside the high windows.

I felt happy too, simply to exist. I left home with a great aim, namely to get to the office on time. But that day, my own vital impulse joined forces with that other worthy impulse by virtue of which the sun rises at the time ordained by one's latitude or longitude on the earth's surface. I felt happy not to be able to feel unhappy. I strolled down the street, feeling full of certainty, because the familiar office and the familiar people in it were themselves certainties. It's hardly surprising, then, that I felt free, though without knowing from what. Beneath the sun, in the baskets placed by the side of the pavement in Rua da Prata, the bananas on sale were a magnificent yellow.

I really need very little to feel content: the rain having stopped, the good sun of the happy South, some yellow bananas, all the yellower for having black spots, the people who chatter as they sell them, the pavements of the Rua da Prata, the blue touched with green and gold, of the Tagus beyond this domestic corner of the Universe.

A day will come when I'll no longer see this, when the bananas by the side of the pavement will continue to exist without me, as will the voices of their canny sellers and the daily newspapers that the young lad has laid out side by side on the corner of the pavement opposite. I know they will not be the same bananas, nor the same sellers; and, for the person bending to look at them, the newspapers will bear a different date from today's. Because they are inanimate, they remain the same even though their form may change; on the other hand, because I live, I will pass on yet remain the same.

I could easily consecrate this moment by buying some bananas, for it seems to me that the natural floodlight of the day's sun has poured all of itself into them. But I feel ashamed of rituals and symbols, of buying things in the street. They might not wrap the bananas properly, they might not sell them to me as they should be sold because I do not know how to buy them as they should be bought. My voice might sound odd when I ask the price. Far better to write than dare to live, even if living means no more than buying . bananas in the sunshine, as long as the sun lasts and there are bananas to sell.

Later, perhaps . . . Yes, later . . . Another, perhaps . . . I don't know . . .

91 [109]

A shaft of grim sunlight burned the physical sensation of looking onto my eyes. A yellow heat stagnated in the black green of the trees. The torpor [. . .]

92 [175]   *18.9.1933*

They say tedium is a sickness that afflicts the inert, or only attacks those who have nothing to do. However, this affliction of the soul is subtler than that: it attacks those with a predisposition towards it and is less lenient on those who work or pretend to work (which comes to the same thing anyway) than on the truly inert.

There is nothing worse than the contrast between the natural splendour of the inner life, with its own Indies and countries still to be explored, and the sordidness, even when it isn't really sordid, of the everydayness of life. Tedium weighs more heavily when it does not have inertia as an excuse. The tedium of the great and the busy is the worst tedium of all.

Tedium is not a sickness brought on by the boredom of having nothing to do but the worse sickness of feeling that nothing is worth doing. And thus, the more one has to do the worse the tedium.

How often have I looked up from the book in which I'm writing and felt my head quite empty of the whole world. It would be better for me if I were inert, doing nothing, with nothing to do, because that tedium, though real, I could at least enjoy. In my present state there is no respite, no nobility, no comfort in feeling discomfort;

there is a terrible dullness in every gesture I make, not a potential weariness in gestures I will never make.

93 [174]   *29.3.1933*

I don't know why – I've only just noticed it – but I'm alone in the office. I had already vaguely sensed it. In some part of my consciousness there was a deep sense of relief, a sense of lungs breathing more freely.

This is one of the odder sensations afforded us by chance encounters and absences: that of finding ourselves alone in a house that is normally full of people and noise or in a house that belongs to someone else. We suddenly have a feeling of absolute possession, of an easy, generous mastery, an ample sense – as I said – of relief and peace.

How good to be all alone! To be able to talk out loud to ourselves, to walk about with nobody's eyes on us, to lean back and daydream with no interruptions! Every house becomes a meadow, every room takes on the amplitude of a country villa.

All the sounds one hears seem to come from somewhere else, as if they belonged to a nearby but independent universe. We are, at last, kings. That's what we all aspire to and, who knows, perhaps the more plebeian among us aspire to it more eagerly than those with false gold in their pockets. For a moment we are the pensioners of the universe, existing on our regular incomes with no needs or worries.

Ah, but in the footstep on the stair, the approach of someone unknown, I recognize the person who will interrupt my enjoyable solitude. My undeclared empire is about to be invaded by barbarians. It isn't that I can tell from the footsteps on the stairs who it is, nor that they remind me of the footsteps of one particular person. It is some secret instinct of the soul telling me that, though they are as yet only footsteps, whoever is approaching up the stairs (which I suddenly see before me just because I am thinking about the person ascending them) is coming here. Yes, it's one of the clerks. He stops, I hear the door open, he comes in. I see him properly now. And as he comes in, he says to me: 'All alone, Senhor Soares?' And I reply: 'Yes, I have been for a while now . . .' And then, peeling off his jacket while he eyes his other one, an old one, hanging on the hook, he says: 'Terrible bore being here all alone, Senhor Soares . . .' 'Oh, yes, a terrible bore,' I say. He has his old jacket on now and, going over to his desk, he says: 'It's enough to make you want to drop off to sleep.' 'It does indeed,' I agree, smiling. Then, reaching out for my forgotten pen, I write my way back into the anonymous health of normal life.

94 [176]

Sometimes, lost in vain meditation, I stand for hours in Terreiro do Paço, by the river. My own impatience tries again and again to tear me away from that quiet state, but inertia holds me fast. Gripped by a physical torpor, which resembles sensuality only to the extent that the whispering of the wind resembles human voices, I meditate on the eternal insatiability of my vague desires and on the perennial instability of my impossible longings. What afflicts me most is a sickness which is really only my capacity for suffering. I lack something I do not want and suffer because this is not true suffering.

The jetty, the evening, the rank sea air all seep in to form part of my anguish. The flutes of impossible shepherds could sound no sweeter than this absence of flutes here that calls them to mind.

In this moment that matches my innermost feelings, the idea of remote idylls on the banks of small streams wounds me. . .

95 [136]   *29.8.1933*

Even the city has its moments of country quiet, especially at midday in high summer, when the country invades this luminous city of

Lisbon like a wind. And even here, in Rua dos Douradores, we sleep well.

How good for the soul it is to observe beneath a high quiet sun the silence of these straw-laden carts, these empty boxes, these slow passers-by, transported here from some village! Watching them from the window of the office, where I'm alone, I too am transformed: I'm in a quiet provincial town, or stagnating in some obscure hamlet and, because I feel other, I'm happy.

I know that I have only to raise my eyes to see before me the sordid skyline of the houses, the unwashed windows of all the offices in the Baixa and the empty windows of the top floor apartments and, above them, around the garret roofs, the inevitable washing hung out to dry in the sun amongst flowerpots and plants. I know this but the golden light that falls is so soft, the calm air that wraps about me so empty, that I lack any visual motive to give up my false village, my provincial town where commerce brings rest and quiet.

I know, I know... It's the time when everyone has lunch or takes a rest or a break. Everything floats blithely by on the surface of life. Even while I lean out over the verandah as if it were a ship's rail looking out over a new landscape, I too sleep. I let go of all tormenting thoughts as if I really were living in the provinces. And, suddenly, something else arises, wraps about me, takes hold of me: behind the midday scene I see the entire life of that provincial town; I see the immense foolish happiness of domesticity, of life in the fields, of contentment in the midst of banality. I see because I see. But then I see no more and I wake up. I look around, smiling, and before I do anything else, I brush down the elbows of my suit, a dark suit unfortunately, made dusty from leaning on the balustrade of the verandah that no one has bothered to clean, not realizing that one day it would be required, if only for a moment, to be the rail (free from all possible dust) of a ship setting sail on an endless cruise.

96 [89]

I asked for so little from life and life denied me even that. A beam of sunlight, a field ... some peace and quiet and a mouthful of bread, not to feel the knowledge of my existence weigh too heavily on me, to demand nothing of others and have them demand nothing of me. That was denied me, like someone denying the shadow not out of malice but merely so as not to have to unbutton his jacket [...]

Sad, in my quiet room, alone as I have always been and as I always will be, I sit writing. And I wonder if that seemingly feeble thing, my voice, does not perhaps embody the substance of thousands of voices, the hunger to speak out of thousands of lives, the patience of millions of souls who, like me, have submitted in their daily lives to vain dreams and evanescent hopes. In moments like these my heart beats faster simply because I am conscious of it. I live more intensely because I live more fully. I feel in my person a religious force, a form of prayer, something like a clamour of voices. But the reaction against myself begins in my intellect ... I see myself in the fourth floor room in Rua dos Douradores and feel drowsy; on the half-written page, I observe my useless life devoid of beauty, the cheap cigarette [...] on the old blotter. Here I am, in this fourth floor room, demanding answers from life! pronouncing on what other souls feel! writing prose [...]

97 [147]   *2.7.1932*

Despite the clear perfection of the day, the sun-filled air stagnates. It isn't the present tension created by a gathering thunderstorm, the unease of bodies lacking all will, a vague dullness in the otherwise true blue sky. It is the perceptible torpor of the promise of leisure, a feather lightly touching a drowsy cheek. Though it's the height of summer, it feels like spring. The countryside seems tempting even to someone who would not usually enjoy it.

If I were someone else, I think, this would be a happy day, for I would just feel it without thinking about it. Full of anticipated pleasure I would finish my day's work, the work that is monotonously abnormal to me each and every day. I'd take the tram out to Benfica with a group of friends. We would dine in the open air just as the sun was going down. Our happiness would seem a natural part of the landscape and be recognized as such by everyone who saw us.

Since, however, I am myself, I squeeze a meagre enjoyment out of the meagre pleasure of imagining myself that other person. Yes, soon he-I, seated beneath a vine or a tree, will eat twice what I can normally eat, drink twice what I dare to drink and laugh twice as much as I could ever imagine laughing. Soon I will be him, for the moment I am me. Yes, for a moment I was someone else: I saw and lived as another that humble, human happiness of existing like a dumb beast in shirtsleeves. What an excellent day to bring me such a dream! Up above it is all blue and sublime like my ephemeral dream of being a hale and healthy clerk off on some after-hours jaunt.

98 [97]

(Written at intervals and much in need of emendation)

Once the last stars had paled into nothingness in the morning sky and the breeze that blew in the slightly orange-yellow light falling on the few low clouds had grown less cold, I could at last, still not yet having slept, slowly raise my body (exhausted after doing nothing) from the bed from which I imagined the universe.

I went over to the window, my eyelids burning from not having closed all night. Amongst the crowded rooftops the light experimented with different shades of pale yellow. I stood there looking at everything with the great stupidity brought on by lack of sleep. On the erect masses of the tall houses the yellow was airy, barely perceptible. Far off in the west, towards which I was turned, the horizon was already a greenish white.

I know today is going to be tedious for me, as tedious as one's inability to understand something. I know that everything I do today will be infected not by the weariness brought on by lack of sleep, but by this night's insomnia. I know that my customary state of somnambulism will be even more marked, even nearer the surface, not just because I didn't sleep, but because I couldn't sleep.

Some days are like whole philosophies in themselves that suggest to us new interpretations of life, marginal notes full of the acutest criticism in the book of our universal destiny. I feel that this is one such day. The foolish thought strikes me that my heavy eyes and my empty head are the absurd pencil shaping the letters of that futile and profound statement.

99 [172]   *25.12.1929*

Once the last of the rain had dwindled until only intermittent drops fell from the eaves of roofs, and the reflected blue of the sky appeared along the cobbled centre of the street, the traffic took up a different song, louder and gayer, and there was the sound of windows being opened to greet the return of the forgetful sun. Then, down the narrow street, from the next corner along, came the loud cry of the lottery seller, and the sound of nails being hammered into boxes in the shop next door reverberated about the bright space.

It was like an optional holiday, quite legal but observed by no one. Rest and work lived alongside one another and I had absolutely nothing to do. I'd got up early and lingered over my preparations for existence. I walked from one side of the room to the other dreaming out loud of unconnected, impossible things – gestures I had forgotten to make, impossible ambitions only randomly realized, long steadfast conversations which, had I had them, would have taken place. And in this reverie devoid of all grandeur and calm, in this hopeless, endless dawdling, my pacing feet wasted away my free morning, and my words, uttered out loud in a quiet voice, multiplied as they reverberated round the cloister of my simple isolation.

Seen from outside, my human figure appeared ridiculous in the way that everything human is when seen in private. Over the simple vestments of abandoned sleep I'd put on an ancient overcoat that I wear for these morning vigils. My old slippers, especially the left one, were badly split. And, with long decisive steps, my hands in the pockets of my posthumous coat, I walked the avenue of my small room, enjoying in those vain thoughts a dream much the same as everyone else's.

In the coolness entering through my one window, you could still hear plump drops falling from the rooftops, the accumulated waters of the rain now gone. There was still a hint of the sweet air it had left behind. The sky, however, was an all-conquering blue and the clouds left behind by the defeated, weary rain withdrew over the castle walls . . .

It was a time to be happy, yet something weighed on me, an obscure longing, an undefined but not entirely despicable desire. Perhaps it just took me time to accustom myself to the sensation of being alive. And, when I leaned out of the high window over the street I looked down at without seeing, I suddenly felt like one of those damp cloths used to clean grimy objects in the house that get taken to the window to dry but instead are left there, screwed up on the sill that they slowly stain.

100 [199]   *21.2.1930*

Suddenly, as if destiny had turned surgeon and, with dramatic success, operated on an ancient blindness, I raise my eyes from my anonymous life to the clear knowledge of the manner of my existence. And I see that everything I have done, everything I have thought, everything I have been is a sort of delusion and madness. I marvel that I did not see it before. I am surprised by everything I have been and that I now see I am not.

I look down on my past life as if it were a plain stretched out beneath the sun just breaking through the clouds, and I notice, with a metaphysical shock, how all my most assured gestures, my clearest ideas and my most logical aims were, after all, nothing but an innate drunkenness, a natural madness, an immense ignorance. I did not act the part. It acted me. I was merely the gestures, never the actor.

Everything that I have done, thought and been has been a series of subordinations either to a false entity I took to be myself, because all my actions came from him, or to the force of circumstance that I took to be the air I breathed. In this visionary moment, I am suddenly a solitary man realizing he is in exile from the country of which he had always considered himself a citizen. In the very heart of everything I thought, I was not me.

I am overwhelmed by a sarcastic terror of life, a dejection that overflows the bounds of my conscious being. I know that I was never anything but error and mistake, that I never lived, that I existed only in the sense that I filled up time with consciousness and thought. And my sense of myself is that of a person waking up after a sleep full of real dreams, or like someone freed by an earthquake from the feeble light of the prison to which he had become accustomed.

It weighs on me this sudden notion of the true nature of my individual being that did nothing but make somnolent journeys between what was felt and what was seen, it weighs on me as if it were a sentence not to death but to knowledge.

It is so difficult to describe the feeling one has when one feels that one really does exist and that the soul is a real entity, that I do not know what human words I can use to define it. I don't know if I'm really as feverish as I feel or if instead I have finally recovered from the fever of slumbering through life. Yes, I am like a traveller who suddenly finds himself in a strange town, with no idea of how he got there and I'm reminded of cases of amnesiacs who, losing all memory of their past lives, for a long time live as other people. For many years – from the time I was born and became a conscious being – I too was someone else and now I wake up suddenly to find myself standing in the middle of the bridge, looking out over the river, knowing more positively now than at any moment before that I exist. But I do not know the city, the streets are new to me and the sickness incurable. So, leaning on the bridge, I wait for the truth to pass so that I can regain my null and fictitious, intelligent and natural self.

It lasted only a moment and has passed now. I notice the furniture around me, the design on the old wallpaper, the sun through the dusty panes. For a moment I saw the truth. For a moment I was, consciously, what great men are throughout their lives. I recall their actions and their words and I wonder if they too were tempted by and succumbed to the Demon Reality. To know nothing about oneself is to live. To know a little about oneself is to think. To know oneself precipitately, as I did in that moment of pure enlightenment, is suddenly to grasp Leibniz's notion of the dominant monad, the magic password to the soul. A sudden light scorches and consumes everything. It strips us naked even of our selves.

It was only a moment but I saw myself. Now I cannot even say what I was. And, after it all, I just feel sleepy because, though I don't really know why, I suspect that the meaning of it all is simply to sleep.

101 [138]

It's just a rather mediocre lithograph. I stare at it without knowing if I actually see it. There are others in the window and there is this one. It's in the middle of the display window on the landing.

She clasps the primrose to her breast and the eyes that stare out at me are sad. Her smile has the same brilliance as the glossy paper and her cheek is touched with red. The sky behind her is bright blue. She has a rather small, curved mouth and above its picture-postcard expression her eyes fix me with a look of terrible sorrow. The arm clutching the flowers reminds me of someone else's arm. The dress or blouse has an open neckline that falls slightly to one side. Her eyes are very sad: they watch me from their background of lithographed reality expressing something like a truth. She arrived with the spring. She has large, sad eyes but that isn't why she seems sad. I drag my feet away from the window. I cross the road and then return in impotent rebellion. She still holds the primrose that they gave her and her eyes reflect the sadness of everything I lack in life. Seen from a distance, the lithograph is more colourful. The figure has a pink ribbon tied round its hair; I hadn't noticed that before. Even in lithographs there is something terrible about human eyes: the unavoidable proof of the existence of a consciousness, the clandestine cry that they too have a soul. With a great effort, I haul myself out of the trance into which I have sunk and, like a dog, shake off the dank darkness of the fog. And above my awakening, in a farewell to something else altogether, those eyes expressive of all of life's sadness, of the metaphysical lithograph we contemplate from afar, regard me as if I had some real notion of God. A calendar is attached to the bottom of the engraving. It's framed above and below by two broad, black, badly painted convex lines. Between the upper and lower boundaries, above the 1929 and the obsolete calligraphy that predictably covers the first of January, the sad eyes smile ironically back at me.

It's strange where I know that figure from. There's an identical calendar, which I've often seen, in the office, in a corner at the back. But by some mystery, to do with both the lithograph and me, the calendar in the office doesn't have sad eyes. It's just a lithograph. (It's printed on shiny paper and sleeps away its dull life above the head of Alves, the lefthanded clerk.)

I'd like simply to laugh this off, but I feel terribly uneasy. I feel the chill of a sudden sickness in my soul. I haven't the strength to rebel against this absurdity. Which window onto which of God's secrets have I unwittingly approached? What does the window on the landing actually look out on? Whose eyes looked out at me from that lithograph? I'm almost trembling. Involuntarily I look over to the far corner of the office where the real lithograph is. Again and again I raise my eyes to look.

102 [139]

Sometimes, when I least expect it, the suffocating quality of the ordinary takes me by the throat and I feel physically sickened by the voices and gestures of my so-called fellow man. That genuine nausea, felt in my stomach and in my head, is the foolish wonderment of an alert sensibility ... Each individual who speaks to me, each face whose eyes meet mine, has the same impact on me as a direct insult or foul language. I overflow with a horror of everything. I grow dizzy feeling myself feel that.

And almost always, when I feel sick to my stomach like that, a man, or a woman, or even a child, rises before me like a representative of the very banality that afflicts me. They are not representative of any subjective, considered emotion of mine, but of an objective truth which, in its outward shape, conforms to what I feel inside and which arises by some analogical magic to provide me with the example for the general rule I happen to be thinking of.

103 [140]   *24.3.1930*

I re-read passively those simple lines by Caeiro*, the natural conclusion he draws from the smallness of the village he lives in, receiving from them what I feel to be both inspiration and liberation. According to him, because his village is small, you can see more of the world there than you can in the city, and in that sense his village is larger than the city ...

> I am equal in size to whatever I see
> Not hemmed in by the size I am.

Lines such as these, which seem to have come spontaneously into existence as if not requiring any human will to dictate them, cleanse me of all the metaphysics I spontaneously add to life. After

---

*Alberto Caeiro, one of Pessoa's heteronyms, represented the latter's existentialist side.

reading them I go to my window that looks out onto the narrow street. I look up at the great sky and the many stars and the beating of the wings of a splendid freedom shakes my whole body.

'I am equal in size to whatever I see!' Each time I think this phrase with every nerve of my being, I'm filled by an even stronger conviction of its ability to reorganize the heavens into new constellations. 'I am equal in size to whatever I see!' What mental energy springs up from the well of deep emotions to the high stars it reflects and which, in some way, inhabit it.

And right now, conscious of my ability to see, I look at the vast objective metaphysics of the skies with a certainty that makes me want to die singing. 'I am equal in size to whatever I see!' And the vague moonlight, entirely mine, begins to mar with its vagueness the almost black blueness of the horizon.

I feel like throwing up my arms and shouting out things of unheard-of savagery, exchanging words with the high mysteries, proclaiming to the vast spaces of empty matter the existence of a new expansive personality.

But I pull myself together and calm myself. 'I am equal in size to whatever I see!' The phrase still fills my whole soul, I rest every emotion I have on it, and the indecipherable peace of the harsh moonlight that begins to spread as night comes, falls on me, into me, as it does on the city beyond.

104 [146]

I can only comprehend the perennial inertia in which I allow my monotonously uneventful life to lie, like a layer of dust or dirt on the surface of a resolute unchangeability, as a lack of personal cleanliness.

We should bathe our destinies as we do our bodies, change our lives just as we change our clothes – not to keep ourselves alive, which is why we eat and sleep, but out of the disinterested respect for ourselves which can properly be called cleanliness.

There are many people in whom a lack of cleanliness is not an act of will but an intellectual shrug of the shoulders. And there are many people for whom the dullness and sameness of their lives is not what they would have chosen for themselves nor a natural conformity with that lack of choice, but rather a snuffing out of self-knowledge, an automatic irony of the understanding.

There are pigs who, however disgusted they may feel at their own filth, fail to remove themselves from it, frozen by the same extremity of feeling that prevents the terrified from removing themselves from the path of danger. There are those, like me, pigs by destiny, who do not attempt to escape the daily banality of life, being mesmerized by their own impotence. They are birds fascinated by the absence of the snake; flies who, unaware, hover above the branches until they come within the sticky reach of the chameleon's tongue.

So each day I promenade my conscious unconsciousness along my particular branch of the tree of routine. I promenade my destiny which trots ahead without waiting for me and my time that advances even when I don't. And the only thing that saves me from the monotony are these brief notes I make about it. I am merely glad that in my cell there are glass panes this side of the bars and in large letters, in the dust of necessity, I write my daily signature on my contract with death.

Did I say my contract with death? No, not even with death. Anyone who lives the way I do does not die: he comes to an end, withers, merely ceases to vegetate. The space he occupied continues to exist without him, the street he walked along remains though he's no longer seen there, the house where he lived is inhabited by not-him. That is all and we call it nothing; but, were we to put it on, not even this tragedy of denial would be guaranteed applause, for we do not know for certain that it is nothing, we who are as much the vegetables of truth as we are of life, the dust that covers the windowpanes both inside and out, the grandchildren of Destiny and the stepchildren of God, who married Eternal Night when she was left a widow by Chaos, our true father.

105 [149]

The sense of smell is like a strange way of seeing. It evokes sentimental landscapes out of a mere sketch in our subconscious minds. I've often felt that. I walk down a street. I see nothing or rather, though I look at everything, I see only what everyone sees. I know that I'm walking down a street but I'm not conscious of it comprising two sides made up of different houses built by human beings. I walk down a street. From a baker's comes the almost sickeningly sweet smell of bread and from a district right on the other side of town my childhood rises up and another baker's appears before me from that fairy kingdom which is everything we have lost. I walk down a street. Suddenly it smells of the fruit on the stand outside a narrow little shop and my short time in the country, I no longer know when or where it was, plants trees and quiet comfort in my heart, for a moment indisputably that of a child. I walk down a street. I'm overcome, quite unexpectedly, by the smell of the wooden crates being made by the box maker: ah, Cesário, you appear before me and at last I am happy because, through memory, I have returned to the one truth that is literature.

106 [121]

I never wanted to be understood by other people. To be understood is akin to prostituting oneself. I prefer to be taken seriously as what I am not and to be, with decency and naturalness, ignored as a person.

Nothing would displease me more than to have my colleagues in the office think me different. I want to savour the irony of their not doing so. I want the penance of having them think me the same as them. I want the crucifixion of their not thinking me any different. There are more subtle martyrdoms than those recorded among saints and hermits. There are torments of the intellect just as there are of the body and of desire. And as in other torments, these contain their own voluptuousness.

107 [120]

Normality is like a home to us and everyday life a mother. After a long incursion into great poetry, into the mountains of sublime aspiration, the cliffs of the transcendent and the occult, it is the sweetest thing, savouring of all that is warm in life, to return to the inn where the happy fools laugh and joke, to join with them in their drinking, as foolish as they are, just as God made us, content with the universe that was given us, and to leave the rest to those who climb mountains and do nothing when they reach the top.

It doesn't shock me that people should say of a man I consider mad or stupid that he is better than some other person whose life and achievements are merely ordinary. When seized by a fit, epileptics are extraordinarily strong; paranoiacs have reasoning powers beyond those of most normal people; religious maniacs in their delirium attract larger crowds of believers than (almost) any demagogue and give an inner strength to their followers that demagogues never can. But all this proves nothing except that madness is madness. I prefer to fail having known the beauty of flowers than to triumph in a wilderness, for triumph is the blindness of the soul left alone with its own worthlessness.

How often has some futile dream left me filled with a horror of the inner life, with a physical nausea for mysticisms and meditations. I rush from my home, where I have dreamed these things, and go to the office where I gaze on Moreira's face like a voyager finally reaching port. All things considered, I prefer Moreira to the astral world; I prefer reality to truth; in fact I prefer life to the God who created it. This is how he presented it to me, so this is how I will live it. I dream because I dream, but I don't insult myself by giving to dreams a value they do not have, apart from that of being my personal theatre, just as I do not call wine (from which I still do not abstain) 'food' or 'one of life's necessities'.

108 [120]

Whenever, under the influence of my dreams, my ambitions reared up above the daily level of my life and I felt myself riding high for a moment, like a child on a swing, like that child I always had to swing back down to the municipal gardens and recognize my defeat with neither fluttering banners to carry into battle nor a sword I would have the strength to unsheath.

I would guess – to judge by the silent movements of their lips and the vague indecisiveness in their eyes or the way they raise their voices when they pray together – that most of the people I pass at random in the streets carry within them similar ambitions to wage vain war with just such a bannerless army. And like me, all of them – I turn round to contemplate their vanquished backs – will meet utter and humiliating defeat, miserable and ignorant amongst the slime and the reeds, with no moonlight shining on the banks nor poetry to be found amidst the marshes.

Like me, they all have sad, exalted hearts. I know them well: some work in shops, others in offices, some have small businesses, others are the heroes of cafés and bars, unwittingly glorious in the ecstasy of the egotistical word [...] But all of them, poor things, are poets and seem to me (as I must to them) to drag with them the same misery of our common incongruousness. Like me, their future is already in the past.

At this moment, alone and idle in the office now that everyone but me has gone to lunch, I'm peering through the grubby window at the old man tottering slowly down the pavement on the other side of the road. He's not drunk, just a dreamer. He's awake to the non-existent; perhaps he still has hopes. The gods, if they are just in their injustice, preserve our dreams for us however impossible and give us good dreams however petty. Today, when I am not yet old, I can dream of South Sea islands and impossible Indias; tomorrow, perhaps the same gods will give me the dream of being the proprietor of a small tobacconist's, or of retiring to a house in the suburbs. All dreams are the same, because they are dreams. May the gods change my dreams, but not my talent for dreaming.

While thinking this, I forgot about the old man. I can't see him now. I open the window to try to catch him but he's out of sight. He's gone. For me he performed the function of a visual symbol; once he'd done that, he simply turned the corner. If someone were to tell me that he had turned a corner of the absolute and that he was never even here, I would accept it with the same gesture with which now I close the window . . .

To succeed? . . .

Poor apprentice demigods who can conquer empires with words and noble intentions but still need money to pay for room and board! They're like the troops of a deserted army, whose commanders had a dream of glory of which all that remains for these soldiers lost amongst the mud in the marshes is the notion of greatness, the knowledge that they were an army and the emptiness of not even having known what the commander they never saw actually did.

Thus everyone at some time dreams of being the commander of the army from whose rearguard they fled. Thus everyone, amidst the mud on the banks, salutes the victory that no one can enjoy and of which all that remained were the crumbs on a stained tablecloth that no one bothered to shake out.

They fill the cracks of daily life the way dust fills the cracks in furniture that doesn't get dusted properly. In the ordinary light of every day they show up against the red mahogany like grey worms. You can scrape them out with a small nail. But no one's in any hurry to do that.

My poor companions with their lofty dreams, how I envy and despise them! I'm on the side of the others, the poorest, who have only themselves to tell their dreams to and make of them what would be poems were they to write them down; poor devils, with only the literature of their own souls [. . .] who die suffocated by the mere fact of existing [. . .]

Some are heroes who took on five men at once on yesterday's street corner. Others are seducers, irresistible even to women who have never existed. They believe it when they say it and they all say it because they believe it. Others [. . .]

Like eels in a bowl they become so entangled with one another that they can never escape. They may occasionally get a mention in the newspapers [. . .] but they never achieve fame.

They are the happy ones because they are given the dream [. . .] of stupidity. But as for those, like me, who have dreams without illusions [. . .]

109 [126]

Even my dreams turn on me. I had achieved such a degree of lucidity in them that I perceived as real everything I dreamed. So, because I dreamed it, was everything I valued just a waste of time?

If I dream of being famous I feel all the indifference that comes with glory, the loss of privacy and anonymity that makes it so painful to us.

110 [128]

Holiday prose

For those three days of holiday, the small beach, forming an even smaller bay cut off from the world by two miniature promontories, was my retreat from myself. You reached the beach by a rough staircase that started as wooden steps but half-way down became mere ledges cut out of the rock, with a rusty iron banister to hold on to. Every time I went down the old steps, especially the ones cut out of the rock, I left my own existence behind and found myself.

Occultists, at least some of them, say that there are supreme moments in the life of the soul when, by way of an emotion or a fragment of memory, it recalls a moment, an aspect or just the shadow of some previous incarnation. Then, since it returns to a time which is closer than the present to the origin and beginning of all things, it feels in some way a child again, it feels a sense of liberation.

You could say that when I slowly descended those rarely used steps to the small, always deserted beach, I was making use of a magical process in order to bring myself closer to the possible monad that is my self. Certain aspects and features of my daily life – represented in my constant self by desires, dislikes, worries – just disappeared from me as if chased away by the night patrol, simply melted into the shadows until one could not even make out their shapes, and I achieved a state of inner distance in which it became difficult even to remember yesterday, or recognize as mine the being that inhabits me from day to day. My usual emotions, my regularly irregular habits, my conversations with other people, my adaptations to the social way of the world – all that seemed to me like things I had read somewhere, the dead pages of a printed biography, details from some novel, those intervening chapters that we read with our mind on something else, leaving the narrative thread to unravel and slither to the ground.

On the beach, where the only sounds were of the waves themselves or the wind passing high above like a great invisible aeroplane, I abandoned myself to new dreams – soft, shapeless things, marvels that impressed without images or emotions, as clear as the sky and the waters, trembling like the crumbling lace on the folds of the sea rising up from the depths of some great truth, a matt blue in the far distance, then, as it reached the shore, its transparency becoming stained by dull greens that shattered, hissing, drawing back a thousand broken arms across the darkened sand, leaving only a dribble of white foam, gathering in to itself all the retreating waves, the returns to an original freedom, divine nostalgias, memories – like my nebulous, painless one of a happier time, happy either because it was genuinely good or simply because it was other, a body of nostalgia with a soul of foam – rest, death, the everything or nothing that, like a great sea, surrounds the island of shipwrecked souls that is life.

And I slept without sleeping, removed from what I saw with my senses, in the twilight of my own self, the sound of water amongst trees, the calm of wide rivers, the cool of sad evenings, the slow rise and fall of the white breast of the child-like sleep of contemplation.

111 [129]

The greater the sensibility and the more subtle the capacity to feel, the more absurdly one trembles and quivers at the small things. It requires prodigious intelligence to be reduced to anguish by a day of lowering skies. Humanity, which is not very sensitive, doesn't get upset by the weather, because the weather is always with us; humanity only feels the rain when it's actually falling on its head.

It's a soft, dull day of humid heat. Alone in the office, I review my life, and what I see is like this day which oppresses and afflicts me. I remember myself as a child made happy by all things, as an adolescent with a hundred ambitions, as a man with no joy and no ambition. And all this happened softly, dully like the day that makes me see or remember it.

Which of us turning to look back down the road along which there is no return, could say that we had walked that road as we should have?

112 [137]

Yesterday I saw and heard a great man. I don't mean someone who is merely considered to be a great man, but a man who truly is. He has value, if there is such a thing in this world; other people know that and he knows they know. He therefore fulfils all the necessary conditions that allow me to call him a great man. And indeed that is what I do call him.

Physically he looks like a worn-out businessman. The signs of weariness on his face could as easily come from leading an unhealthy life as from thinking too much. His gestures are utterly unremarkable. There's a certain sparkle in his eyes – the privilege of one not afflicted with myopia. His voice is a little slurred as if a general paralysis were beginning to attack that particular manifestation of his soul, a soul that expressed views on party politics, the devaluation of the escudo and the more despicable aspects of his colleagues in greatness.

Had I not known who he was, I would never have guessed from his appearance. I know perfectly well that one should not succumb to the heroic ideas about great men that appeal to simple people: that a great poet should have Apollo's body and Napoleon's face or, rather less demanding, that he be a man of distinction with an expressive face. I know that such ideas are absurd, if natural, human foibles. However, it is not unreasonable to expect some sign of greatness. And when one moves from physical appearance to consider the utterances of the soul, whilst one can do without spirit and vivacity, one does expect intelligence with at least a trace of grandeur.

All this, all these human disappointments, make us question the truth of what we take to be inspiration. It would seem that this body destined to be that of a businessman and this soul destined to be that of a man of culture are mysteriously invested with an outer and an inner quality respectively and, though they do not speak, something speaks through them and that voice utters words which, if said by the body or the soul alone, would be falsehoods.

But these are just vain, indolent speculations. I almost regret having indulged in them. I've neither diminished the value of the man nor improved his physical appearance by my remarks. The truth is that nothing changes anything and what we say or do only brushes the tops of the mountains in whose valleys all things sleep.

113 [163]

Everything is absurd. One man spends his life earning money which he then saves even though he has no children to leave it to nor any hope that a heaven somewhere will offer him a divine reward. Another puts all his efforts into becoming famous so that he will be remembered once dead, yet he does not believe in a survival of the soul that would give him knowledge of that fame. Yet another wears himself out looking for things he doesn't even like. Then there is the man who . . .

One man reads in order to know, all in vain. Another enjoys himself in order to live, again all in vain.

I'm riding a tram and, as is my habit, slowly absorbing every detail of the people around me. By 'detail' I mean things, voices, words. In the dress of the girl directly in front of me, for example, I see the material it's made of, the work involved in making it – since it's a dress and not just material – and I see in the delicate embroidery around the neck the silk thread with which it was embroidered and all the work that went into that. And immediately, as if in a primer on political economy, I see before me the factories and all the different jobs: the factory where the material was made; the factory that made the darker coloured thread that ornaments with curlicues the neck of the dress; and I see the different workshops in the factories, the machines, the workmen, the seamstresses. My eyes' inward gaze even penetrates into the offices, where I see the managers trying to keep calm and the figures set out in the account books, but that's not all: beyond that I see into the domestic lives of those who spend their working hours in these factories and offices . . . A whole world unfolds before my eyes all because of the regularly irregular dark green edging to a pale green dress worn by the girl in front of me of whom I see only her brown neck.

A whole way of life lies before me.

I sense the loves, the secrets, the souls of all those who worked just so that this woman in front of me on the tram should wear around her mortal neck the sinuous banality of a thread of dark green silk on a background of light green cloth.

I grow dizzy. The seats on the tram, of fine, strong cane, carry me to distant regions, divide into industries, workmen, houses, lives, realities, everything.

I leave the tram exhausted, like a sleepwalker, having lived a whole life.

114 [156]   *12.6.1930*

There are times when everything wearies us, even those things that
would normally bring us rest. Obviously what wearies us does so
because it's tiring; what is restful tires us because the thought of
having to obtain it is tiring. Behind all anguish and pain lie certain
debilities of the soul; the only people who remain unaware of these
are, I believe, those who shrink from human anguish and pain and
tactfully conceal from themselves their own tedium. Since in this
way they armour themselves against the world, it is not surprising
that at some stage in their self-consciousness they feel suddenly
crushed by the whole weight of that armour, and life is revealed to
them as an anguish in reverse, an absent pain.

That's how I feel now, and I write these lines like someone
struggling to know that he is at least alive. Up till now I've worked
the whole day as if half-asleep, dreaming my way through accounts,
writing out of my own listlessness. All day I've felt life like a weight
on my eyelids and temples – my eyes heavy with sleep, constant
pressure on my temples, an awareness of all this in the pit of my
stomach, feelings of nausea and despair.

Living seems to me a metaphysical mistake on the part of matter,
an oversight on the part of inaction. I do not even look to see what
kind of day it is, to see if there might be something to distract me
from myself and, by describing it here, cover with words the empty
cup of my self-love. I do not even look out at the day but sit,
shoulders hunched, not knowing whether or not there's sun out
there in the subjectively sad street, in the deserted street where
nonetheless I hear the sounds of people walking by. I know
nothing and my heart aches. I've finished work but I don't want to
move from here. I look at the off-white expanse of blotter glued at
the corners to the ancient surface of the sloping desk. I stare
attentively at the blur of doodles, the result of self-absorption or of
simple distraction. My signature appears several times upside
down and back to front, as do certain figures and a few
meaningless sketches, the creations of my distracted mind. I look at
all this like a yokel who has never seen a blotter before, like

someone staring at the latest novelty, with my whole brain inert (except for the areas to do with seeing).

I feel an inner drowsiness so great it overflows the bounds of self. And I want nothing, prefer nothing, there is nothing I can escape into.

115 [177]   *5.2.1930*

It isn't the shabby walls of my meagre room, or the old writing desks in the office, or even the poverty of the Baixa streets that separate room and office (and which I've walked so often they already seem to me to have achieved a fixity beyond that of mere irreparability) that provoke in me my frequent feelings of disgust for the grubby everydayness of life. It's the people around me who leave this knot of physical disgust in my spirit, the souls who know nothing about me but, in their daily contact and conversations with me, treat me as if they did. It's the monotonous squalor of these lives that run parallel to my own external life, it's their inner certainty of being my equal that straps me in the straitjacket, locks me in the prison cell, makes me feel apocryphal and beggarly.

There are moments when every detail of the ordinary interests me in its own right and I feel affectionate towards everything because I can read it all so clearly. Then – as Sousa* describes Vieira saying – I perceive the singularity of the ordinary, and I am a poet with the kind of soul that amongst the Greeks produced the intellectual age of poetry. But there are also moments, like now, when I feel too oppressed and too aware of myself to be conscious of external things and everything then becomes for me a night of rain and mud, alone and lost in an abandoned railway station, where the last third-class train left hours ago and the next has yet to arrive.

---

*Frei Luis de Sousa (*c.* 1555–1632) was a Dominican friar, a writer and biographer.

In common with all virtues and indeed all vices, my inner virtue – my capacity for objectivity that deflects me from thoughts of self — suffers from crises of confidence. Then I wonder at my ability to survive, at my cowardly presence here amongst these people, on terms of perfect equality, in genuine accord with all their trite illusions. All the solutions spawned by my imagination flash upon my mind like beams from a distant lighthouse: suicide, flight, renunciation, in short, the grand aristocratic gestures of our individuality, the cloak-and-dagger of existences like mine with no balconies to climb.

But the ideal Juliet of the finest reality has closed the high windows of literary discourse on the fictitious Romeo in my blood. She obeys her father; he obeys his. The feud between the Montagues and the Capulets continues; the curtain falls on what did not happen; and, my office worker's collar turned unselfconsciously up around the neck of a poet, my boots, which I always buy in the same shop, instinctively skirting the puddles of cold rain water, I return home (to that room where the absent mistress of the house is as sordid a reality as the rarely seen children and the office colleagues I will meet again tomorrow) feeling a slight, confused concern that I may have lost for ever both my umbrella and the dignity of my soul.

116 [166]   *28.9.1932*

For some time now – it may be days or months – I haven't really noticed anything; I don't think, therefore I don't exist. I've forgotten who I am; I can't write because I can't be. Under the influence of some oblique drowsiness I have been someone else. The knowledge that I do not remember myself awakens me.

I fainted away a little from my life. I return to myself with no memory of what I have been and the memory of the person I was before suffers from that interruption. I am aware only of a confused notion of some forgotten interlude, of my memory's futile efforts to find the other me. But I cannot retie the knots. If I did live, I've forgotten how to know that I did.

It isn't this first real autumn day – the first cold rather than cool day to clothe the dead summer in a lesser light – whose alien transparency leaves me with a sense of dead ambitions or sham intentions. It isn't the uncertain trace of vain memory contained in this interlude of things lost. It's something more painful than that, it's the tedium of trying to remember what cannot be remembered, despair at what my consciousness mislaid amongst the algae and reeds of some unknown shore.

Beneath an unequivocally blue sky, a shade lighter than the deepest blue, I recognize that the day is limpid and still. I recognize that the sun, slightly less golden than it was, gilds walls and windows alike with liquid reflections. I recognize that, although there's no wind, nor any breeze to recall or deny the existence of a wind, a brisk coolness nonetheless hovers about the hazy city. I recognize all this, unthinkingly, unwillingly, and feel no desire to sleep, only the memory of that desire, feel no nostalgia, only disquiet.

Sterile and remote, I recover from an illness I never had. Alert after waking, I prepare myself for what I dare not do. What kind of sleep was it that brought me no rest? What kind of caress was it that would not speak to me? How good it would be to take one cold draught of heady spring and be someone else! How good, how much better than life, to be able to imagine being that other person, whilst far off, in the remembered image, in the absence of even a breath of wind, the reeds bend blue-green to the shore.

Recalling the person I was not, I often imagine myself young again and forget! And were they different those landscapes that I never saw; were they new but non-existent the landscapes I did see? What does it matter? I have spent myself in chance events, in interstices, and now that the cool of the day and the cooling sun are one, the dark reeds by the shore sleep their cold sleep in the sunset I see but do not possess.

117 [463]

Litany

We never truly realize ourselves. We are like two chasms – a well staring up at the sky.

118 [322]   *1.12.1931*

Since I'm so given to tedium, it's odd that until today I've never really thought much about what it actually consists of. Today I'm in that intermediate state of mind in which I feel no interest in life or in anything else. And I take advantage of the sudden realization that I've never really thought about this feeling to dream up an inevitably somewhat artificial analysis of it, using my thoughts and half-impressions on the subject.

I don't honestly know if tedium is just the waking equivalent of the somnolence of the inveterate idler or something altogether nobler than that particular form of listlessness. I often suffer from tedium but, as far as I can tell, it follows no rules as to when and why it appears. I can spend a whole vacuous Sunday without once experiencing tedium, yet sometimes, when I'm hard at work, it comes over me, suddenly, like a cloud. I can't link it to any particular state of health or lack of health; I can't see it as the product of causes in any apparent part of myself.

To say that it is a metaphysical anguish in disguise, an ineffable disappointment, a secret poem of the bored soul leaning out of the window that opens on to life, to say that, or something similar, might lend colour to the tedium, the way a child draws something then clumsily colours it in, blurring the edges, but to me it's just words echoing around the cellars of thought.

Tedium . . . It is thinking without thinking, yet requires all the effort involved in having to think; it is feeling without feeling, yet stirs up all the anguish that feeling normally involves; it is not wanting something but wanting it, and suffering all the nausea involved in not wanting. Although tedium contains all of these things, they are not themselves tedium, they provide only a paraphrase, a translation. Expressed as direct sensation, it is as if the drawbridge over the moat around the soul's castle had been pulled up, leaving us with but one power, that of gazing impotently out at the surrounding lands, never again to set foot there. We are isolated within ourselves from ourselves, an isolation in which what separates us is as stagnant as us, a pool of dirty water surrounding our inability to understand.

Tedium . . . It is suffering without suffering, wanting without will, thinking without reason . . . It's like being possessed by a negative demon, bewitched by nothing at all. They say that witches and some minor wizards, by making images of us which they then torment, can reproduce those same torments in us by means of some sort of astral transference. Tedium arises in me, in the transposed feeling of such an image, like the malign reflection of some fairy demon's spell cast not upon the image but upon its shadow. It is on my inner shadow, on the surface of the interior of my soul, on which they glue papers or stick pins. I am like the man who sold his shadow or, rather, like the shadow of the man who sold it.

Tedium . . . I work quite hard. I fulfil what practical moralists would call my social duty, and fulfil that duty, or that fate, with no great effort nor noticeable difficulty. But sometimes, right in the middle of work or leisure (something which, according to those same moralists, I deserve and should enjoy), my soul overflows with the bile of inertia and I feel weary, not of work or leisure, but of myself.

And why weary of myself, if I wasn't even thinking about myself? What else would I be thinking about? The mystery of the universe descending upon me while I toil over accounts or recline in a chair? The universal pain of living crystallized suddenly in the intermediary of my soul? Why thus ennoble someone who doesn't even know who he is? It's a feeling of utter vacuity, a hunger with no desire to eat, about as noble as the feelings you experience in your brain or stomach from having smoked or eaten too much.

Tedium ... Perhaps, it's basically an expression of a dissatisfaction in our innermost soul not to have been given something to believe in, the desolation of the child all of us are deep down not to have been bought the divine toy. It is perhaps the insecurity of someone in need of a guiding hand, conscious of nothing on the black road of deep feeling but the silent night of one's inability to think, the deserted road of one's inability to feel ...

Tedium ... No one with a god to believe in will ever suffer from tedium. Tedium is the lack of a mythology. To the unbeliever, even doubt is denied, even scepticism does not give the strength to despair. Yes, that's what tedium is: the loss by the soul of its capacity to delude itself, the absence in thought of the non-existent stairway up which the soul steadfastly ascends towards the truth.

119 [337]

May I at least carry toward the possible vastness of the abyss of all things the glory of my disillusion, as if it were that of a great dream, the splendour of unbelief as if it were a flag of defeat ... a flag carried by feeble hands, a flag dragged through the mud and the blood of the weak ... but raised on high as we plunge ourselves into the quicksands, whether as a protest, a challenge or a gesture of despair, no one knows ... No one knows, because no one knows anything and the quicksands as readily swallow up those with flags as those without ...

And the sands cover everything, my life, my prose, my eternity.

I carry with me, like a victory flag, the knowledge of my defeat.

120 [338]

The great anguishes of the soul always come upon us like cosmic cataclysms. When they do, the sun errs from its course and the stars are troubled. A day will come to every feeling soul when Fate stages an apocalypse of anguish, an upturning of all known heavens and universes over the soul's desolation.

To feel oneself superior and yet find oneself treated by Fate as inferior to the least significant of beings – who can feel proud to be a man in such circumstances?

If one day I were to achieve a power of expression so great as to concentrate all art in me, I would write an apotheosis of sleep. I know of no greater pleasure in the whole of life than that of sleep. The wholesale blotting out of life and soul, the complete removal of all other beings, all other people, a night without memory or illusion, possessed of neither past nor future [. . .]

121 [340]   23.3.1930

There is such a thing as a weariness of the abstract intelligence, which is the most terrible of all wearinesses. It does not weigh on you like physical weariness, nor does it trouble you like a weariness of the emotions. It is the consciousness of the weight of the whole world, an inability in the soul to breathe.

In that moment, as if they were clouds blown by the wind, every idea through which we have experienced life, all the ambitions and plans on which we have founded our hopes for the future, are torn apart, ripped open, carried far off like the grey remnants of mists, the tatters of what never was nor ever could be. And in the wake of that defeat arises the black, implacable solitude of the deserted, starry sky in all its purity. Life's mystery wounds and frightens us in many ways. Sometimes it comes to us as a formless phantasm, the monstrous incarnation of non-being, and our soul trembles in the most terrible of fears. At other times it – the whole truth in all the horror of our inability ever to know it — lurks behind us, visible only so long as we do not turn round to see it.

But the horror that racks me today is at once less noble and more corrosive. It is a wish not to think, a desire never to have been anything, a conscious despair in every cell of my soul. It is a sudden sense of being locked up in an infinite prison. Where can one even think of fleeing, if the prison cell is all there is?

And then there comes over me an absurd and irresistible desire, a kind of satanism predating Satan, that one day – a day outside of all time and matter – we might find a way of fleeing beyond God in order that whatever constitutes the deepest part of us might cease entirely (though how I don't know) to participate in either being or non-being.

122 [352]   *28.9 1932*

No one has as yet produced an exact definition of tedium, at least not in language comprehensible to someone who has never experienced it. What some people call tedium is nothing more than boredom; others use the word to mean a certain physical malaise; for still others tedium is simply tiredness. Tedium does contain tiredness, malaise and boredom but only in the way water contains the hydrogen and oxygen of which it is composed. It includes them without resembling them.

If some give tedium a restricted, incomplete sense, others lend it an almost transcendental significance, as, for example, when the word 'tedium' is used to describe someone's deep sense of spiritual nausea at the randomness and uncertainty of the world. Boredom makes one yawn; physical malaise makes one fidget; tiredness prevents one from moving at all; none of them is tedium. Neither is it that profound sense of the emptiness of things, out of which frustrated aspirations struggle free, a sense of thwarted longing arises and in the soul is sown the seed from which is born the mystic or the saint.

Yes, tedium is boredom with the world, the malaise of living, the weariness of having lived; in truth, tedium *is* the feeling in one's flesh of the endless emptiness of things. But, more than that, tedium is a boredom with other worlds, whether they exist or not; the malaise of living, even if one were someone else, with a different life, in another world; a weariness not just with yesterday or today but with tomorrow too, with all eternity (if it exists) and with nothingness (if that is what eternity is). It isn't just the emptiness of things and beings that hurts the soul when it is immersed in tedium, it's the emptiness of something else too, the emptiness of the soul experiencing that emptiness and feeling itself to be empty, the emptiness that provokes a sense of self-disgust and repudiation.

Tedium is the physical sensation of chaos and of the fact that chaos is everything. Someone who is bored, uncomfortable or tired feels himself to be imprisoned in a tiny cell. Someone disenchanted with the narrowness of life feels himself to be chained up in a large cell. But someone afflicted by tedium feels himself the prisoner of a futile freedom, in a cell of infinite size. The walls of the cell surrounding the bored, uncomfortable or weary prisoner might crumble and bury him beneath them. The chains may fall from the limbs of the prisoner disenchanted with the narrowness of the world and allow him to flee; or, unable to free himself from them, the chains may hurt him and the experience of that pain may revive in him his appetite for life. But the walls of an infinite cell cannot crumble and bury us, since they do not exist, nor can we claim as proof of our existence the pain caused by handcuffs no one has placed round our wrists.

These are my feelings as I stand before the placid beauty of this immortal but dying evening. I look up at the high, clear sky where vague, pink shapes, like the shadows of clouds, are the impalpable down on the wings of distant life. I look down at the river where the water, shimmering slightly, is of a blue that seems the mirror image of a deeper sky. I look up again at the sky and already, in the invisible air, amongst the vague colours that unravel without quite disintegrating, there is an icy dull whiteness, as if in all things, at their highest and most incorporeal level, there were some malaise, a tedium in matter itself, a sense of the impossibility of something just being what it is, an imponderable nexus of anxiety and desolation.

But what if there is? What else is there in the high air but the high air, which is nothing? What else is there in the sky but borrowed colour? What is there in these tiny scraps, barely clouds, whose presence I already doubt, but a little reflected light scattered by a submissive sun? What is there in all this but myself? Ah, but in that and only that lies tedium. It's the fact that in all this – sky, earth, world – there is never anything but myself!

123 [332]

What I feel above all else is weariness and the disquiet that is the twin of weariness when it has no other reason to exist than the fact of existence itself. I feel a deep dread of gestures as yet unmade, an intellectual timidity about words as yet unspoken. Everything seems doomed in advance to insignificance.

The unbearable tedium of all these faces, foolish with intelligence or the lack of it, grotesque to the point of nausea in their happiness or unhappiness, horrific in the mere fact of their existence, a separate tide of living things quite alien to me . . .

124 [350]

I've reached the point where tedium has become a person, the fiction made flesh of my life with myself.

125 [291]

True wealth is closing one's eyes and puffing on an expensive cigar.

With the aid of a cheap cigarette I can return, like someone revisiting a place where they spent their youth, to the time in my life when I used to smoke. The light tang of that cigarette smoke is enough for me to relive the whole of my past life.

At other times a certain type of sweet might serve the same purpose. One innocent chocolate can rack my nerves with the profusion of memories it provokes. Childhood! And as my teeth bite into the soft, dark mass, I bite into and savour my humble joys as contented companion to a lead soldier, as competent horseman with a stick for a horse. Tears fill my eyes and the taste of chocolate mingles with the taste of my past happiness, my lost childhood, and I cling voluptuously to that sweet pain.

The simplicity of this ritual tasting does not detract from the solemnity of the occasion.

But it is cigarette smoke that most subtly rebuilds past moments for me. It just barely touches my consciousness of having a sense of taste and that's why, more than anything else [. . .] it evokes hours to which I am now dead, makes far-off times present, makes them mistier the closer they wrap about me, more ethereal when I make them flesh. A mentholated cigarette, a cheap cigar can bathe in tenderness almost any moment from my past. With what subtle plausibility I use that combination of taste and smell to reconstruct dead scenes and once more borrow [. . .] from a past, as distant, bored and malicious as the eighteenth century, as irredeemably lost to me as the middle ages.

126 [171]   *25.7.1932*

Generally speaking, the classifiers of the world, those men of science whose only knowledge consists in their ability to classify, are ignorant of the fact that what is classifiable is infinite and therefore unclassifiable. But what amazes me most is that they know nothing of the existence of certain unknown classifiable categories, things of the soul and the consciousness that live in the interstices of knowledge.

Perhaps because I think or dream too much I simply cannot distinguish between existent reality and the non-existent reality of dreams. And so I interleave in my meditations on the sky and earth things that neither gleam in the sun nor are trodden under foot: the fluid marvels of the imagination.

I clothe myself in the gold of imagined sunsets, but what is imagined lives on in the imagination. I gladden myself with imaginary breezes, but the imaginary lives when it is imagined. Various hypotheses furnish me with a soul and since each hypothesis has its own soul, each gives me the soul it possesses.

There is only one problem: reality, and that is insoluble and alive. What do I know about the difference between a tree and a dream? I can touch the tree; I know I have the dream. What does that really mean?

What does it mean? That I, alone in the deserted office, can live and imagine without detriment to my intelligence. My thoughts can continue untroubled by the presence of the abandoned desks and the despatch section with its paper and balls of twine. I've left my own high stool and, enjoying in advance a hypothetical promotion, I lean back in Moreira's curve-armed chair. Perhaps it's the influence of the place anointing me with the balm of abstraction. These very hot days make one sleepy; I sleep without sleeping, for lack of energy. That's why I have these thoughts.

127 [173]   *14.3.1930*

The silence that emanates from the sound of the falling rain spreads in a crescendo of grey monotony along the narrow street I gaze down at. I'm sleeping on my feet, standing by the window, which I lean against as if there were nothing else in the world. I search myself to find out what feelings I have before this unravelling fall of dark luminous water standing out clearly against the grubby façades and, even more clearly, against the open windows. And I don't know what I feel, I don't know what I want to feel, I don't know what I think or what I am.

Before my unfeeling eyes, the repressed bitterness of my whole life peels off the suit of natural joy it wears in the prolonged randomness of every day. I realize that I'm always sad, however happy or content I may often feel. And the part of me that realizes this stands a little behind me, as if it were leaning over me standing at the window, and stares out, with more piercing eyes than mine, over my shoulder and over my head at the slow, slightly undulating rain that filigrees the brown, evil air.

One should abandon all duties, even those not demanded of us, reject all cosy hearths, even those that are not our own, live on what is vague and vestigial, amongst the extravagant purples of madness and the false lace of imagined majesties . . . To be something that does not feel the weight of the rain outside, or the pain of inner emptiness . . . To wander with no soul, no thoughts, just pure impersonal sensation, along winding mountain roads, through valleys hidden amongst steep hills, distant, absorbed, ill-fated . . . To lose oneself in landscapes like paintings. To be nothing in distance and in colours . . .

Safe behind the window panes, I do not feel the soft gust of wind that tears and fragments the perpendicular fall of the rain. Somewhere a section of the sky clears. I know this because behind the half-cleaned window immediately opposite I can just make out the calendar on the wall that I couldn't see before.

I forget. I stop seeing, stop thinking.

The rain stops but lingers a moment longer in a cloud of tiny diamonds like crumbs shaken off a great blue tablecloth somewhere up above. You can sense now that part of the sky is already blue. Through the window opposite I can see the calendar more clearly now. It bears the face of a woman and I easily recognize it as an advertisement for one of the more popular brands of toothpaste.

But what was I thinking about before I lost myself in looking? I don't know. The will? Effort? Life? From the spreading light I can tell that the sky must be almost completely blue again. But there is no peace – nor will there ever be! – in the depths of my heart, that old well at the far corner of the estate long since sold, the memory of childhood locked up under the dust of an attic in someone's else's house. There is no peace and, alas for me, not even a desire to find it . . .

128 [178]   *7.10.1931*

The sunset is scattered with stray clouds that fill the whole sky. Soft reflected lights of every colour fill the multifarious upper air and float, oblivious, amongst the great disquiet above. On the very tops of the tall roofs, lying half in light, half in shade, the last slow rays of the setting sun take on shades of colours that belong neither to them nor to the things on which they alight. A vast peace hovers above the noisy surface of the city that is itself slowly settling into quietness. Beyond all the colour and sound everything takes in a deep, dumb breath of air.

The colours on the stuccoed houses out of sight of the sun gradually take on their stone-grey tones. There's something cold about that diversity of greys. A mild unease slumbers in the false valleys of the streets. It slumbers and grows quiet. And little by little the light on the lowest of the clouds begins to turn to shadow; only on one small cloud, which hovers above everything like a white eagle, does the sun still smile, golden, distant.

Everything I searched for in life, I gave up precisely because I had to search for it. I am like someone distractedly looking for something which he sought in dreams, having since forgotten what exactly it was. The present gesture of visible hands – that actually exist each with their five long, white fingers – seeking, turning things over, picking things up and putting them down, becomes more real than the object of my search.

Everything I have ever had is like this lofty sky, diversely uniform, full of scraps of nothing touched by a distant light, fragments of a false life that death, from afar, touches with gold, with the sad smile of the whole truth. Yes, everything I have been came from my inability to look and find: the feudal lord of twilight marshes, the deserted prince of a city of empty tombs.

In these thoughts of mine and in the abrupt fall from light of that one high cloud, everything I am or was or whatever I think of what I am or was suddenly loses its grasp on the secret, the truth, perhaps even the danger there might be in whatever lies beneath life. This, like a truant sun, is all that remains to me; the changing light lets its hands slip from the tall roofs and the inner shadow of all things slowly appears on the rooftops.

Far off the first tiny star – a hesitant, tremulous drop of silver – begins to shine.

129 [182]

It is a rule of life that we can and must learn from everyone. There are serious matters in life to be learned from charlatans and bandits, there are philosophies to be gleaned from fools, real lessons of fortitude that come to us by chance and from those who depend on chance. Everything contains everything else.

In certain very lucid moments of meditation, like those times when, as evening sets in, I wander through the streets looking about me, each person offers me some snippet of news, each house some novelty, each poster some advice.

My silent walk is one long conversation, and all of us, men, houses, stones, posters and sky, are one great comradely crowd, elbowing each other with words in the great procession of Fate.

130 [190]

I'm always astonished whenever I finish anything. Astonished and depressed. My desire for perfection should prevent me from ever finishing anything; it should prevent me even from starting. But I forget that and I do begin. What I achieve is a product not of the application but of a giving in of the will. I begin because I do not have the strength to think; I finish because I do not have the heart just to abandon it. This book represents my cowardice.

The reason I so often break off from a thought to insert a description of a landscape, which in some real or imagined way fits in with the general scheme of my impressions, is that the landscape is a door through which I can escape from the knowledge of my own creative impotence. In the middle of the conversations with myself that make up this book, I often feel a sudden need to talk to someone else, so I address the light hovering, as it does now, above the roofs of the houses that shine as if damp or the tall trees, apparently so near, swaying gently on a city hillside rehearsing the possibility of their own silent downfall, or the posters pasted one on top of the other on the walls of the steep houses with windows for words, where the dead sun turns the still wet glue golden.

Why write if I can't manage to write any better? But what would become of me if I didn't write what I do manage to write, however far below my own standards I fall? I'm a plebeian in my aspirations because I try to create; I fear silence the way others fear entering a dark room alone. I'm like those people who value the medal more than the effort it took to win it and see glory in the gold braid on dress uniforms.

For me, to write is to despise myself, but I can't stop writing. Writing is like a drug I detest but keep taking, a vice I despise and for which I live. There are necessary poisons and there are very subtle ones made up of ingredients of the soul, herbs gathered in the corners of ruined dreams, black poppies found near tombs [. . .] the long leaves of obscene trees that wave their branches on the noisy banks of the infernal rivers of the soul.

Yes, to write is to lose myself, but everyone gets lost, because everything in life is loss. But unlike the river flowing into the estuary for which, unknowing, it was born, I feel no joy in losing myself, but lie like the pool left on the beach at high tide, a pool whose waters, swallowed by the sands, never more return to the sea.

131 [196]

Like Diogenes of Alexander*, all I asked of life was that the sun should not be taken away from me. I had desires, but the reason for having them was denied me. As for what I found, it would have been better if I had really found it. The dream [. . .]

I hesitate before doing anything, often without knowing why.

---

*When Alexander visited Diogenes (whom he greatly admired) and asked if there was anything he could do for him, the latter replied: 'Stand a little out of my sun' (Plutarch, *Lives: Alexander*, chapter 12, sec. 2).

How often, like the straight line appropriate to my nature (conceiving this in my head as the ideal straight line) I deliberately seek out the longest distance between two points. I've never had a talent for the active life. I always bungled the gestures no one else gets wrong; what others were born to do, I always had to struggle not to forget to do. I always want to achieve what others achieved almost casually. Between myself and life there have always been panes of opaque glass, undetectable to me by sight or touch; I never actually lived life according to a plan, I was the daydream of what I wanted to be, my dream began in my will, my goal was always the first fiction of what I never was.

I never knew if my sensibility was too advanced for my intelligence or my intelligence too advanced for my sensibility. I was always too late, for which I don't know, perhaps for both, for one or the other at any rate. Or perhaps it was a third thing that came late.

132 [198]   *7.4.1933*

Though I walked amongst them a stranger, no one noticed. I lived amongst them as a spy and no one, not even I, suspected. Everyone took me for a relative, no one knew that I had been switched at birth. Thus I was like yet unlike the others, everyone's brother but never one of the family.

I came from prodigious lands, from landscapes more beautiful than life itself, but I never spoke of those lands, except to myself, and told no one of the landscapes glimpsed in dreams. On wooden floors and on paving stones my steps echoed just like theirs, but, however near my heart seemed to beat, it was always far away, the false lord of a strange, exiled body.

No one recognized me beneath the mask of equality, nor did they once guess that it was a mask, because no one knew masked players existed in this world. No one imagined that there was always another by my side, the real me. They never doubted my identity with myself.

Their houses sheltered me, their hands shook mine, they saw me walk down the street as if I were really there; but the person I am was never there in those rooms, the person living in me has no hands to be shaken by others, the person I know myself to be has no streets to walk along nor can anyone see him there, unless those streets are all streets and the person who sees him all people.

We all live such distant and anonymous lives; disguised, we suffer the fate of strangers. To some, however, this distance between another being and themselves is never revealed; to others it is revealed only every now and then, through horror or pain, lit by a limitless lightning flash; for yet others it is the one painful constant of their daily lives.

Knowing clearly that who we are has nothing to do with us, that what we think or feel is always in translation, that perhaps what we want we never wanted – to know this every moment, to feel all this in every feeling, is not this what it means to be a stranger in one's own soul, an exile from one's own feelings?

But, on this last night of Carnival, the man in the mask whom I had been passively staring at and who was standing on the corner talking to an unmasked man, at last held out his hand and, laughing, said goodbye. The man without a mask turned left up the lane at the corner of which they'd been standing and the masked man – in unimaginative domino – walked on ahead, moving between the shadows and the occasional lights, in a definitive farewell that was quite different from what I was thinking about. Only then did I notice that there was something else in the street apart from the streetlamps: a diffuse moonlight, hidden and silent, full of nothing, like life. . .

133 [200]   *20.12.1931*

I'm almost convinced now that I'm never truly awake. I'm not sure if it's that I don't dream when I live, or don't live when I dream, or if dream and life commingle and overlap in me and out of that interpenetration is formed my conscious being.

Sometimes, right in the middle of my active life, when I'm evidently as clear about myself as anyone is, a strange feeling of doubt enters my imagination; I do not know if I exist, it seems possible to me that I might be someone else's dream; the idea occurs to me, with an almost carnal reality, that I might be a character in a novel, moving through the long waves of someone else's literary style, through the created truth of a great narrative.

I've often noticed that certain characters in novels take on for us an importance that our acquaintances and friends, who talk and listen to us in the real and visible world, could never have. And this thought provokes the dream question: is everything in the whole world just a series of interlocking dreams and novels like smaller boxes fitting inside larger ones – each one inside another – stories within a story, like *The Thousand and One Nights*, unwinding falsely into the eternal dark?

If I think, everything seems absurd to me; if I feel, everything seems strange; if I want, what I want is something in myself. Whenever something happens in me, I realize that it wasn't me it happened to. If I dream, I feel as if someone were writing me; if I feel, it's as if someone were painting me. If I want something, I feel as if I had been put in a cart, like merchandise to be transported, and simply let myself be carried along, rocked by a motion apparently my own, until we reach a place I did not know I wanted to go to until after I had arrived.

How confusing everything is! Seeing is so superior to thinking, and reading so superior to writing! I may be deceived by what I see but at least I never think it's mine. What I read may depress me, but at least I'm not troubled by the thought that I wrote it. How painful everything is if we think of it conscious of having the thought, like spiritual beings who have passed through that second evolution of consciousness by which we know that we know! However lovely the day, I can't help thinking like this... To think or to feel, or is there some third possibility between the sets pushed to the side of the stage? Feelings of tedium brought on by twilight and neglect, fans clicked shut, the weariness of having had to live...

134 [202]

One's life should be so arranged that it remains a mystery to other people, so that those who know one best in fact know one as little as anyone else, only from a slightly nearer vantage point. That is how, almost without thinking, I have designed my life, but such was the instinctive art I put into it that even to myself my individuality is not entirely clear-cut or precise.

135 [203]

Having seen with what lucidity and logical coherence certain madmen (with method in their madness) justify their crazed ideas to themselves and to others, I have lost for ever any real confidence in the lucidity of my own lucidity.

136 [205]

I look for myself but find no one. I belong to the chrysanthemum hour of bright flowers placed in tall vases. I should make an ornament of my soul.

I do not know which particular magnificent details I would choose to define the essence of my spirit. Doubtless I love the decorative because I sense in it something that resembles the substance of my own soul.

137 [206]

I'm not sure whether my recognition of the human aridity of my heart makes me sad or not. I care more about an adjective than about any real cry from the soul. My master Vieira [. . .]

But sometimes I'm different and I weep real tears, hot tears, the tears of those who do not have or never had a mother; and my eyes, burning with those dead tears, burn too inside my heart.

I don't remember my mother. She died when I was only one year old. If there is anything harsh or disjointed about my sensibility, it has its roots in that absence of warmth and in a vain nostalgia for kisses I cannot even recall. I'm a fraud. I always awoke on other breasts, warmed only obliquely.

Ah, it's the longing for the other person I could have been that unsettles and troubles me. Who would I be now had I but received the affection that wells up naturally from the womb to be bestowed as kisses on a baby's face?

Whether I like it or not, in the confused depths of my fatal sensibility I am all these things.

Perhaps the nostalgia that comes from never having been someone's son has contributed to my emotional indifference. The person who clasped me to them when I was a child could not truly clasp me to their heart. The one person who could have done that was far away, laid in a tomb – the mother who would have been mine, had Fate wished it so.

They say that later, when told that my mother had been pretty, I said nothing. I was already grown in body and soul but ignorant of emotions, and for me speech was not yet mere information lifted from the inconceivable pages of another's book.

My father, who lived a long way from us, killed himself when I was three and I never knew him. I still don't know why he lived so far away. I never particularly wanted to know. I remember his death as a great cloak of seriousness over the first meals after we heard the news. I remember that every now and then they would look at me and I would look back, in clumsy comprehension. Then I would eat my food more carefully just in case, without my knowing it, the others continued to look at me.

138 [208]   *16.9.1931*

Fluidly, the departing day dies amidst spent purples. No one will tell me who I am, nor knows who I was. I came down from the unknown mountain to the equally unknown valley and my steps in the slow evening were just tracks left in the clearings of the forest. Everyone I loved abandoned me to the shadows. No one knew the time of the last boat. In the post there was no sign of the letter no one would write.

Yes, everything was false. No tales were told that others might have told before, and no one had any firm information about the person who left earlier in the hope of embarking on some illusory boat, child of the coming fog and of indecision. Amongst the latecomers I have a name but that, like everything else, is mere shadow.

139 [211]

Now and then something happens in me, and when it does it usually happens suddenly, a terrible weariness with life imposes itself on all other feelings, a weariness so terrible as to defy all remedy. Suicide seems too uncertain and death, even if one assumes it guarantees oblivion, merely insignificant. What this weariness aspires to is not simply to cease to exist – which might or might not be possible – but, far more horrifying, far deeper than that, it wants never to have existed at all, and that, of course, cannot be.

I have caught occasional hints of something similar to this ambition (which outdoes in negativity even the void itself) in the often confused speculations of the Indians. But either they lack the keenness of feeling that would enable them to explain what they think or the acuity of thought to feel what they feel. The fact is that what I glimpse in them I cannot actually see. More to the point, I believe I am the first to put into words the sinister absurdity of this irremediable feeling.

Yet I exorcise it by writing about it. Provided it comes also from the intellect and is not just pure emotion, there is no truly deepseated affliction that will not succumb to the ironic cure of being written about. For the few this might be one of literature's uses, assuming, that is, that it has no other use.

Unfortunately, the suffering of the intellect is less painful than that of the emotions, and that of the emotions, again unfortunately, less than that of the body. I say 'unfortunately' because human dignity would naturally demand the opposite. No anguished sense of the mystery of life hurts like love or jealousy or longing, chokes you the way intense physical fear can or transforms you like anger or ambition. But neither can any of the pains that lacerate the soul ever be as real a pain as that of toothache, or colic or (I imagine) childbirth . . .

I write like someone asleep, and my whole life is like a receipt awaiting signature.

Inside the chicken coop from whence he will go to be killed, the cock sings hymns to freedom because they gave him two perches all to himself.

140 [212]   *2.9.1931*

Unknowingly, I have been a witness to the gradual wasting away of my life, to the slow shipwreck of everything I ever wanted to be. I can say, with the truth that requires no wreaths to remind it of its own demise, that there is not one thing I have wanted or in which I have even for a moment placed my momentary dream that has not fallen and shattered beneath my window and lain like the dusty remains of a clump of soil fallen from a flowerpot on a balcony high above the street. It even seems that Fate has always tried, first and foremost, to make me love or want the very thing that, the following day, Fate itself has ordained I will see that I did not and would not have.

However, as an ironic spectator of myself, I have never lost my interest in observing life. And now, knowing beforehand that each tentative hope will be crushed, I suffer the special pleasure of enjoying the disillusion together with the pain, a bittersweetness in which the sweetness predominates. I am a sombre strategist who has lost every battle and now, on the eve of each new engagement, draws up the details of the fatal retreat, savouring the plan as he does so.

That fate of being unable to desire without knowing beforehand that I will not be granted my desire, has pursued me like some malign creature. Whenever I see the figure of a young girl in the street and just for a moment wonder, however idly, how it would be if she were mine, every time, just ten paces on from my daydream, that girl meets a man who is obviously her husband or her lover. A romantic would make a tragedy of this, a stranger a comedy; I, however, mix the two things, for I am both a romantic and a stranger to myself, and I simply turn the page to enjoy the next irony.

Some say there's no life without hope, others that hope makes life meaningless. For me, bereft of both hope and despair, life is just a picture in which I am included but that I watch as if it were a play with no plot, performed merely to please the eye – an incoherent ballet, the stirring of leaves on a tree, clouds that change colour with the changing light, random networks of old streets in odd parts of the city.

I am, for the most part, the very prose that I write. I shape myself in periods and paragraphs, I punctuate myself and, in the unleashed chain of images, I make myself king, as children do, with a crown made from a sheet of newspaper or, in finding rhythms in mere strings of words, I garland myself, as madmen do, with dried flowers that in my dreams still live. And, above all this, I am as calm as a doll stuffed with sawdust which, becoming conscious of itself, every now and then gives a nod so that the bell on top of the pointed hat sewn to its head rings out: the jingle of life in a dead man, a tiny warning to Fate.

How often, though, right in the midst of my quiet dissatisfaction, has not a sense of the emptiness and tedium of this way of thinking crept slowly into my conscious emotions! How often, like someone hearing voices emerging from amongst other intermittent noises, have I not felt the essential bitterness of this life so alien to human life, a life in which the only thing that happens is its own consciousness of itself. How often, waking from myself, have I not glimpsed from the exile that is me, how much better to be the ultimate nobody, the fortunate man who at least feels real bitterness, the contented man who feels tiredness not tedium, who suffers rather than merely imagining he suffers, who actually kills himself instead of just slowly dying.

I've become a character in a book, a life already read. Quite against my wishes what I feel is felt in order for me to write it down. What I think appears later set down in words, mixed up with images that merely undo it all, set out in rhythms that mean something else altogether. With all this rewriting, I have destroyed myself. With all this thinking, I am now just my thoughts, not myself. I plumbed the depths of myself but dropped the plumbline; I spend my life wondering whether or not I am deep, with only my own eyes to gauge the depth, and all they show me, clearly in the black mirror of the great well, is my own face watching me watching it.

I'm like a playing card that belongs to some ancient and unknown suit, the only remnant of a lost pack. I have no meaning, I do not know my value, I have nothing to compare myself with in order to find myself, I have no purpose in life by which to know myself. And thus, in the successive images I use to describe myself – not untruthful but not truthful either – I become more image than me, talking myself out of existence, using my soul as ink, whose only purpose is to write. But that reaction fades and I resign myself again. I return to myself as I am, even though that is nothing. And something like dry tears burns in my wide open eyes, something like a never-felt anxiety catches in my dry throat. But, alas, I don't know what I would have wept for if I had cried, nor why it was I did not weep. The fiction cleaves close to me as my shadow. All I want is to sleep.

141 [214]

I envy in everyone the fact that they are not me. Of all impossibilities, and this always seemed the greatest, this was the one that made up the greater part of my daily dose of anguish, the despair that fills every sad hour.

142 [215]

Painful interlude

Like something tossed into a corner, a rag discarded in the street, my ignoble being, confronted by life, pretends its own self.

143 [219]

I experience time as a terrible ache. I get ridiculously upset whenever I have to leave anything: the miserable little rented room where I spent a few months, the table in the provincial hotel at which I dined on each of my six days there, even the waiting room at the railway station where I wasted two hours waiting for the train. But the good things of life, when I have to leave them and think, with all the sensitivity my nerves can muster, that I will never see or have them again, at least not as they are in that exact, precise moment, hurt me metaphysically. An abyss yawns open in my soul and a cold blast from the hour of God brushes my pale face.

Time! The past! [...] What I was and will never be again! What I had and will never have again! The Dead! The dead who loved me when I was a child. When I remember them my whole soul grows cold and I feel myself to be an exile from every heart, alone in the night of my own self, crying like a beggar at the closed silence of every door.

144 [220]

God created me to be a child and left me to be a child forever. But why did he let life beat me and take away my toys and leave me alone at playtime, to crumple up in feeble hands the blue pinafore streaked with tearstains? Since I cannot live without affection, why was that affection taken from me? Whenever I see a child in the street crying, a child exiled from the others, it hurts me more than the sadness of the child I see in the unsuspected horror of my exhausted heart. I hurt in every inch of my lived life, and the hands crumpling the hem of the pinafore, the mouth twisted by real tears, the weakness and the solitude are all mine, and the laughter of passing adults is like the flame of a match struck on the sensitive tinder of my own heart.

145 [221]

. . . like a child, breathing hard, who stops running and leaves behind him the sound of small feet pounding hard on the ground . .

146 (222)

Everything becomes mixed up in me. When I think I have remembered something, I'm actually thinking something else; if I look, I see nothing, yet when distracted, I see everything clearly.

I turn my back on the grey window, on the glass panes cold to the touch, and, by some trick of the penumbra, I carry with me the interior of the old house where, in the nearby courtyard, a parrot used to call; and my eyes close sleepily on the irreparable fact of having actually lived.

It's been raining for two days now and the rain that falls from the cold, grey sky is of a colour that grieves the soul. Two days . . . I'm sad from too much feeling and reflect that back onto the window to the sound of water dripping and rain falling. My heart feels heavy and all my memories have turned to anguish . . .

What made me think about that parrot now? The fact that I'm sad and my far-off childhood reminds me of that? No, I really thought of it because right now from the courtyard on the borders of this present moment, I can hear the voice of a parrot calling out incomprehensible words. . . . that imaginative episode we call reality.

147 [225]

Day by day, in my deep but ignoble soul I record the impressions that form the external substance of my consciousness of myself. I put them into errant words that desert me as soon as they're written and wander off independently down hills and across lawns of images, along avenues lined with conceits and lanes of confusions. This is of no use to me, for nothing is of any use. But it calms me to write, the way an invalid may breathe more easily even though his sickness has not passed.

Some people when they're distracted scribble lines and absurd names on the blotter on their desk. These pages are the doodles of my intellectual unconsciousness of myself. I set them down in a torpor of feeling, like a cat in the sun, and re-read them at times with a dull, belated pang, as if remembering something I had always previously forgotten.

Writing is like paying myself a formal visit. I have special rooms, recalled in the interstices of the imagination by someone else, where I enjoy myself analysing what I do not feel and peer at myself as at a painting hung in the shadows.

I lost my ancient castle even before I was born. The tapestries of my ancestral palace were all sold before I even came into being. My mansion built before I lived has now crumbled into ruins and, only at certain times, when the moon rises in me over the reeds, do I feel the chill of nostalgia emanating from that site where the toothless remains of the walls stand silhouetted black against the sky whose dark blue gradually pales into milky yellow.

I divide myself up, sphinx-like. And the forgotten skein of my soul falls from the lap of the queen I lack, like a scene taken from her futile tapestry. It rolls beneath the inlaid chest and something of myself follows it, as if that something were my eyes, until the skein is lost amongst a general horror of tombs and endings.

148 [226]

My self-imposed exclusion from the aims and directions of life, my self-imposed rupture with any contact with things, led me precisely to what I was trying to flee. I did not want to feel life or touch things, knowing from my experience of what happened when my temperament came into contact with the world that the sensation of living was always painful to me. But in avoiding that contact, I isolated myself and, in isolating myself, exacerbated my already excessive sensibility, for which the best thing, were it possible, would be to end all contact with anything. But such total isolation is not possible. However little I do, I still breathe, however little there is to do, I still move. And thus, with my sensibility heightened by isolation, I find that the tiniest things, which before would have had no effect even on me, buffet and bruise me like the worst catastrophe. I chose the wrong method of flight. I took an awkward short cut that led me right back to where I was, compounding the horror of living there with the exhaustion of the journey.

I never considered suicide a solution, because I only hate life out of love for it. It took me a long time to be convinced of the lamentable error in which I live with myself. Once convinced, I felt displeased, as always happens when I convince myself of something, because it means the loss of another of my illusions.

By analysing my will, I killed it. What I'd give to go back to my childhood before I learned how to analyse, even to the time before I had a will!

A heavy sleep fills my gardens, pools lie somnolent beneath the noonday sun, the noise of insects throngs the hour and life weighs on me, not like a grief, but like an unending physical ache.

Distant palaces, dreaming parks, the narrow lines of avenues far off, the graveyard grace of the stone benches built for those who once were – dead splendours, ruined elegance, lost baubles. Sweet longing sliding slowly into forgetting, if only I could recover the pain with which I dreamed you.

149 [229]   *16.10.1931*

I've always been an ironic dreamer, unfaithful to promises I made to myself. I've always savoured the shipwreck of my daydreams as if I were someone else, a stranger, as if I were a chance participant in what I thought I was. I never gave much credence to any of my beliefs. I filled my hands with sand and called it gold then let it all slip away through my fingers. The sentence was the only truth. Once the sentence was formed everything was done; the rest was the sand it always had been.

Were it not for the fact that I am always dreaming and live in a state of perpetual foreignness to my own self, I could happily call myself a realist, that is, an individual for whom the external world is an independent nation. However, I prefer not to label myself but to be only obscurely who I am and to enjoy the piquancy of being unpredictable even to myself.

I have a kind of duty always to dream, for, since I am nothing more, nor desirous of being anything more, than a spectator of myself, I must put on the best show I can. So I deck myself in gold and silks and place myself in imaginary rooms on a false stage with ancient scenery, a dream created beneath the play of soft lights, to the sound of invisible music.

Like the recollection of a sweet kiss, I treasure the childhood memory of a theatre in which the blue, lunar scenery represented the terrace of an impossible palace. Painted round it was a vast park and I put my whole heart into living all that as if it were real. The music that played quietly on that imaginary occasion in my experience of life lent the gratuitous scene a feverish reality.

The scenery was definitively blue and lunar. I don't remember who appeared on the stage but the play I choose to set in that remembered landscape comes to me now in lines from Verlaine and Pessanha*; it's not the play, now long forgotten, that was acted out on the real stage beyond that reality of blue music. It's my own play, a vast, fluid, lunar masquerade, an interlude in silver and fading blue.

Then life intervened. That night they took me to have supper at the Leão†. On the palate of my nostalgia I can still remember the taste of the steaks – steaks, I know or imagine, the like of which no one cooks today and the like of which I never eat. And all those things mingle in me – my childhood, lived somewhere in the distance, that night's delicious meal, the lunar scenery, the future Verlaine and the present me – in a diffuse refraction, in a false space between what I was and what I am.

150 [157]   18.7.1916

No problem is soluble. None of us unties the Gordian knot; we either give up or cut it. We brusquely resolve with our feelings problems of the intellect and do so because we are tired of thinking, because we are too timid to draw conclusions, because of an absurd need for support, or because of our gregarious impulse to rejoin the others and rejoin life.

Since we can never know all the factors involved in an issue, we can never resolve it.

To reach the truth we lack both the necessary facts and the intellectual processes that could exhaust all possible interpretations of those facts.

---

*Camilo Pessanha (1871–1926) was a Portuguese symbolist poet who spent a large part of his life in Macau where he died.

†A famous café in Lisbon, frequented by intellectuals.

151 [233]

In those occasional moments of detachment in which we become aware of ourselves as individuals whom other people perceive as other, it has always bothered me to imagine the sort of moral and physical figure I must cut in front of those who see and talk to me whether daily or from time to time.

We are all accustomed to think of ourselves as essentially mental realities and of others as merely physical realities; because of the way others respond to us, we do vaguely think of ourselves as physical beings; we vaguely think of other people as mental beings, but only when we find ourselves in love or conflict with another do we really take in the fact that others have a soul just as we do.

That's why I sometimes lose myself in futile imaginings about the kind of person I am for those who see me, what my voice sounds like, what kind of impression I leave on the involuntary memory of others, how my gestures, my words, my outward life engrave themselves on the retina of other people's interpretations. I've never managed to see myself from outside. There is no mirror that can show us to ourselves as exteriors, because no mirror can take us outside ourselves. We would need another soul, another way of looking and thinking. If I were an actor captured on film or could record my speaking voice on disc I'm sure that I would still be a long way from knowing how I seem from outside because, whether I like it or not, record what I will of myself, I remain stuck here inside the high-walled garden of my consciousness of me.

I don't know if other people feel the same, or if the science of life does not indeed consist essentially in being so alienated from oneself that one instinctively achieves the alienation necessary to be able to participate in life as if unaware of one's own consciousness; or if others, even more inward-looking than me, are not entirely given over to the brutishness of just being themselves, living entirely outwardly through that miracle whereby bees form societies better organized than any human nation and ants communicate amongst themselves in a language of tiny twitching antenna far superior to our complex ability to misunderstand one another.

The geography of our consciousness of reality is one of complicated coastlines, lakes and rugged mountains. And to me, if I think about it too long, it begins to seem like the sort of map one finds in the *Pays du Tendre** or in *Gulliver's Travels*, a joke drawn up with precision in some fantastic or ironic book for the diversion of superior beings who know where lands are really lands.

For those who think, everything is complex, and thought, no doubt purely for its own pleasure, only complicates things further. But any thinking person has a need to justify his abdication with a vast manifesto of understanding, embellished, like the excuses given by liars, with the excess of detail which, when shaken off like earth from a plant, reveals the root of the lie.

Everything is complex or perhaps it's just me who is. But in the end it doesn't matter because nothing really matters. All this, all these considerations that have strayed from the main highway, vegetate in the gardens of the excluded gods like climbing plants growing too far from the walls they should be climbing. And in this night that sees the end but not the conclusion of my disjointed thoughts, I smile at the essential irony that causes them to arise in a human soul orphaned since before the stars were made from Destiny's grand motives.

152 [234]

In order to understand, I destroyed myself. To understand is to forget to love. I know nothing at once so false and so meaningful as that saying of Leonardo da Vinci that one can only love or hate something once one has understood it.

Solitude torments me; company oppresses me. The presence of another person distracts me from my thoughts; I dream their presence in a peculiarly abstracted way that none of my analytical powers can define.

---

*The 'Carte du Tendre', an allegorical map showing the region of the 'tender sentiments', drawn up by Madeleine de Scudéry (1607–1701).

153 [235]

Isolation made me in its own image. The presence of another person – one person is all it takes – immediately slows down my thinking and, just as in a normal person contact with others acts as a stimulus to expression and speech, in me that contact acts as a counter-stimulus, if such a word exists. When I'm alone I can come up with endless bon mots, acerbic ripostes to remarks no one has made, sociable flashes of wit exchanged with no one; but all this disappears when I'm confronted by another human being. I lose all my intelligence, I lose the power of speech and after a while all I feel like doing is sleeping. Yes, talking to people makes me feel like sleeping. Only my spectral and imagined friends, only the conversations I have in dreams, have reality and substance and in them the spirit is present like an image in a mirror.

The whole idea of being forced into contact with someone oppresses me. A simple invitation to supper from a friend produces in me an anguish difficult to put into words. The idea of any social obligation – going to a funeral, discussing something with someone at the office, going to meet someone (whether known or unknown) at the station – the mere idea blocks that whole day's thoughts and sometimes I even worry about it the night before and sleep badly because of it. Yet the reality, when it comes, is utterly insignificant, and certainly doesn't justify so much fuss, yet it happens again and again and I never learn.

'My habits are those of solitude not of men.' I don't know if it was Rousseau or Senancour who said that, but it was some spirit belonging to the same species as me, though I could not perhaps say of the same race.

154 [237]   *13.4.1930*

I think what creates in me the deep sense I have of living out of step with others is the fact that most people think with their feelings whereas I feel with my thoughts.

For the average man, to feel is to live, and to think is to know that one lives. For me, to think is to live, and to feel just provides food for thought.

My capacity for enthusiasm being minimal, it's odd that I'm more drawn to those opposed to me in temperament than to those of the same spiritual species as myself. In literature I admire no one more than the classical writers with whom I have least in common. If I had to choose as my only reading between either Chateaubriand or Vieira, I wouldn't think twice about choosing Vieira.

The more different someone is from me, the more real they seem, because they depend less upon my subjectivity. That is why the constant object of my close study is precisely that vulgar humanity I reject and from which I distance myself. I love it because I hate it. I enjoy observing it because I hate actually feeling it. The landscape one admires so much as a picture generally makes for an uncomfortable bed.

155 [239]   *18.9.1931*

Just as, whether we know it or not, we all have a metaphysics, so also, whether we like or not, we all have a morality. I have a very simple morality – to do neither good nor evil to anyone. To do no evil because I not only recognize in others the same right I judge myself to have, which is not to be bothered by them, but also because I think there are enough natural evils in the world without my adding to them. In this world we're all travellers on the same ship that has set sail from one unknown port en route to another equally foreign to us; we should treat each other therefore with the friendliness due to fellow travellers. And I choose to do no good because I don't know what good is, nor whether I really am doing good when I think I am. How am I to know what evils I may cause when I give alms, or if I attempt to educate or instruct? In case of doubt, I abstain. I believe, moreover, that to help or clarify is, in a way, to commit the evil of intervening in someone else's life. Kindness is a temperamental caprice and we do not have the right to make others the victims of our caprice however humane or tender-hearted. Favours are things imposed on others; that's why I so thoroughly detest them.

If, for moral reasons, I choose to do no good, neither do I demand that anyone else should do good to me. What I hate most when I fall ill is obliging someone to look after me because it's something I would hate to do for someone else. I've never once visited a sick friend. Whenever I've been ill and people have visited me, I felt each visit to be an inconvenience, an insult, an unjustifiable violation of my chosen privacy. I don't like people giving me things; they seem then to be obliging me to give them something too – to them or to others, it doesn't matter to whom.

I'm extremely sociable in an extremely negative manner. I'm inoffensiveness incarnate. But I'm no more than that, I don't want to be more than that, nor can I be more than that. I feel for everything that exists a visual tenderness, an intelligent affection, but nothing heartfelt. I have no faith in anything, no hope in anything, no charity for anything. I feel nothing but aversion and disgust for the sincere adherents of every kind of sincerity and for the mystics of every kind of mysticism or rather for the sincerities of all sincere people and for the mysticisms of all mystics. I feel an almost physical nausea when those mysticisms turn evangelical, when they try to convince another intelligence or another will to find the truth or change the world.

I consider myself fortunate no longer to have any relatives, for I am thus free of the obligation, which would inevitably weigh on me, of having to love someone. My only nostalgias are literary ones. My eyes fill with tears at the memory of my childhood but they are rhythmical tears in which some piece of prose is already in preparation. I remember it as something external to me and remember it through external things; I remember only external things. It isn't the cosy warmth of provincial evenings that fills me with tender feelings for my childhood but the way the table was laid for tea, the shapes of the furniture placed around the house, people's faces and physical gestures. My nostalgia is for certain pictures of the past. That's why I feel as much tenderness for my own childhood as for someone else's: lost in some indefinite past, they are both purely visual phenomena that I perceive with my literary mind. I do feel tenderness, not because I remember, but because I see.

I've never loved anyone. What I have loved most have been sensations – the scenes recorded by my conscious vision, the impressions captured by attentive ears, the perfumes by which the humble things of the external world speak to me and tell me tales of the past (so easily evoked by smells) – that is, their gift to me of a reality and emotion more intense than the loaf baking in the depths of the bakery as it was on that far-off afternoon on my way back from the funeral of the uncle who so adored me and when all I felt was the vague tenderness of relief, about what I don't know.

That is my morality or my metaphysics or me myself: a passer-by in everything, even in my own soul. I belong to nothing, I desire nothing, I am nothing except an abstract centre of impersonal sensations, a sentient mirror fallen from the wall but still turned to reflect the diversity of the world. I don't know if this makes me happy or unhappy, and I don't much care.

156 [241]

When I examine my own pain I do so with that uncertain and almost imponderable malice that enlivens any human heart when confronted by other people's pain or discomfort; I take this to such lengths that I even enjoy those occasions when I'm made to feel ridiculous or mean-spirited as if they were happening to someone else. By some strange and fantastic transformation of my feelings I do not feel any spiteful and all too human joy at other people's pain and absurdity. Confronted by other people's misfortunes I do not experience pain but a feeling of aesthetic discomfort and a furtive irritation. This has nothing to do with kindness, it is simply because when someone is made to feel ridiculous, they appear ridiculous not only to me but to others too and it is that that irritates me; it hurts me that any animal of the human species should laugh at someone else's expense when they have no right to do so. I don't care if others laugh at me, because I'm protected by an efficient armour of scorn.

To mark the boundaries of the garden of my being I put up high railings, more daunting than any wall, so that whilst I can see others quite clearly, at the same time I exclude them and keep them other.

All my life I have concentrated all my attention and every moral scruple on finding ways of avoiding action.

I submit myself neither to the state nor to men; I put up an inert resistance. The only thing the state would want me for is to perform some action. If I refuse to act, the state can get nothing out of me. Since there's no capital punishment these days, all the state can do is make life difficult for me. Were this to happen I would simply renew the armour about my spirit and entrench myself still further in my dreams. But this has never happened. The state has never bothered me. I think good fortune must have protected me.

157 [243]

Lucid diary

My life: a tragedy booed off the stage by the gods after only the first act.

Friends: none. Just a few acquaintances who think they get on with me and would perhaps be sorry if I got knocked down by a train or it rained on the day of the funeral.

The natural reward for my withdrawal from life has been an inability, which I created in others, to sympathize with me. There's an aura of cold around me, a halo of ice that repels others. I still haven't managed not to feel the pain of my solitude. It is so difficult to achieve the distinction of spirit that makes isolation seem a haven of peace free from all anguish.

I never believed in the friendship shown me, just as I would not have believed in their love, which was anyway impossible. So complex and subtle is my manner of suffering that, although I never had any illusions about the people who called themselves my friends, I still managed to feel disillusioned by them.

I never doubted for a moment that they would all betray me and yet I was always shocked when they did. Even when what I was expecting to happen did happen, for me it was always unexpected.

As I never found in myself qualities that might be attractive to another person, I could never believe that anyone could feel attracted to me. That could be dismissed as the considered opinion of a foolish modesty if fact after fact – those unexpected facts I confidently expected – had not always proved it correct.

I can't even imagine them feeling compassion for me since, though I'm physically awkward and unacceptable, I don't have that degree of batteredness which would make me a likely candidate for other people's compassion, nor the sympathy that attracts it even when not obviously deserved; and there can be no compassion for the quality in me that might merit pity, because there is no pity for spiritual cripples. So I was drawn instead into the gravitational field of other people's scorn where I am unlikely to attract anyone's sympathy.

I've spent my whole life trying to adapt to this without feeling too deeply the cruelty and vileness of it all.

One needs a certain intellectual courage to recognize unflinchingly that one is no more than a scrap of humanity, a living abortion, a madman not yet crazy enough to be locked up; but, having recognized that, one needs even more spiritual courage to adapt oneself perfectly to one's destiny, to accept without rebellion, without resignation, without a single gesture or attempt at a gesture of protest, the elemental curse Nature has laid upon one. Wanting to feel no pain at all is to want too much, because it is not in human nature to accept evil, recognize it for what it is and call it good; and if you accept it as an evil then you cannot but suffer.

My misfortune – a misfortune for my own happiness – lay in my imagining myself from outside. I saw myself as others saw me and I began to despise myself, not because I recognized in myself qualities deserving of scorn, but because I saw myself as others saw me and felt the kind of scorn they would feel for me. I suffered the humiliation of knowing myself. Since this was a calvary lacking in all nobility and was not to be followed some days later by a resurrection, all I could do was suffer with the ignobility of it all.

I understood then that only someone lacking all aesthetic sense could possibly love me and if they did, I would despise them for it. Even liking me could be no more than the caprice born of another's indifference.

To see clearly into ourselves and into how others see us! To see this truth face to face! Thence comes the final cry of Christ on the cross when he saw, face to face, *his* truth: My God, my God, why hast thou forsaken me?

158 [244]   *18.9.1917*

Everywhere I have been in my life, in every situation, wherever I've lived and worked alongside people, I've always been considered by everyone to be an intruder or, at the least, a stranger. Amongst my relatives as amongst acquaintances, I've always been considered an outsider. Not that even once have I been treated like that consciously, but the spontaneous response of others to me ensured that I was.

Everyone everywhere has always treated me kindly. Very few people, I think, have had so few raise their voice against them, or been so little frowned at, so infrequently the object of someone else's arrogance or irritability. But the kindness with which I was treated was always devoid of affection. For those who would naturally be closest to me, I was always a guest who, as such, was well treated but only with the attentiveness due to a stranger and the lack of affection which is the lot of the intruder.

I'm sure that all this, I mean other people's attitudes towards me, lies principally in some obscure intrinsic flaw in my own temperament. Perhaps I communicate a coldness that unwittingly obliges others to reflect back my own lack of feeling.

I get to know people quickly. It doesn't take long for people to grow to like me. But I never gain their affection. I've never experienced devotion. To be loved has always seemed to me an impossibility, as unlikely as a complete stranger suddenly addressing me familiarly as 'tu'.

I don't know if this makes me suffer or if I simply accept it as my indifferent fate into which questions of suffering or acceptance do not enter.

I always wanted to please. It always hurt me that people should be indifferent towards me. As an orphan of Fortune I have, like all orphans, a need to be the object of someone's affection. I've always been starved of the realization of that need. I've grown so accustomed to this vain hunger that, at times, I'm not even sure I still feel the need to eat.

With or without it life still hurts me.

Others have someone who is devoted to them. I've never had anyone who even considered devoting themselves to me. That is for others: me, they just treat decently.

I recognize in myself the capacity to arouse respect but not affection. Unfortunately I've done nothing that in itself justifies that initial respect and so no one has ever managed fully to respect me either.

I sometimes think that I enjoy suffering. But the truth is I would prefer something else.

I don't have the right qualities to be either leader or follower. I don't even have the merit of being contented which, if all else fails, is all that remains.

Other people of lesser intelligence are in fact much stronger than me. They are better than I am at carving out their lives amongst other people, more skilled at administering their intelligence. I have all the necessary qualities to influence others but not the art with which to do so, nor even the will to want to do so.

If one day I were to love someone, I would not be loved in return.

It's enough for me to want something for that thing to die. My destiny, however, is not powerful enough to prove deadly to just anything. It has the unfortunate disadvantage of being deadly only to those things I want.

159 [263]

It is not love itself but the outskirts of love that matter. . .

The sublimation of love illuminates the phenomena of love much more clearly than the actual experience of it. There are some very wise virgins in the world. Action has its compensations but it confuses the issue. To possess is to be possessed and therefore to lose oneself. Only in ideas does one achieve, without spoiling it, a knowledge of reality.

160 [264]

Be pure, not in order to be noble or strong, but to be oneself. If you give love, you lose love.

Abdicate from life so as not to abdicate from oneself.

Woman is a rich source of dreams. Never touch her.

Learn to separate the concepts of voluptuousness and pleasure. Learn to take pleasure not in what something actually is, but in the ideas and dreams it provokes. For nothing is what it is: dreams are always dreams. That's why you must touch nothing. If you touch your dream it will die and the touched object will then fill your senses.

Seeing and hearing are the only noble things in life. The other senses are plebeian and carnal. True aristocracy means never touching anything. Never go too near – that is true nobility.

161 [275]

In me all affections are superficial, but sincerely so. I've always been an actor, and a good one. Whenever I have loved, I've only pretended to love, even to myself.

162 [276]

Letter not to be sent

I excuse you from having to appear in my idea of you. Your life [...]
   This is not my love; it is just your life.
   I love you as I do the sunset or the moonlight, wanting the moment to stay, but wanting nothing more than the feeling of possessing that moment.

163 [277]

If only our life were one long standing at the window, if only we could just stay there, like an unmoving curl of smoke, frozen at that one moment in the evening that paints the curve of the mountains with painful colour. If only we could stay there beyond forever! If, at the very least, on this shore of the impossible, we could stay like that, without undertaking one single action, without our pale lips committing the sin of uttering more words!
   Look, it grows dark! ... The positive peace of everything fills me with rage, with something which is the bitter aftertaste of the air I breathe. My soul aches ... In the distance a slow ribbon of smoke rises and disperses ... A restless tedium blocks further thoughts of you ...
   How unnecessary it all is! Us and the world and the mystery of both.

164 [279]

ANTEROS*

---

*Anteros was the brother of Eros, said to be either the avenger of unrequited love or the opposer of love.

The visual lover

I have a superficial, decorative concept of deep love and its useful employment. I'm subject to visual passions. I keep whole a heart given over to unreal destinies.

I can't recall ever having loved in someone anything more than the 'image' of them, not what portrait painters depict but the purely exterior, into which the soul enters only to lend animation and life.

This is how I love: I fix on the image of a woman or a man – where desire is absent, gender is irrelevant – because they are beautiful, attractive or lovable and that image obsesses, binds, grips me. However, all I want is to see it [. . .] nothing more [. . .] than to be able to come to know and speak with the real person of whom that image is the outward manifestation.

I love with my eyes and not with my fantasy. I don't fantasize about the image that obsesses me. I don't imagine myself connected to it in any other way [. . .] I have no interest in finding out what this creature, who presents to me only their external aspect, is or does or thinks.

The endless procession of people and things that forms the world is for me an interminable gallery of pictures whose content bores me. It doesn't interest me because the soul is a monotonous thing and is always the same in everyone; it differs only in its personal manifestations and the best part of it is that which overflows into dreams, into mannerisms and gestures, and thus becomes part of the image that so captures my interest [. . .]

This is how I experience the animate exteriors of things and beings, in pure vision, indifferent as a god from another world to their content, to their spirit. I only go deep into the surface of other people, if I want profundity I look for it in myself and in my concept of things.

What would I gain from personal knowledge of the creature I love as a decorative object? Not disappointment, because, since what I love in her is only her appearance and since I have no fantasies about her, her stupidity or mediocrity is irrelevant as I was only ever interested in her outward appearance from which I expected nothing anyway, and that outward appearance is still there. Moreover personal knowledge of someone is harmful because useless and what is useless in the material world is always harmful. What good would it do me to know the creature's name? And yet that is the first thing I find out on being introduced to her.

Personal knowledge ought to mean freedom of contemplation, which is precisely what my idea of love also desires. We cannot freely regard or contemplate someone we know personally.

Superfluous knowledge is useless to the artist because, by disturbing him, it lessens the effect he seeks.

My natural destiny is to be an unconfined and passionate observer of the appearances and manifestations of things, the objective observer of dreams, the visual lover of every form and aspect of nature.

It is not a case of what psychiatrists call psychic onanism, nor even erotomania. I don't, as is the case with psychic onanism, indulge in fantasies; I don't dream of making a lover or even a friend of the creature I contemplate and remember: I have no fantasies about her. Nor, like the erotomane, do I idealize her and transport her beyond the sphere of pure aesthetics: to fulfil my desires and my thoughts, I want nothing more from her than what she offers to my eyes and to the pure direct memory of what my eyes saw.

165 [283]

I was only ever truly loved once. Everyone has always treated me kindly. Even the most casual acquaintance has found it difficult to be rude or brusque or even cool to me. Sometimes with a little help from me, that kindness could – or at least might – have developed into love or affection. I've had neither the patience nor the concentration of mind to want to make that effort.

When I first noticed this in myself – so little do we know ourselves – I attributed it to some shyness of the soul. But then I realized that this wasn't the case; it was an emotional tedium, different from the tedium of life; an impatience with the idea of associating myself with one continuous feeling, especially if that meant steeling myself to make some sustained effort. Why bother? thought the unthinking part of me. I have enough subtlety, enough psychological sensitivity to know how, but the why has always escaped me. My weakness of will always began by being a weakness of the will even to have a will. The same happened with my emotions, my intelligence, my will itself, with everything in my life.

But on the one occasion that malicious fate caused me to believe I loved someone and to recognize that I really was loved in return, it left me at first as stunned and confused as if my number had come up on the lottery and I had won a huge amount of money in some inconvertible currency. Then, because I'm only human, I felt rather flattered. However, that most natural of emotions soon passed, to be overtaken by a feeling difficult to define but one in which tedium, humiliation and weariness predominated.

A feeling of tedium as if Fate had imposed on me a task to be carried out during some unfamiliar evening shift. As if a new duty – that of an awful reciprocity – were given to me, ironically, as a privilege over which I would have to toil, all the time thanking Fate for it. As if the flaccid monotony of life were not enough to bear without superimposing on it the obligatory monotony of a definite feeling.

And humiliation, yes, I felt humiliated. It took me a while to understand the justification for such an apparently unjustifiable feeling. The love of being loved no doubt surfaced in me. I probably felt flattered that someone had taken the time to consider my existence and conclude that it was that of a potentially lovable being. But apart from that brief moment of pride – and I'm still not entirely sure that astonishment did not outweigh pride – the feeling that welled up in me was one of humiliation. I felt as if I had been given a prize intended for someone else, a prize of great worth to the person who truly deserved it.

And, above all else, I felt weary – the weariness that surpasses all tedium. Only then did I understand something Chateaubriand wrote and which until then, because I lacked the necessary self-knowledge, had always puzzled me. Of his character René* he says: 'on le fatiguait en l'aimant,' (people wearied him with their love) and I realized with a shock that this was exactly my experience, the truth of which I could not deny.

How wearisome it is to be loved, to be truly loved! How wearisome to be the object of someone else's bundle of emotions! To be changed from someone who wanted to be free, always free, into an errand boy with a responsibility to reciprocate those emotions, to have the decency not to run away, so that the other person will not think one is acting with princely disdain and rejecting the greatest gift the human soul can offer. How wearisome to let one's existence become something absolutely dependent on someone else's feelings; to have no option but to feel, to love a little too, whether or not it is reciprocated.

That episode passed me by just as it had come to me, in the shadows. Now not a trace of it remains either in my intelligence or in my emotions. It brought me no experience that I could not have deduced from the rules of human life, an instinctive knowledge of which I hold inside me simply by virtue of being human. It gave me neither pleasure that I could later remember with sadness, nor grief to be recalled with equal sadness. It feels like something I read somewhere, something that happened to someone else, in a novel of which I read only half, the other half being missing, not that I cared that it was missing, because what I had read up till then was enough and, although it made no sense, it was already clear that, however the plot turned out, the missing part would clarify nothing.

All that remains is a feeling of gratitude towards the person who loved me. But it's a stunned, abstract gratitude, more intellectual than emotional. I'm sorry that someone should have suffered because of me; I regret that, but nothing else.

It's unlikely that life will bring me another encounter with

---

*Chateaubriand's *René* was published in 1805.

natural emotions. I almost wish it would just to see how I would feel the second time around, now that I have thoroughly analysed that first experience. I might feel less; I might feel more. If Fate decrees it should happen, so be it. I feel curious about emotions. About facts, whatever they might be, I feel no curiosity whatsoever.

166 [284]   *5.10.1932*

The death of the Prince

Why shouldn't the truth turn out to be something utterly different from anything we imagine, with no gods or men or reasons why? Why shouldn't it be something that we can't even conceive of not conceiving, a mystery from another world entirely? Why shouldn't we – men, gods and world – be someone's dreams, someone's thoughts, marooned forever outside existence? And why shouldn't that someone who dreams or thinks us be someone who does not dream or think, but is himself subject to the void and to fiction? Why shouldn't everything be simultaneously something else and nothing, and what is not be the only thing that truly exists? Where am I that I can perceive all this as a possible truth? On what high bridge do I stand and look down on the lights of all the cities of this world and the next, on the clouds of undone truths that hover above them, all seeming to seek something to embrace?

I'm feverish but not sleepy and I see without knowing what I see. There are great plains all around and, in the distance, rivers and mountains ... But at the same time there is nothing and I stand at the very dawn of the gods, with a sense of utter horror at the idea of leaving or staying, of where and what I should be. And this room where I hear you seeing me is something that I know and seem to see; and all these things are together and separate and none of them is that other thing I'm trying to see.

Why did they give me a kingdom to rule over if there is no better kingdom than this hour in which I exist between what I was not and what I will not be?

167 [285]   *18.5.1930*

They were strange hours, successive unconnected moments, that I spent on the walk I took at night by the solitary shore of the sea. In my walking meditation, all the thoughts that have made men live, all the emotions that men have allowed to exist, passed through my mind like an obscure summary of history.

I suffered in myself, with myself, the aspirations of every era and all the unrest of all time strolled alongside me by the thunderous shore. What men wanted to do but did not and what they destroyed in so doing, what became of their souls and was never spoken of – all that formed part of the sensitive soul accompanying me along the night shore. And what lovers found wanting in each other, the truth about herself that the wife always hid from her husband, what the mother thought of the child she never had, things that found expression only in a smile or an opportunity, in a moment that was not the right one or in an absent emotion – all of this came with me on my walk and returned with me whilst the vast waves crashed out the accompaniment that lulled me to sleep.

We are who we are not and life is swift and sad. The sound of waves at night is a nocturnal sound, and how many have heard it in their own soul like the constant hope breaking in the dark in a dull thud of dense foam! What tears were shed by those who failed, what tears were spent by those who reached their goal! In my stroll by the sea, all this came to me like the secrets of the night, the whispered confidences of the abyss. How many we are, how many of those selves we deceive! What seas break in us, in the night of our being, along beaches that we only sense in the full flood of our emotion!

What we lost, what we should have loved, what we got and were, by mistake, contented with, what we loved and lost and, once lost, saw that we had not loved but loved it still just because we had lost it; what we believed we thought when we felt something; what we believed to be an emotion and was in fact only a memory; and, as I walked, the whole sea came rolling in, cool and clamorous, from the deepest reaches of the dark, to etch itself delicately along the sands . . .

Who knows what he thinks or what he desires? Who knows what meaning he really has for himself? How many things are suggested to us by music and how comforting to know those things can never be! How many things the night recalls and how we weep for them though they never were! Like a voice unleashed from the long peaceful line of the sea, the wave arches, crashes and dies, leaving behind the sound of its waters licking the invisible shore.

How I die if I allow myself to feel for all things! How much I feel if I let myself drift, incorporeal and human, my heart quiet as a beach, and, in the night in which we live, in my endless nocturnal walk along its shore, the sea of all things beats loud and mocking, then grows calm.

168 [290]   *2.5.1932*

I never sleep: I live and I dream or rather I dream both whilst I live and whilst I sleep, which is also life. There is no break in my consciousness: I sense what is around me even when I'm not quite asleep or when I don't sleep well. I start to dream as soon as I'm properly asleep. I'm a perpetual unfolding of connected and disconnected images, always disguised as something external, that stand between men and the light if I'm awake, or between ghosts and the visible dark if I'm asleep. I really do not know how to distinguish one from the other, nor would I venture to affirm that I'm not sleeping when I'm awake, or that I'm not on the point of waking when I'm asleep.

Life is like a ball of wool that someone has tangled up. There would be some sense in it were it unravelled and pulled out to its full length, or else properly rolled up. But, as it is, it's a problem no one has bothered to roll into a ball, a muddle with nowhere to go.

I feel now what I will later write down, for I'm already dreaming the phrases I will use, I sense through this night of half-sleeping the landscapes of vague dreams and the noise of the rain outside making them even vaguer. They are guesses made in the void, trembling on the brink of the abyss, and through them vainly trickles the plangent sound of the constant rain outside, the abundant detail of the landscape of the heard. Hope? None. A windborne watery grief falls from the invisible sky. I sleep on.

Doubtless the tragedy out of which life was created occurred along the avenues of the garden. There were two of them and they were beautiful and they wanted to be something else; love waited for them far off in the tedious future and the nostalgia for what would be arrived as the child of the love they had never felt. Thus, beneath the moonlight in the nearby woods, for the light trickled through the trees, they would walk hand in hand, feeling no desires or hopes, across the desert of abandoned avenues. They were just like children, precisely because they weren't. From avenue to avenue, silhouetted like paper cut-outs amongst the trees, they strolled that no-man's-land of a stage. And so, ever closer and more apart, they disappeared beyond the fountains, and the noise of the gentle rain — almost stopping now — is the noise of the fountains they moved towards. I am the love that was their love and that's why I can hear them in this sleepless night and why I'm capable of living unhappily.

169 [292]

It's Captain Nemo's final death. Soon I too will die.

My whole childhood, in that moment, was robbed of its ability to survive.

170 [293]   *10.3.1931*

Just as some people work because they're bored, I sometimes write because I have nothing to say. My writing is just like the reverie in which someone avoiding thought would naturally immerse himself with the difference that I am able to dream in prose. And I extract a great deal of sincere feeling and much legitimate emotion out of not feeling.

There are moments when the vacuity that comes with one's sense of being alive takes on the density of something concrete. Amongst the saints, who are the truly great men of action, for they act with all their emotions not just some of them, this sense of the nothingness of life leads to the infinite. They garland themselves in night and stars, anoint themselves with silence and solitude. Amongst the great men of inaction, to whose ranks I humbly belong, the same feeling leads to the infinitesimal; feelings are pulled taut, like elastic bands, the better to observe the pores of their false, flabby continuity.

At such moments, both types of men long for sleep, just like the most ordinary of men, that mere reflection of the generic existence of the human species, who neither acts nor doesn't act. Sleep is fusion with God, Nirvana, or however you choose to define it; sleep is the slow analysis of sensations, whether applied like an atomic science of the soul or experienced through sleep like a music of the will, a slow anagram of monotony.

I write and linger over the words as if over window displays I can't quite see, and all that remains to me are half-meanings, quasi-expressions like the colours of fabrics I can't identify, a harmonious display composed of unknown objects. I rock myself as I write, like the crazed mother of a dead child.

I found myself in this world one day, I don't know when, and until then, from birth I presume, I had lived without feeling. If I asked where I was, everyone deceived me, everyone contradicted everyone else. If I asked them to tell me what to do, everyone lied and told me something different. If I became lost and stopped along the road, everyone was shocked that I did not just continue on to wherever the road led (though no one knew where that was), or did not simply retrace my steps – I, who did not even know whence I came, having only woken up at the crossroads. I realized that I was on a stage and did not know the words that everyone else picked up instantly even though they did not know them either. I saw that though I was dressed as a page they had given me no queen to wait on and blamed me for that. I saw that I had in my hands a message to deliver and when I told them the paper was blank, they laughed at me. I still don't know if they laughed because all such pieces of paper are blank or because all messages are only hypothetical.

At last, as if before the hearth I did not have, I sat down on the milestone at the crossroads and, all by myself, began to make paper boats out of the lie they had given me. No one took me seriously, not even as a liar, and I had no lake on which to test my truth.

Lost, lazy words, random metaphors, linked to the shadows by a vague anxiety . . . Traces of happier times, lived out in some avenue somewhere . . . An extinguished lamp whose gold shines in the dark, a memory of the lost light . . . Words scattered not to the winds but on the ground, dropped from fingers that can no longer grip, like dry leaves fallen from a tree invisibly infinite . . . A nostalgic longing for the fountains that play in other people's gardens . . . A feeling of tenderness for what never happened . . .

To live! To live! with just the suspicion that perhaps only in Proserpina's* bed would I sleep well.

171 [294]

During one of those periods of sleepless somnolence in which we entertain ourselves intelligently enough without recourse to our intelligence, I re-read some of the pages which, when put together, will make up my book of random impressions. And there rises from them, like a familiar smell, an arid sense of monotony. I feel that in describing all my different moods, I always use the same words; I feel that I am more like myself than I would like to think; that, when the final accounts are drawn up, I have tasted neither the joy of winning nor the excitement of losing. I am my own absence of balance, of an involuntary equilibrium that torments and weakens me.

---

*The Roman goddess of the underworld (her Greek counterpart was Persephone).

Everything I wrote is so grey. It's as if my life, even my mental life, were a day of slow rain in which everything is eventlessness and half-shadow, empty privilege and forgotten reason. I mourn in torn silks. I don't recognize myself in this light and tedium.

My humble attempt simply to say who I am, to set down, like a feeling machine, the tiniest details of my sharp, subjective life, all this emptied out of me like an overturned bucket and soaked the earth just like water. I painted myself in false colours and ended up with an attic room for an empire. Today, re-reading with a different soul what I wrote on these distant pages, my heart, out of which I spawn the great events of my lived prose, seems to me like a pump in some provincial garden, installed by instinct and set going by duty. I was shipwrecked beneath a stormless sky in a sea shallow enough to stand up in.

In this confused series of intervals between things that do not even exist, I ask of what remains of my consciousness: what possible use was it to me to fill so many pages with words I believed to be mine, with emotions I felt to have been thought by me, with the flags and banners of armies that are, after all, just scraps of paper with which the beggar's daughter decorates the eaves? . . .

I address what remains of me and ask what is the point of these useless pages, destined for the rubbish heap and for ruin, lost even before they come into being amongst the torn pages of Fate.

I ask and I continue. I write down the question, I wrap it up in new sentences, unravel it to form new emotions. And tomorrow I will return to my foolish book to set down coldly further thoughts on my lack of conviction.

Let them continue, just as they are. When the last domino is played and the game is won or lost, all the pieces are turned over and the game ends in darkness.

172 (298)   *19.6.1934*

When we live constantly in the abstract – whether it be abstractness of thought or of feelings one has thought – it soon comes about that contrary to our own feelings and our own will the things in real life which, according to us, we should feel most deeply turn into phantasms.

However good or genuine a friend I might be to someone, hearing that he is ill or has died leaves me with such a vague, uncertain, dull impression that I'm ashamed to feel it. Only seeing the event itself, finding its landscape laid out before me would move me. Living so much on one's imagination actually erodes one's ability to imagine, especially one's ability to imagine the real. Living mentally on what is not and cannot be, we are, in the end, unable even to ponder what might really be.

I learned yesterday that an old friend of mine, whom I haven't seen for a long time but whom I always think of with what I take to be nostalgia, has gone into hospital for an operation. The only clear, positive feeling I had was what a bore it would be to have to go and visit him, with the ironic alternative that, if I couldn't be bothered to visit him, I would only regret not having done so.

That's all . . . After years of wrestling with shadows, I've become one myself, in what I think, feel, am. Then the nostalgia for the normal person I never was enters the very stuff of my being. But that and only that is all I feel. I don't really feel sorry for the friend who's going to be operated on. I don't really feel sorry for all the others who are going to be operated on, all those who suffer and grieve in this world. I just feel sorry that I do not know how to be someone who feels sorry.

And, inevitably, the next moment, driven by some unknown impulse, I'm already thinking about something else. And then, as if in a delirium, the murmur of trees, the sound of water flowing into pools, a non-existent garden all intermingle with what I didn't manage to feel and what I could not be . . . I try to feel but I no longer know how. I've become a shadow of myself to whom I've surrendered my whole being. Unlike the character Peter Schlemihl*

---

*The eponymous hero of the novel by Adelbert von Chamisso (1781–1838).

in the German story, it was not my shadow I sold to the Devil but my very substance. I suffer because I do not suffer, because I do not know how to suffer. Am I alive or am I only pretending? Am I asleep or awake? A light breeze, cool in the heat of the day, makes me forget everything. My eyelids feel pleasantly heavy ... I imagine that this same golden sun is falling on the fields where I am not and where I do not wish to be ... A great silence emerges from the bustle of the city ... How gentle it is! But how much gentler, perhaps, if I could really feel it!

173 [299]

One of the great tragedies of my life – though it is one of those tragedies that take place amidst shadows and subterfuge – is that of being unable to feel anything naturally. I am as capable as anyone of love and hate, of fear and enthusiasm, but neither my love nor my hate, neither my fear nor my enthusiasm are exactly what they seem. They either lack some element or have had something added to them. What's certain is that they are something else, and what I feel is out of step with life.

In those spirits we so aptly call 'calculating', feelings are defined and limited by calculation and by selfish scruples, and they therefore seem different. You can see the same dislocation of natural instincts in those we call 'scrupulous'. In me there is the same muddying of clear feelings yet I'm neither calculating nor scrupulous. I have no excuse for being bad at feeling. This denaturing of instincts is utterly instinctive in me. Without even wanting to, I want mistakenly.

174 [300]   *16.7.1930*

You can feel life like a sickness in the pit of the stomach, the existence of your own soul like a muscular cramp. Desolation of the spirit, when sharply felt, creates distant tides in the body and hurts by proxy.

I am conscious that in myself today the pain of consciousness is, as the poet says:

> languidez, mareo
> y angustioso afán.*

175 [302]

Sometimes I think with ambivalent pleasure of the possibility of creating in the future a geography of our consciousness of ourselves. As I see it, the future historian of feelings will perhaps be able to reduce to an exact science his own attitude towards his consciousness of his own soul. Meanwhile we are very much beginners in this difficult art, for it is still only an art, a chemistry of the feelings that has not yet got much beyond alchemy. This scientist of tomorrow's world will have a special sensitivity to his own inner life. He will create out of himself the precision instrument necessary for its analysis. I see no great difficulty in making an instrument for self-analysis out of the steels and bronzes of thought alone. I mean by that, real steels and bronzes but ones that are forged in the spirit. Perhaps that's how it really should be made. It may be necessary to come up with the idea of a precision instrument and physically see that idea before being able to proceed with any rigorous analysis of oneself. And naturally it will also be necessary to reduce the spirit to some sort of physical matter surrounded by a space in which it can exist. All this depends on a great refinement of our inner feelings which, taken to its limit, will no doubt reveal or create in us a genuine space like the space in which physical things exist but which, in fact, does not itself exist as a thing.

*'langour, confusion/and anguished desire' (in Spanish in the original)

I don't quite know if this inner space will be just another dimension of the other space. Perhaps future scientific research will discover that everything, whether physical or spiritual, is just a dimension of the same space. In one dimension we live as body, in the other as soul. And perhaps there are other dimensions in which we experience other equally real aspects of ourselves. Sometimes I enjoy letting myself be carried away by this futile meditation on just how far this research might lead.

Perhaps they'll discover that what we call God, and which is clearly on another level from that of logic and spatial and temporal reality, is just one of our ways of being, one of the ways we experience ourselves in another dimension of existence. This doesn't strike me as impossible. Dreams may also be another dimension in which we live or even an overlapping of two dimensions. Just as a body exists in height, width and length who knows but that our dreams may exist simultaneously in space, in the ideal world and in the ego: their physical representation in space; their non-physical representation in the ideal world; their role as an intimate aspect of ourselves in the ego. Even each person's 'I' may perhaps be another divine dimension. All this is very complex but doubtless in time it will be resolved. Today's dreamers are perhaps the great precursors of the ultimate science of the future, not that I believe in any such ultimate science. But that has nothing to do with the case in hand.

Sometimes I invent a metaphysics like this with all the respectful scrupulousness of attention of someone engaged in real scientific work. As I've said before it reaches the point where I may really be doing just that. The important thing is not to pride myself too much on all this for pride is prejudicial to the precise impartiality of scientific exactitude.

176 [303]

The simplest things, the truly simple things that nothing can make anything other than simple, are made complex just by my experiencing them. I feel intimidated sometimes by having to say good morning to someone. My voice dries up, as if to pronounce the words out loud were an act of extraordinary audacity. It's a kind of embarrassment at my own existence – there are no other words for it.

Constant analysis of our feelings creates a new way of feeling that seems artificial to anyone who analyses only with his intellect rather than with feeling itself.

All my life I have been metaphysically frivolous and playfully earnest. I never did anything seriously, however much I may have wanted to. A mischievous Destiny has made of me its playground.

How I'd like to have emotions made of chintz or silk or brocade! How I'd like to have emotions as easily describable as that, to have emotions that could at least be described!

There rises in my soul a feeling of regret that is God's regret for everything, a dumb, tearful fury at the condemnation of dreams in the very flesh of those who dreamed them ... And I hate without hatred the poets who wrote verses, all the idealists who realized their ideals, all those who got what they wanted.

I wander aimlessly through the quiet streets, I walk until my body is as tired as my soul, until I feel that familiar pain that revels in being felt, a maternal compassion for oneself, set to music, indefinable.

Oh to sleep, finally to sleep! To find some peace! To be an abstract consciousness of one's own quiet breathing, with no world, no stars, no soul – a dead sea of emotion reflecting only an absence of stars!

177 [309]

As a slave loves a beloved tyrant I love the vague tipsiness brought on by a slight fever, the flaccid, cold, penetrating discomfort in the very marrow of one's aching bones, one's burning eyes and pounding temples. It provides me with that tremulous, exhausted passivity in which I glimpse visions, turn the corner of certain ideas only to be disconcerted by colliding feelings.

Thinking, feeling, wanting, become one confused emotion. Beliefs, feelings, things imagined and real become jumbled, like the contents of several drawers upturned on the floor.

178 [310]

That's how I am, frivolous and sensitive, capable of impulses that can be violent and all-consuming, good and bad, noble and base, but never contain any lasting feeling, any enduring emotion that really penetrates the substance of my soul. Everything in me is a tendency to be about to become something else; an impatience of the soul with itself, as if with an importunate child; a disquiet that is always growing, always the same. Everything interests me and nothing holds my attention. I listen to everything while constantly dreaming; I notice the tiniest facial tics of the person I'm talking to, pick up minimal changes in the intonation of what they say; but when I hear, I do not listen, for I'm thinking about something else, and I come away from any conversation with little idea of what was said, either by me or by the other person. So I often find myself repeating to someone something I've already told him or asking again the very thing he's just told me; yet I can describe in four photographic words the set of his facial muscles as he said the words I no longer remember, or the attentive way he looked at me as I told him the story I now have no recollection of having told. I'm two people who mutually keep their distance — Siamese twins living separate lives.

179 [312]   3.9.1931

The most painful feelings, the most piercing emotions are also the most absurd ones – the longing for impossible things precisely because they are impossible, the nostalgia for what never was, the desire for what might have been, one's bitterness that one is not someone else, or one's dissatisfaction with the very existence of the world. All these half-tones of the soul's consciousness create a raw landscape within us, a sun eternally setting on what we are. Our sense of ourselves then becomes a deserted field at nightfall, with sad reeds flanking a boatless river, bright in the darkness growing between the distant shores.

I don't know if these feelings are some slow madness brought on by hopelessness, if they are recollections of some other world in which we've lived – confused, jumbled memories, like things glimpsed in dreams, absurd as we see them now but not in their origin if we but knew what that was. I don't know if we once were other beings, whose greater completeness we sense only incompletely today, being mere shadows of what they were, beings that have lost their solidity in our feeble two-dimensional imaginings of them amongst the shadows we inhabit.

I know that these thoughts born of emotion burn with rage in the soul. The impossibility of imagining something they might correspond to, the impossibility of finding some substitute for what in visions they embrace, all this weighs on one like a judgement given one knows not where, by whom, or why.

But what does remain of all this is a distaste for life and all its manifestations, a prescient weariness with all its desires and ways, an anonymous displeasure with all feeling. In these moments of subtle pain, it becomes impossible for us, even in dreams, to be a lover or a hero, even to be happy. It is all empty, even the idea of its emptiness. It is all spoken in another language, incomprehensible to us, mere sounds of syllables that find no echo in our understanding. Life, the soul and the world are all hollow. All the gods die a death greater than death itself. Everything is emptier than the void. It is all a chaos of nothing.

If I think this and look around me to see if reality will quench my thirst, I see inexpressive houses, inexpressive faces, inexpressive gestures. Stones, bodies, ideas – everything is dead. All movement is a kind of standing still, everything lies in the grip of stasis. Nothing means anything to me. Everything looks unfamiliar, not because I find it strange but because I don't know what it is. The world is lost. And in the depths of my soul – the only reality of the moment – there is an intense, invisible pain, a sadness like the sound of someone weeping in a dark room.

180 [313]

A breath of music or of a dream, anything that might make me almost feel, anything that might make me stop thinking.

181 [314]

The burden of feeling! The burden of having to feel!

182 [316]   *16.7.1932*

Convalescence, especially if the preceding illness affected one's nerves, has a sort of gay sadness about it. There is a touch of autumn in all one's emotions and thoughts, or rather one feels like one of those early spring days when the air and sky seem more like autumn than spring, except, of course, that no leaves fall.

We experience a pleasant tiredness but our sense of well-being also hurts a little. Whilst still in life, we feel somewhat apart from it, as if standing on the verandah of the house of life. We are contemplative but think no thoughts, we feel but feel no definite emotion. The will grows quiet, because we have no need of it.

It's then that certain memories, certain hopes, certain vague desires slowly ascend the ramp of our consciousness, like distant travellers seen from a mountain peak. Memories of futile things, hopes for things that never came to pass and about which we no longer care, desires that were neither violent by nature nor in intention and that could never really have wanted to exist.

When the day is right for such feelings, when, like today, even though it is still summer, the blue sky is striped with clouds and the light wind feels cold simply because it isn't warm, then that state of mind grows more noticeable in the way we think, feel or experience these impressions. It isn't that the memories, hopes or desires we had are any clearer, they are simply more present and, however absurd it may seem, the uncertain sum of their parts weighs a little on one's heart.

There is something distant about me just now. I stand on the verandah of life but it's not quite of this life. I'm both in the midst of life and observing it from where I stand. It lies before me, descending in ledges and slopes, like a varied landscape, down to the smoke rising from the white houses of the villages in the valley. If I shut my eyes I continue to see it just because I can't see it. If I open my eyes I see no more, because I never really saw anything. Every part of me is a vague nostalgia neither for the past nor for the future: the whole of me is a nostalgia for the anonymous, prolix, unfathomable present.

183 [319]

Millimetres (the observation of infinitesimal things)

I believe that the present is very ancient simply because everything, when it did exist, existed in the present, and accordingly I feel for all things, because they belong to the present, both the fondness of the antiquarian and the fury of the thwarted collector to whom the former dismisses my errors about things with well-founded, plausible, possibly even true, scientific explanations.

To my astonished eyes the various, successive poses of a butterfly as it flies through the air seem like separate moments made visible in space. My recollections are so vivid that [. . .]

But I experience intensely only the tiny feelings of the tiniest things. This must come from my love of the frivolous or perhaps my passion for detail. But I think – I don't know because these are things I never analyse – that it's probably because what is tiny has absolutely no social or practical value and is, for that very reason, absolutely free of any sordid associations with reality. To me all tiny things savour of unreality. The useless is beautiful because it is less real than the useful, which enjoys a continuing and lasting existence; while the marvellously useless, the gloriously infinitesimal remains where it is, never goes beyond being what it is, and lives free and independent. The useless and the futile create intervals of humble static in our real lives. The mere insignificant existence of a pin stuck in a piece of ribbon provokes in my soul all manner of dreams and wondrous delights! I pity those who do not recognize the importance of such things!

One of the most complex and widespread of those feelings that hurt one almost to the point of being pleasurable, is the disquiet aroused by the mystery of life. That mystery is never so easy to spot as in the contemplation of tiny things which, because they do not move, are perfectly translucent to it, they stop to let it pass. It is more difficult to experience any sense of mystery when contemplating a battle (while pondering on the absurdity of there being people and societies and battles between them), or any sense of what it is in our thoughts that unfurls the flag of victory, than in the contemplation of one small stone on the road, which, because it does not evoke any idea in us beyond the fact of its existence, cannot, if we pursue our thought, fail to evoke in us the thought that immediately follows on from there, that is: the mystery of its existence.

Blessed be moments, millimetres and, even humbler than these, the shadows of all tiny things! Moments [. . .] Millimetres – their existence side by side, so close together on the ruler provokes in me such an impression of wonder and daring. Sometimes such things cause me both pain and joy. I feel a kind of rough pride in this.

I am an endlessly sensitive photographic plate. In me every tiny detail is recorded and magnified in order to form part of a whole. I concern myself only with myself. For me the external world is pure sensation. I never forget what I feel.

184 [321]

Lucidly, slowly, piece by piece, I re-read everything I have written. And I find it all worthless and feel it would have been better never to have written it. The very fact of completing or achieving anything, be it an empire or a sentence, contains what is worst about all real things: our knowledge that they will perish. But, as I slowly re-read these pages, that isn't what I feel or what hurts me about what I've created. What hurts me is that it wasn't worth doing, and that all I gained from the time I wasted is the now shattered illusion that it *was* worth doing.

In seeking anything, we do so out of ambition, but we either fail to achieve that ambition and are the poorer, or we think we have achieved it and are merely rich madmen.

What hurts me is that even the best of it is bad and that someone else (if they existed and of whose existence I dream) would have done it better. Everything we do, in art and life, is the imperfect copy of what we intended. It betrays both external and internal ideals of perfection; it fails not only our concept of what it should have been, but also of what it could have been. We are hollow inside and out, pariahs of anticipation and promise.

Where did I find the strength in my solitary soul to write page after lonely page, to live out syllable by syllable the false magic not of what I was writing but of what I imagined I was writing? What spell of ironic witchery led me to believe myself the poet of my own prose, in the winged moment in which it was born in me, faster than my pen could write, like a sly revenge on life's insults! And re-reading it today I watch my precious dolls ripped apart, see the straw burst out of them and see them scattered without ever having been . . .

185 [326]

Fragments of an autobiography

I devoted myself first to metaphysical speculations, then to scientific ideas. Finally I was drawn to sociological theories. But at no point in the various stages of my search for the truth did I find security or relief. I read little in any of these fields, but in what I did read of all these theories it wearied me to see how contradictory they were, though all were based on a convincing line of argument, all equally probable and in accord with certain chosen facts that seemed to stand for *all* the facts. If I raised my weary eyes from the books, or if my restless attention wandered off to the outside world, I saw one thing that negated the usefulness of all reading and thinking, that plucked off one by one all the petals from the idea of that effort: the infinite complexity of things, the immense sum [. . .], the infinite unattainability of the few facts one needs in order to create a science.

186 [327]

Little by little I discover in myself the pain of finding nothing. I found neither reason nor logic only a scepticism that makes not the slightest attempt to create a logic with which to defend itself. I never thought of trying to rid myself of this illness: why should I? What does being healthy mean? How could I be so sure my state of mind was an unhealthy one? Who can say that just because it is an illness, that illness is not more desirable, more logical, more [. . .] than health? If health were preferable, why did I fall ill in the first place unless it was natural to do so, and if it was natural, why go against Nature which for some reason, assuming Nature has reasons, apparently wanted me to be ill?

All the arguments I come up with are merely justifications for inertia. Increasingly, with each passing day, the dark realization has filtered through to me that I have the inert soul of a born abdicator . . . I have stopped reading; I have abandoned the chance caprices of this or that aesthetic way of life. From the little I read I learned to extract only those elements I could use in dreams. From the little I saw, I took care to take only what could, after mature reflection, be put to use in my inner life. I struggled hard in order that all my thoughts, every daily chapter of my experience supplied me only with sensation. I gave my life the tenor of an aestheticism. And I tailored that aestheticism to suit my personality. I made it mine alone.

Then, in the course of my pursuit of an inner hedonism, I applied myself to avoiding social niceties. I gradually armoured myself against the fear of appearing ridiculous. I taught myself to be insensitive both to the appeals of the instincts and to social blandishments [. . .]

I reduced my contact with others to a minimum. I did my best to lose all fondness for life [. . .] Like some very weary person getting undressed before bed, I slowly disrobed myself of any desire for glory.

187 [331]

I wonder how many people have contemplated as it deserves to be contemplated a deserted street with people in it. Even putting it that way makes it seem as if I were trying to say something else, which in fact I am. A deserted street is not one along which no one walks, but a street along which people walk as if it were deserted. It isn't a difficult concept to grasp once one has seen it, after all, to someone whose experience of the equine is restricted to mules, a zebra must seem inconceivable.

Feelings adjust themselves within us to certain degrees and types of comprehension of them. There are ways of understanding that dictate the ways they are to be understood.

Sometimes there arises in me, as if it rose up from the alien ground through my body to my head, a tedium, a grief, an anxiety about life that only seems bearable to me because I do in fact bear it. It's a suffocation of life in my own self, a desire in every pore of my being to be another person, a brief warning that the end is near.

188 [333]

We are death. This thing we think of as life is only the sleep of real life, the death of what we truly are. The dead are born, they do not die. These worlds have become reversed for us. When we think we are alive, we are dead; we live even while we lie dying.

The relation that exists between sleep and life is the same as exists between what we call life and what we call death. We are asleep and this life is a dream, not in any metaphorical or poetic sense, but really a dream.

Everything we consider important in our active lives participates in death, is all death. What are ideals but a confession that life is not enough? What is art but the negation of life? A statue is a dead body, sculpted in order to fix death in incorruptible matter. Even pleasure, which seems to immerse us in life, is in fact an immersion in ourselves, a destruction of the relationship between us and life, a troubled shadow of death.

Living is in itself dying because every new day we enjoy is another day of our lives lost.

We people dreams, we are shadows wandering through impossible forests in which the trees are houses, habits, ideas, ideals and philosophies.

Never to find God, never to know even if God exists! To pass from world to world, from incarnation to incarnation, nursed always by the same illusion, cossetted always by the same errors.

Never to find truth or peace! Never to know union with God! Never to be completely at peace, but instead to be always troubled by the suggestion of what peace is and by our desire for it!

189 [345]

To live a dispassionate, cultured life beneath the dewfall of ideas, reading, dreaming and thinking about writing, a life slow enough to be always just on the edge of tedium, but considered enough not to slip into it. To live a life removed from emotions and thoughts, enjoying only the thought of emotions and the emotion of thoughts. To stagnate, golden, in the sun like a dark lake surrounded by flowers. To entertain in the shadows that noble individuality of mind that consists in not expecting anything from life. To be in the turning of the worlds like the dust of flowers that an unknown wind lifts through the evening air, and that the torpor of nightfall lets fall randomly, to lie unnoticed amongst larger things. To be all this with an assured knowledge, neither happy nor sad, grateful to the sun for its brilliance and to the stars for their distance. To be nothing more, to have nothing more, to want nothing more . . . The music of the hungry man, the song of the blind man, the relic of the unknown traveller, the footsteps in the desert of the empty camel with nowhere to go . . .

190 [348]

My conscious mind is filled by a drowsiness that I can't explain but which frequently attacks me, if something so shadowy can be said to attack. I walk along a street as if I were in fact still seated in an armchair and my attentive mind, though alert to everything, is still filled by the inertia of a body in repose. I would be incapable of avoiding an oncoming passer-by. I would be unable to respond in words, or even formulate an answer in my head, to a question put to me by some casual passer-by taking advantage of my chance presence in the street. I would be incapable of harbouring a desire, a hope, or anything that could be construed as a movement not necessarily of the will of my whole being but, if I can put it this way, of the partial and individual will of each of the elements I can be broken down into. I would be incapable of thinking, feeling, wanting. And yet I walk, I move on, I drift. Nothing in my movements (I know this because no one else seems to notice) betrays my stagnant state. And this lack of soul which would be comfortable, even correct, in someone lying down or recumbent, is singularly uncomfortable, even painful, in a man walking down a street.

It's like being drunk on inertia, a drinking spree as utterly joyless in itself as in its cause. It's an illness from which there is no hope of recovery. It is a cheerful death.

191 [349]   *5.4.1933*

To consider our greatest anguish an incident of no importance, not just in terms of the life of the universe, but in terms of our own souls, is the beginning of knowledge. To reflect on this whilst in the midst of that anguish is the whole of knowledge. When we suffer, human pain seems infinite. But not even human pain is infinite, because nothing human is infinite, nor is our pain ever anything more than a pain that we have.

How often, weighed down by a tedium that verges on madness, or an anguish that seems to go beyond all anguish, do I stop and hesitate before I rebel, do I hesitate and stop before making myself a god. The pain of not understanding the mystery of life, the pain of being unloved, the pain of others' injustice to us, the pain of life crushing us, suffocating and imprisoning us, the pain of toothache, of pinching shoes – who can say which pain he finds the worse, let alone which is worse for others, or worse for others in general?

To some people who speak and listen to me I must seem an insensitive person. However, I am, I think, more sensitive than the vast majority of men. I am, moreover, a sensitive man who knows himself and therefore knows what sensitivity is.

It isn't true that life is painful, or that it's painful to think about life. What is true is that our pain is only as serious and important as we pretend it to be. If we lived naturally, it would pass as quickly as it came, it would fade as quickly as it bloomed. Everything is nothing, and our pain is no exception.

I write this beneath the weight of an oppressive tedium that seems about to burst the bounds of my being or rather seems to need some larger space than my soul to exist in. Everyone and everything oppresses me, chokes and maddens me; I am troubled by a crushing physical sense of other people's lack of comprehension.

But I look up at the blue sky, bare my face to the unconsciously cool breeze, then lower my eyelids having seen the sky, and forget my own cheek once I have felt the breeze. I don't feel better, I feel different. Seeing myself frees me from myself. I almost smile, not because I understand myself, but because, having become other, I'm no longer able to understand myself. High up in the sky, like a visible void, hangs one tiny cloud, a pale forgotten fragment of the whole universe.

192 [354]

The label that best defines my spirit today is that of creator of indifferences. More than anything else I would like my role in the world to be to educate others to feel more and more for themselves and less and less according to the dynamic law of the collectivity...

To educate others in that spiritual asceticism, which would preclude the contagion of vulgarity, seems to me the highest destiny of the teacher of the inner life I would like to be. That all those who read me should learn – little by little, as the subject demands – to feel utter indifference before the critical gaze and opinions of others, such a destiny would be reward enough for the scholastic stagnation of my life.

In me, the inability to act was always an affliction that had its origins in metaphysics. According to my way of experiencing things, any gesture always implied a perturbation, a fragmentation, of the external world; I always feared that any movement on my part would dislodge the stars or alter the skies. That's why the metaphysical importance of even the smallest gesture rapidly took on an extraordinary importance for me. I acquired with regard to action a transcendental honesty which, ever since I became aware of it, has inhibited me from having any strong links with the tangible world.

193 [357]

All effort is a crime because every gesture is but an inert dream.

194 [358]

An aesthetics of indifference

What the dreamer should try to feel for any object is the utter indifference that it, as object, provokes in him.

To know, immediately and instinctively, how to abstract from every object and event only what is suitable dream material and to leave for dead in the External World any reality it contains, that is what the wise man should aim to achieve in himself.

Never to feel one's feelings wholeheartedly and then to elevate that wan victory to the point of being able to regard one's own ambitions, longings and desires with indifference; to pass by one's joys and griefs as one would a person in whom one feels no interest . . .

The greatest self-discipline one can achieve is indifference towards oneself, believing one's self, body and soul, to be merely the house and garden in which Destiny has ordained one should spend one's life.

One should treat one's own dreams and intimate desires with the haughty indifference of a great lord [. . .] showing the highest degree of delicacy in not even noticing them. One should have a sense of modesty before oneself and understand that in the presence of ourselves we are never alone, we are witness to ourselves, and it is therefore important to act always as we would before a stranger, adopting a studied and serene exterior, indifferent because aristocratic and cold because indifferent.

In order not to demean ourselves in our own eyes, it is enough that we should become accustomed to harbouring no ambitions, passions, desires, hopes, impulses or feelings of restlessness. To achieve this, we must remember that we are always in the presence

of ourselves, that we are never alone, can never be at ease. We must .
master all passions or ambitions because passions and ambitions
render us defenceless; equally we must nurture neither desires nor
hopes because they are merely low, inelegant gestures; nor must we
be prone to sudden impulses or to restlessness because, in the eyes
of others, precipitate behaviour is rude and impatience is always
vulgar.

An aristocrat is someone who is always conscious of the fact that
he is never alone; that's why custom and protocol come naturally to
the aristocracy. We must internalize the aristocrat. We must drag
him away from his drawing rooms and gardens to enter instead our
soul and our consciousness of our existence. Let us always treat
ourselves with due custom and protocol and with gestures studied
and used for the benefit of others.

Each one of us is a whole society […] it is as well then at least to
bring a certain elegance and distinction to life in our part of town,
to make sure that the celebrations held by our senses show good
taste and reserve, and […] sober courtesy in the banquets of our
thoughts. Let other souls build their poor, shabby dwellings
around us but let us clearly mark where ours begin and end, and
make sure that from the façades of our houses to the inner
sanctums of our timidities, everything is noble and serene,
sculpted out of sobriety and discretion. We must find for every
feeling the most serene mode of expression; reduce love to a mere
shadow of a dream of love, a pale and tremulous interval between
the crests of two small waves gleaming in the moonlight; make of
desire something vain and inoffensive, the delicate, private smile of
a soul to itself; make of it something that never even considers
announcing its presence, let alone realizing itself. We must lull
hatred to sleep like a captive snake and order fear to preserve the
agony only in its eyes and in the eyes of our soul, the only fitting
expression for an aesthete.

195 [360]   *15.5.1930*

There was a time when the very things that today make me smile used to irritate me intensely. One of them, of which I am reminded almost every day, is the way normal, active men persist in laughing at poets and artists. Although newspaper philosophers would have us believe otherwise, ordinary men do not always laugh at us with an air of superiority. They often do so affectionately. But it's always rather like the pat on the head an adult would give a child, someone unconvinced of life's certainty and exactitude.

This used to irritate me because I thought ingenuously, for I was ingenuous then, that the smile they bestowed on other people's preoccupation with dreaming and with describing their dreams was the effluvium of a deep sense of superiority. In fact it's just a blunt recognition of difference. And whilst I used to consider that smile an insult because it implied some kind of superiority, now I consider it to be the admission of an unconscious doubt; just as grown men often recognize in children a sharper wit than their own, so they recognize in us, in those who dream and speak of our dreams, a difference that they distrust because it is strange. I'd like to think that often the more intelligent among them glimpse our superiority and, thus, smile in order to conceal that fact.

But our superiority is not what many dreamers have considered it to be. The dreamer is not superior to the active man because dreaming is essentially superior to reality. The superiority of the dreamer lies in the fact that dreaming is much more practical than living, and in the fact that the dreamer derives a greater and more multifarious pleasure from life than the man of action. To put it more succinctly, it's the dreamer who is the true man of action.

Since life is essentially a mental state and everything that we do or think is only as valuable as we think it is, it depends on us for any value it may have. The dreamer is a distributor of banknotes and these notes are passed around the city of his spirit just as they would be in reality. What does it matter to me if the paper money of my soul can never be converted into gold, since there is no gold in the factitious alchemy of life? After us the deluge, but only after all of us. The truly superior (and the happiest) men are those who, perceiving that everything is a fiction, make up their own novel before someone else does it for them and, like Machiavelli, don courtly robes in order to write in secret.

196 [361]

The pleasure of praising ourselves . . .

197 [363]

Apocalyptic feeling

Believing that each step of my life would mean contact with the horror of the New and that each new person I met was a new and living fragment of the unknown to be placed before me on the table for my daily horrified contemplation, I decided to abstain from everything, to go nowhere, to reduce action to the minimum, to avoid as far as possible meeting either men or events, to perfect abstinence and cultivate renunciation. That's how much living frightens and torments me.

Coming to a decision, ending something, finally leaving the doubt and the darkness behind, are things that seem catastrophic to me, like universal cataclysms.

That is how I experience life, as apocalypse and cataclysm. Each day brings an increasing inability in myself to make the smallest gesture, even to imagine myself confronting clear, real situations.

The presence of others – always such an unexpected event for the soul – grows daily more painful and distressing. Talking to others makes me shudder. If they show any interest in me, I flee. If they look at me, I tremble. If [. . .]

I am constantly on the defensive. Life and other people bruise me. I can't look reality in the eye. The sun itself leaves me feeling discouraged and desolate. Only at night, by myself, alone, forgotten and lost – with no links with reality, no need to participate in anything useful – only then can I find and comfort myself.

Life chills me. My existence is all damp caves and dark catacombs. I am the great defeat of the final army that sustained the final empire. I taste of the fall of some ancient master civilization. I am alone and abandoned, I who was accustomed to give orders to others. I am without a friend, without a guide, I whose path was always smoothed by others.

Something in me pleads eternally for compassion and weeps over itself as over a dead god stripped of all his altars, when the pale coming of the barbarians dawned at the frontiers and life came to call the empire to account, to ask what it had done with happiness.

I'm always afraid people will talk about me. I've failed in everything. I've never even dared think of making something of myself; I never even dreamed of thinking of desiring something because in my own dreams, even in my visionary state of mere dreamer, I recognized that I was unsuited for life.

Not one feeling could make me raise my head from the pillow in which I bury it because I can't cope with my body nor with the idea that I'm alive, nor even with the absolute idea of life itself.

I don't speak the language of reality. I totter amongst the things of life like a long bedridden patient getting up for the first time. I only feel part of normal life when I'm in bed. I feel pleased when I succumb to a fever because it seems appropriate and natural [. . .] to my recumbent state. Like a flame in the wind I stutter and grow faint. Only in the dead air of closed rooms do I breathe the normality of my life.

Nothing remains of the shells I found by the shores of seas, not even nostalgia. I likened my state to having made of my soul a monastery and myself to autumn over a dry, deserted field where the only spark of life is a bright reflection like a light dying in the endovelate* dark of pools, with no more force or colour than the

---

*'endevolada' is a neologism created by Pessoa to suggest dark, veiled depths.

violet splendour, the spent exile of the sunset on the mountains.

At bottom there is no greater pleasure than that of analysing one's own pain, no more sensual pleasure than the liquid, sickly meanderings of feelings as they crumble and rot: light steps in the uncertain shadows, so gentle on the ear we do not even turn to find out whose they are; vague, distant songs, whose words we do not try to catch but are lulled all the more by not knowing what they say or whence they come; the tenuous secrets of pale waters, filling the night with fragile distances; and, inaudible from here, somnolent in the warm torpor of the afternoon where summer slides into autumn, the rattle of far-off carts, returning from where and carrying what joys inside them? The flowers in the garden died and, withered, became different flowers, older, nobler, more in keeping in their dead yellows with mystery, silence and abandon. The watersnakes that surface in the pools have their reasons for their dreams. Is that the distant croaking of frogs? Ah the dead fields of my self! The rustic peace known only in dreams! My futile life like that of a vagabond who does not work but sleeps by the roadside with the smell of the fields seeping like mist into his soul, lulled by a cool, translucent sound, deep and rich with the understanding that nothing connects with nothing, a nocturnal, unknown, weary nomad beneath the cold compassion of the stars.

I follow the path of my dreams, making of the images steps up to other images; opening out like a fan the chance metaphors to be found in the great paintings of my inner visions; I divest myself of life and lay it to one side like a suit that's grown too tight. I hide amongst trees far from the roads. I lose myself. For light fleeting moments I manage to forget the taste of life, to leave [. . .] life and noise behind and die, feelings first, consciously, absurdly, like an empire of anguished ruins, a grand entrance amidst flags and victorious drums into a vast final city where I will weep for nothing, want nothing and not even ask to be myself.

The blue surfaces of the pools that I created in dreams wound me. The paleness of the moon I envision shining on forest landscapes is mine alone. The autumn of stagnant skies that I recall without ever having seen is nothing but my own weariness. My whole dead life weighs on me, all my failed dreams, everything I had that was never mine, the blue of my inner skies, the visible murmur of the rivers of my soul, the vast, troubled peace of wheatfields on plains that I see and yet do not see.

A cup of coffee, a cigarette, the penetrating aroma of its smoke, myself sitting in a shadowy room with eyes half-closed ... I want no more from life than my dreams and this ... It doesn't seem much? I don't know. What do I know about what is a little and what is a lot?

Summer evening out there, how I would love to be someone else ... I open the window. Everything outside is so gentle, yet it pierces me with an indefinable pain, a vague feeling of discontent.

And one last thing pierces me, tears at me, leaves my soul in tatters. It's that I, at this moment, at this window, looking out at these sad, gentle things, ought to present an aesthetic figure, beautiful, like someone in a picture – and I don't, I don't even do that ...

May this hour pass and be forgotten ... May the night approach, grow, descend on all things and never end. May this soul be my eternal tomb ...

198 [367]

The sweetness of having neither family nor companions, the gentle pleasure akin to that of exile, in which we feel the pride of distance shade into a hesitant voluptuousness, into the vague disquiet that comes with being far from home – yes, in my own indifferent way I enjoy all that. For one of the characteristics of my mental outlook is the belief that one should not over-cultivate one's attention, even a dream should be treated with condescension, with an aristocratic awareness that it owes its existence to oneself. Giving too much importance to a dream would, after all, be giving too much importance to something that has merely broken away from us and, as best it could, made a place for itself in reality, thereby losing the absolute right to be treated by us with any delicacy.

Imaginary figures have more substance and truth than real ones.

My imaginary world has always been the only true world for me. I never knew loves so real, so full of passion and life as I did with the characters I myself created. What a shame! I miss them because, like all loves, they too end . . .

199 [369]   *5.6.1934*

I grow still at last. Any remaining debris or detritus of disquiet vanishes from my soul as if it had never been. I sit alone and calm. The moment just past was like a moment of religious conversion, except that nothing draws me heavenwards, just as nothing before drew me down. I feel free, as if I had ceased to exist but yet retained my consciousness.

Yes, I grow still. With the sweetness of the utterly useless, a great calm penetrates the depths of my being. Pages read, duties performed, the actions and chance events of my life – all this has become for me a vague penumbra, a barely visible halo surrounding some strange and tranquil thing unknown to me. The effort I sometimes put into forgetting my soul; the thought I occasionally put into abandoning all action – both come back to me now in the form of an unsentimental tenderness, a bland, empty compassion.

It's not this slow, sweet day, cloudy and soft. It's not the barely existent breeze, scarcely more insistent than the air I feel on my skin. It isn't the anonymous colour of the sky, touched feebly here and there with blue. It isn't that. Because I feel nothing. I simply see without intention, without remedy, the attentive spectator of a non-existent spectacle. I cannot feel my soul and yet I'm quite calm. Everything in the external world, even those things that move, has grown clear and motionless, and it seems to me as the world must have seemed to Christ when he looked down at the city spread before him and was tempted by Satan. These things are nothing and I understand why Christ wasn't tempted. They are as nothing and I can't understand how an old hand like Satan could possibly have imagined they could prove a temptation.

Flow lightly, life that does not even feel itself, a silent, supple stream beneath forgotten trees! Flow softly, soul that does not know itself, a murmur hidden from view by great fallen branches! Flow vainly, aimlessly, consciousness conscious of nothing, a vague, distant glimmer through leafy clearings, with no known source or destination. Flow on, flow on and leave me to forget!

Faint breeze of all that never dared to live, dumb breath of all that did not want to feel, vain murmur of all that did not want to think, go slowly, lazily down into the whirlpools that inevitably await you and down the slippery slopes placed there for you, go into the shadows or into the light, brother of the world, go forward into glory or into the abyss, son of Chaos and of Night, always remembering in some corner of your being that the Gods came later, and that the Gods too pass away.

200 [373]

(a child's hand playing with cotton-reels, etc.) *

All I've ever done is dream. That, and only that, has been the meaning of my existence. The only thing I've ever really cared about is my inner life. My greatest griefs faded to nothing the moment I opened the window onto my inner self and lost myself in watching.

I never tried to be anything other than a dreamer. I never paid any attention to people who told me to go out and live. I belonged always to whatever was far from me and to whatever I could never be. Anything that was not mine, however base, always seemed to me to be full of poetry. The only thing I ever loved was pure nothingness. I only ever desired what was beyond my imaginings. All I ever asked of life was that it should pass me by without my even noticing it. Of love I demanded only that it never be anything more than a distant dream. In my own inner landscapes, all of them

---

*The title is in English in the original.

unreal, it was always the far-off that attracted me, and the blurred
outlines of aqueducts, almost lost in the far distance of my dream
landscapes, imposed a dreamy sweetness on other parts of them, a
sweetness that enabled me to love them. My mania for creating a
false world is still with me and will leave me only when I die. I no
longer line up in my desk drawers cotton reels and pawns – with the
occasional bishop and knight thrown in – but I regret not doing so
. . . and instead, like someone in winter, cosily warming themselves
by the fire, I line up in my imagination the ranks of constant, living
characters who inhabit my inner world. For I have a whole world of
friends inside me, each with his or her own real, defined and
imperfect life.

Some go through hard times, others lead bohemian lives,
picturesque and humble. Others are travelling salesmen (dreaming
myself as a travelling salesman was always one of my greatest
ambitions – unfortunately never realized!). Others live in villages
and towns near the frontier of a Portugal I carry within me; they
come to the city where I chance to meet and recognize them,
warmly embracing them. . . And when I'm dreaming all this,
walking up and down in my room, talking out loud, gesticulating
. . . when I dream this and imagine myself meeting them, I'm filled
with happiness, I feel complete, I leap for joy, my eyes shine, I open
my arms to them and feel an immense, inexpressible felicity.

Ah, there is no more painful longing than the longing for things
that never were! What I feel when I think of the past I lived in real
time, when I weep over the corpse of my lost childhood . . . even this
does not compare with the painful, tremulous fervour with which I
weep for the unreality of the humble figures who people my
dreams, even minor characters I recall having glimpsed only once,
by chance, in my false life, as they turned a corner in my imaginary
scenario, entering a door on a street I had walked along during that
dream.

The rage that pure longing is incapable of reviving and
resurrecting the past is never more tearfully vented against the God
who created these impossibilities than when I think that my dream
friends, with whom I have shared so many details of my imagined

life, with whom I have enjoyed so many brilliant conversations in imagined cafés, have never had a space of their own where they could be truly independent of my consciousness of them!

Ah, the dead past that I carry with me and that never was except in me! The flowers in the garden of the small country house that existed only inside me! The vegetable gardens, the orchards and the pine forest of the estate that was only one of my dreams! The imaginary summer resorts, my walks through a countryside that never was! The trees by the side of the road, the country paths, the stones, the peasants passing by . . . all this, which was never more than a dream, is shut away in my memory where it lies aching and I, who spent hours dreaming it all, spend as many hours afterwards remembering having dreamed it and then it is a genuine nostalgia I feel, a real past I weep for, a real life that is dead and that I stare at solemnly as it lies in its coffin.

Then there are the landscapes and the lives that had a real existence outside of me. For example, after spending many hours in the company of certain pictures or lithographs (none of any great artistic merit) that hung on the walls of certain rooms, those pictures became part of my inner reality. The pain I felt then was different, sharper and sadder. Regardless of whether the scene was real or not, I suffered not to be included in the small engraving in a room I never in fact slept in when I was younger, I suffered not to be, at the very least, an additional figure sketched in at the edge of the moonlit wood. It pained me not to be able to imagine myself hidden there, in the wood by the river, in that eternal (albeit ill-drawn) moonlight, watching the man pass in a boat beneath the drooping branches of the willow. I felt hurt by my inability to dream it all. My nostalgia took on other characteristics. My despairing gestures were different. The impossibility that tortured me produced quite a different degree of anguish. If only this could find some meaning in God, some realization suited to the spirit of our desires, where I don't know, perhaps in some sort of vertical time, consubstantiate with the aims of all my longings and daydreams. If only I could have my own personal paradise tailor-made for this purpose. If only I could meet the friends I dreamed, or walk along the streets I created, or wake up to the sounds of cockerels and chickens and the morning noises of the house, the country house I imagined myself in . . . and have all of this even more perfectly arranged by God and placed by him in perfect order to exist purely for my benefit in that precise form, unattainable even in my dreams, lacking only [. . .] awareness of the inner space occupied by those poor realities.

I raise my head from the paper I'm writing on . . . It's still early, just gone midday, and it's Sunday. The sickness of life, the affliction of consciousness, enter my body and trouble me. Why are there not islands for those who feel uncomfortable here, ancient avenues for the lonely to dream in that others cannot find? Having to live and, however feebly, to act; being bruised by the fact that in life there are other people, themselves real. Having to be here writing this, because my soul demands it, and being unable simply to dream it, to express it without words, even without consciousness, through some self I could construct out of music and evanescence, and bring tears to my eyes just to feel that expression of myself, and to feel myself flow, like an enchanted river, past the slow banks of my own self, ever closer to the unconscious and the Distant, with no meaning or direction except God.

201 [515]

The visual lover

It is not my custom to weave any kind of fantastic plot about the figures I amuse myself in contemplating. I just see them and their value lies purely in the fact that I can see them. Anything else I might add would diminish them, because it would diminish what I term their 'visibility'.

Whatever I fantasized about them would from the start inevitably ring false to me; and, whilst dreams please me, I find falseness repugnant. Pure dream delights me, the dream that has no connections, no point of contact with reality. The imperfect dream, with its roots in reality, displeases me or rather it would if I ever bothered with it.

For me humanity is one vast decorative motif, existing through one's eyes and ears and through psychological emotion. I demand nothing more from life than to be a spectator of it. I demand nothing more from myself than to be a spectator of life.

I'm like a being from another existence who passes, endlessly curious, through this one to which I am in every way alien. A sheet of glass stands between it and me. I always try to keep that glass as clean as possible so I can examine this other existence without smudges or smears spoiling my view; but I choose to keep that glass between us.

For any spirit of a scientific bent, seeing more in something than is actually there is actually to see less. What you add in substance, you take away in spirit.

I attribute to this state of mind my distaste for art museums. For me, the museum is the whole of life, in which the painting is always exact and the only possible inexactitude is in the imperfect eye of the beholder. I either try to diminish any imperfection or, if I can't, then simply accept it the way it is since, as with everything, it cannot be other than it is.

202 [467]

The government of the world begins in ourselves. It is not the sincere who govern the world but neither is it the insincere. It is governed by those who manufacture in themselves a real sincerity by artificial and automatic means; that sincerity constitutes their strength and it is that which shines out over the less false sincerity of the others. A marked talent for self-deception is the statesman's foremost quality. Only poets and philosophers have a practical vision of the world since only to them is given the gift of having no illusions. To see clearly is to be unable to act.

203 [480]   *8.4.1931*

The whole desolate day, filled with light, warm clouds, was taken up with the news that there had been a revolution. Whether true or false, such news always fills me with a peculiar unease, a mixture of scorn and physical nausea. It pains my intelligence that someone should think they can alter anything through political agitation. I've always considered violence, of any type, a particularly cock-eyed example of human stupidity. All revolutionaries are stupid as are all reformers, albeit to a lesser degree, because less discomfiting.

Revolutionaries and reformers all make the same mistake. Lacking the power to master and reform their own attitude towards life, which is everything, or their own being, which is almost everything, they escape into wanting to change others and the external world. Every revolutionary, every reformer is an escapee. To fight is proof of one's inability to do battle with oneself. To reform is proof that one is oneself beyond all help.

If a man of real sensitivity and correct reasoning feels concerned about the evil and injustice of the world, he naturally seeks to correct it first where it manifests itself closest to home and that, he will find, is in his own being. The task will take him his whole lifetime.

For us everything lies in our concept of the world; changing our concept of the world means changing our world, that is, the world itself, since it will never be anything other than how we perceive it. The inner sense of justice that allows us to write one beautifully fluent page, the true reformation by which we bring to life our dead sensibilities – these are the truth, our truth, the only truth. All the rest is landscape, picture frames for our feelings, bindings for our thoughts. And that is the case whether the landscape is full of colourful things and people — fields, houses, posters and suits – or a colourless landscape of monotonous souls rising to the surface for a moment to utter clichéd phrases or sketch tired gestures, only to sink back again to the bottom of the fundamental stupidity of all human expression.

Revolution? Change? What I most want, with every particle of my soul, is for the sluggish clouds that fill the sky with grubby lather to be gone; I want to see the blue beginning to show between them, a bright, clear truth, because it is nothing and wants nothing.

204 [456]

Freedom is the possibility of isolation. You are only free if you can withdraw from men and feel no need to seek them out for money, or society, or love, or glory, or even curiosity, for none of these things flourish in silence and solitude. If you cannot live alone, then you were born a slave. Though you may be possessed of every superior quality of spirit and soul, you are still nothing more than a noble slave or an intelligent serf, you are not free. But that is not your tragedy, for the tragedy of being born like that is not yours but Destiny's. Woe betide you, though, if the very weight of life itself makes you a slave. Woe betide you if, having been born free and capable of providing for yourself and leading a separate existence, penury forces you into the company of others. That tragedy is yours alone, which you alone must bear.

To be born free is Man's greatest quality; it is what makes the humble hermit superior to kings, superior even to the gods, who are sufficient unto themselves only by virtue of their power but not by virtue of their disdain for it.

Death is a liberation because to die is to need no one else. The poor slave finds himself prised free from all his pleasures, his griefs, from the uninterrupted life he so desired. The king finds himself free of dominions he had no wish to leave. The women who freely offered their love find themselves free of the conquests they so adore. Those who conquered find themselves free of the victories to which their lives predestined them.

Death ennobles and clothes the poor absurd cadaver in unaccustomed finery. There you have a free man, though admittedly it was not a freedom he sought. There you have a man set free from slavery, though he wept to lose his servitude. A king may be laughable as a man and the only splendid thing about him be his title but, by virtue of that title, he is nonetheless a superior being, just as, however monstrous he may seem, the dead man is superior, because death has set him free.

Weary, I close the shutters on my windows; I exclude the world and for a moment I am free. Tomorrow I will return to being a slave; but now, alone, not needing anyone, fearful lest some voice or presence should disturb me, I have my own small freedom, my moment of exaltation.

In the chair in which I sit, I forget the life that so oppresses me. The only pain I feel is that of having once felt pain.

205 [377]

Anyone reading the earlier part of this book will doubtless have formed the opinion that I'm a dreamer. If so, they're wrong. I don't have enough money to be a dreamer.

The great melancholies, the sadnesses filled with tedium, can exist only in an atmosphere of comfort and sober luxury. Thus Poe's Egaeus sits in his ancient ancestral castle, immersed in long hours of morbid meditation, whilst beyond the door of the great hall ordinary life goes on, invisible major-domos organize the meals and the household chores.

The great dream demands certain social circumstances. One day, captivated by a musical plaintiveness in what I had written, I imagined myself to be another Chateaubriand but brought myself up sharply with the realization that I was neither a viscount nor a Breton. On another occasion when I seemed to notice in my own words a similarity to Rousseau, again it did not take me long to see that I did not have the advantage of being a nobleman or a castellan and, moreover, was neither Swiss nor a vagabond.

But, after all, the universe also exists here in Rua dos Douradores. Even here God ensures the continuing presence of the enigma of life. And that's why, though poor, like the landscape of carts and packing cases, the dreams I manage to extract from amongst the wheels and planks, are what I have and what I'm able to have.

No doubt there are real sunsets elsewhere. But even in this fourth floor room above the city one can ponder on the infinite. An infinite built over warehouses, it's true, but with stars above it . . . These are the thoughts that occur to me standing at my high window watching the slow end of evening, feeling the dissatisfaction of the bourgeois I am not and the sadness of the poet I can never be.

206 [374]

Part 2

In me the habit of dreaming and the ability to dream are primordial. Ever since I was a quiet, solitary child, the circumstances of my life, along perhaps with other obscure hereditary forces that have moulded me from afar and cut me to their own sinister pattern, have made of my spirit a constant flow of daydreams. Everything that I am is bound up in this and even the part of me that seems farthest removed from the dreamer belongs without a doubt to the soul of one who only dreams, a soul raised to its highest level.

As best I can, and purely for the pleasure self-analysis affords me, I would like to put into words all the mental processes that in me are but one thing, a life devoted to dreaming, a soul brought up only to dream.

When, as I almost always do, I look at myself from outside, I recognize that I am entirely unsuited to action, easily perturbed by the need to take steps or make gestures, uneasy when talking to others, with insufficient insight to entertain myself by grappling with spiritual matters and lacking the necessary physical coordination to apply myself to any merely physical work.

It's only natural that I should be like that. It's accepted that all dreamers are like that. Any reality troubles me. Other people's conversation throws me into a state of terrible anguish. The reality of other people's souls is a constant surprise to me. The vast unconscious network that lies behind all actions seems an absurd illusion, with no plausible coherence, nothing.

But if you think that I must therefore be ignorant of other people's complex psychological processes, that I must lack a clear understanding of other people's intimate thoughts and motives, you're mistaken.

For I'm not merely a dreamer, I am exclusively a dreamer. The singlemindedness with which I cultivate the habit of dreaming has given me an extraordinary clarity of inner vision. Not only do I see in frightening and at times disturbing relief the figures and backdrops of my dreams but, just as clearly, I see my abstract ideas, my human feelings – what's left of them – my secret impulses, my psychological attitudes toward myself. I mean that I see my own abstract ideas in me, I see them with real internal vision inhabiting a genuine inner space. And thus the smallest detail of their meanderings is visible to me.

That's how I have come to know myself so completely and, knowing myself completely, I know humanity just as completely. There is no base impulse, no noble instinct that has not flashed upon my soul; I know the gestures that accompany each one. I know evil ideas for what they are, whatever masks of goodness or indifference they put on. I know what it is in ourselves that struggles to delude us. And so I know most of the people I see around me better than they do themselves. I often apply myself to studying them in depth, because that way I can make them mine. I conquer the psyche I analyse, because for me to dream is to possess. And so you see that it is only natural that a dreamer like myself should also possess these powers of analysis.

That's why one of the few things I enjoy reading are plays. Every day I put on plays inside myself and I know all there is to know about drawing up a Mercator projection of the soul. But the truth is I derive little entertainment from this; dramatists constantly make the same gross, vulgar mistakes. I've never found a play yet that satisfied me. Having seen human psychology with the clarity of a lightning flash illuminating every corner at a glance, I find most dramatists' clumsy construction and character analysis painful, and the little I've read in the genre is as displeasing to me as an inkblot on a page in one of my account books.

Things form the very stuff of my dreams; that's why I pay such distracted attention to certain details of the external world.

To give vividness to my dreams I need to know how it is that real landscapes and real-life characters appear so vivid to us. Because the vision of the dreamer is not like that of someone who sees things. In dreaming one does not rest one's gaze equally on the important and unimportant aspects of a real object. The dreamer sees only the important part. The true reality of an object lies only in a part of it; the rest is the heavy tribute it pays to the material world in exchange for its existence in space. Similarly, certain phenomena that have a palpable reality in dreams have no reality in space. A real sunset is imponderable and transitory. A dream sunset is fixed and eternal. The person who can write knows how to see his dreams clearly (for that is what it means), to see life as if in dreams, to see life immaterially, taking photographs of it with the camera of his daydreams, on which the rays of anything boring, utilitarian and circumscribed have no effect, registering only as black on the photographic plate of the spirit.

This attitude, which all my excessive dreaming has only made worse, means that I see only the dream part of reality. My vision of things suppresses in them anything that is of no use to my dream. And thus I live always in dreams, even when I'm living in the real world. To me looking at a sunset within myself or a sunset in the real world are one and the same thing, because I always see in the same way, because my vision is cut to the same pattern.

That's why the idea I have of myself is an idea that to many will seem mistaken. In a way it is. But I dream myself and I select out what is dreamable in me, composing and recomposing myself in every possible way until I fit my own requirements for what I should or should not be. Sometimes the best way to see an object is to destroy it, for it survives, I can't explain how, in its own negation and destruction; that's what I do to large areas of my own being which, once painted out from my portrait of myself, lead to a transfiguration of myself within my own reality.

How can I be so sure that I'm not deceiving myself about these inner processes of illusion? Because the process that draws one aspect of the world or a figure from a dream into a heightened reality, draws with it an emotion or a thought; it therefore divests it of all claims to nobility and purity which, as is almost always the case, it has no right to anyway. You will notice that my objectivity is of the most absolute. I create the absolute object and give absolute qualities to its physical reality. I did not flee from life exactly, in the sense of seeking a softer bed for my soul, I simply changed lives and found in my dreams the same objectivity I found in life. My dreams – which I will deal with elsewhere – exist independently of my will and often shock and wound me. Often what I find inside myself distresses, shames (some persistent shred of humanity in me perhaps – what is shame after all?) and frightens me.

Attentiveness has been replaced in me by uninterrupted daydreaming. I now superimpose on things I have seen, even things seen in dreams, other dreams I carry with me. Once I became sufficiently inattentive to perform well what I referred to as 'seeing as if in dreams', for that inattentiveness was motivated by perpetual daydreaming and by an (again rather inattentive) preoccupation with the course taken by my dreams, I could superimpose what I dream on the dream I see and interweave the reality now stripped of its material reality with the absolutely immaterial.

From this comes my ability to pursue several ideas at once, to observe something and at the same time dream a great diversity of other things; to dream a real sunset over a real river Tagus at the same time as I dream a dreamed morning on some inner Pacific Ocean. The two dreamed things mingle without mixing, without really confusing the different emotional state each one gives rise to. Thus I am like someone watching a lot of people passing by on the street and being simultaneously in each person's soul (which presupposes a complete unity of feeling) and at the same time seeing their bodies (which must of necessity be perceived separately) passing one another in a street of walking legs.

207 [194]

The generation to which I belong was born into a world devoid of certainty for anyone possessed of both an intellect and a heart. The destructive work of previous generations meant that the world into which we were born had no security to offer us as regards religion, no anchor as regards morality, no stability as regards politics.

We were born into a state of anguish, both metaphysical and moral, and of political disquiet. Drunk on external formulae, on the mere processes of reason and science, the preceding generations destroyed the foundations of the Christian faith because their Biblical exegesis, which shifted from the textual to the mythological, reduced the gospels and the earlier hierography of the Jews to a collection of hypothetical myths and legends, to mere literature. Their scientific criticism gradually found out all the mistakes and wild ingenuities of the primitive 'science' of the gospels and, at the same time, the freedom of debate threw open all metaphysical problems including religious questions. Under the influence of a vague theory they called 'positivism', these generations criticized all morality and scrutinized all rules for living. All that remained from this clash of doctrines was uncertainty and the pain of that uncertainty. Naturally, a society so confused in its cultural foundations could not but be a victim, politically, of that confusion; and thus we woke to a world avid for social change that went forward with joy to the conquest of a freedom whose meaning it did not understand and an idea of progress it had never clearly defined.

Whilst our forefathers' crude criticism bequeathed the impossibility of being Christians, it left us bereft of all possibility of contentment. Whilst they bequeathed to us a dissatisfaction with the established moral formulae, they did not bequeath to us an indifference to morality and to rules for living. Whilst they left political problems in a state of uncertainty, they did not leave our spirits indifferent to how these problems might be resolved. Our forefathers destroyed all this with a good conscience because they lived in an era that could still count on fragments of a past solidity.

What they destroyed was the very thing that gave society its strength and allowed them to destroy it without even noticing the cracks in the walls. We inherited the destruction and its consequences.

In modern life the world belongs to the stupid, the insensitive and the disturbed. The right to live and triumph is today earned with the same qualifications one requires to be interned in a madhouse: amorality, hypomania and an incapacity for thought.

208 [192]   *29.3.1930*

I was born at a time when most young people had lost their belief in God for much the same reason that their elders had kept theirs – without knowing why. And so, because the human spirit tends naturally to criticize because it feels rather than because it thinks, most of those young people chose Humanity as a substitute for God. I belong, however, to that species of man that is always on the edge of the thing they belong to, that sees not only the crowd they form a part of but also the great spaces all around. That's why I did not abandon God as wholeheartedly as they did, nor did I ever accept Humanity as a replacement. I considered that God, because unlikely, just might exist and might therefore deserve to be adored, but that Humanity, being a mere biological idea designating nothing more than the human race itself, was no more deserving of adoration than any other animal species. This worship of Humanity, with its rituals of Liberty and Equality, always struck me as being like a revival of the ancient cults, in which animals were gods or the gods bore the heads of animals.

Thus, not knowing how to believe in God and being unable to believe in a herd of animals, I maintained, like others on the sidelines of the crowd, that attitude of distance towards everything, which is commonly called Decadence. Decadence is the total absence of unconsciousness, for unconsciousness is the very foundation of life. If the heart could think it would stop beating.

To someone like myself, and to the few like me who live without knowing they live, what remains except renunciation as a way of life and contemplation as destiny? Ignorant of the meaning of a religious life and unable to discover it through reason, unable to have faith in the abstract concept of man and not even knowing what to do with it, all that remains for us as a justification for having a soul is the aesthetic contemplation of life. And so, insensitive to the solemnity of the world, indifferent to the divine and despising humankind, we gave ourselves vainly over to a purposeless sensationism crossed with a refined form of epicurianism suited to our cerebral nerves.

From science we took only its central precept that everything is subject to laws of fate against which no independent action is possible because all action is merely reaction. We observed that this law fitted in well with that other more ancient law of the divine fatality of things and, like feeble athletes abandoning their training, we gave up the struggle and, with all the scrupulous attention of genuine erudition, we concentrated instead on the book of sensation.

Unable to take anything seriously and believing that we were given no other reality than that of our feelings, we took shelter in them and explored them as if they were great undiscovered lands. And if we work assiduously not just at aesthetic contemplation but at finding expression for its modes and consequences, it is because the prose or poetry we write, stripped of the desire to influence another's perceptions or change someone else's mind, has become rather like someone reading out loud in order to give a heightened objectivity to the subjective pleasure of reading.

We know only too well that every work is doomed to imperfection and that there is no aesthetic contemplation less assured than the aesthetic contemplation of what we ourselves write. But everything is imperfect; there is no sunset, however lovely, that could not be more so, no gentle breeze lulling us to sleep that could not lull us into a still sweeter sleep. Thus, equally contented contemplating mountains or statues, poring over the days as if they were books, above all dreaming everything in order to convert it into something intimately ours, we too will write descriptions and analyses which, once written, will become alien objects that we can enjoy as if they had simply arrived along with the dusk.

This is not the thinking of pessimists like Vigny*, for whom life was a prison in which he wove straw to pass the time. To be a pessimist one has to view life as a tragedy, which is an exaggerated, uncomfortable attitude to take. It's true that we do not have any concept of value that we can place on the work we produce. It's true we produce that work in order to pass the time, but we do so not like the prisoner weaving straw to distract himself from his destiny, but like the little girl embroidering pillowcases to entertain herself and nothing more.

For me life is an inn where I must stay until the carriage from the abyss calls to collect me. I don't know where that carriage will take me because I know nothing. I could consider this inn to be a prison since I'm compelled to stay here; I could consider it a kind of club, because I meet other people here. However, unlike others, I am neither impatient nor sociable. I leave those who shut themselves in their rooms and wait, lying limply on their beds unable to sleep; I leave those who chatter in the living room, from where the cosy sound of music and voices reaches me. I sit at the door and fill my eyes and ears with the colours and sounds of the landscape and slowly, just for myself, I sing vague songs that I compose while I wait.

Night will fall on all of us and the carriage will arrive. I enjoy the breeze given to me and the soul given to me to enjoy it and I ask no more questions, look no further. If what I leave written in the visitors' book is one day read by others and entertains them on their journey, that's fine. If no one reads it or is entertained by it, that's fine too.

---

*Alfred de Vigny (1797–1863), the French Romantic poet and novelist, was the author of *Chatterton* (1835). For him the world was a place of suffering, life a constant process of abnegation, and God (if he existed) a harsh Old Testament deity.

209 [195]

I belong to a generation that inherited a disbelief in the Christian faith and that created within itself a disbelief in all other faiths. Our forefathers still felt an impulse to believe, which they transferred from Christianity onto other forms of illusion. Some were enthusiasts for social equality, others were simply in love with beauty, others put their faith in science and its benefits whilst others, even more Christian than ever, went off to East and West in search of other religions with which they could fill their consciousness of merely living, which seemed hollow otherwise.

We lost all this and were orphaned at birth of all these consolations. Every civilization cleaves to the intimate contours of the religion that represents it: to go after other religions is to lose that first religion and ultimately to lose them all.

We lost both our religion and all others.

We remained each of us abandoned to ourselves, amidst the desolation of merely knowing ourselves to be alive. A boat would seem to be an object whose one purpose is to travel, but its real purpose is not to travel but to reach harbour. We found ourselves on the high seas, with no idea of which port we should be aiming for. Thus we represent a painful version of the argonauts' bold motto: the journey is what matters, not life.

Bereft of illusions, we live on dreams, which are the illusions of those who cannot have illusions. Living off ourselves alone, we diminish ourselves, because the complete man is he who is unaware of himself. Without faith, we have no hope and without hope we do not really have a life. With no idea of the future, we can have no real idea of today, because, for the man of action, today is only a prologue to the future. The fighting spirit was stillborn in us, because we were born with no enthusiasm for the fight.

Some of us stagnated in the foolish conquest of the everyday, contemptible, vulgar beings scrabbling for our daily bread and wanting to get it without working for it, without feeling the effort involved, without the nobility of achievement.

Others, of better stock, abstained from public life, wanting and desiring nothing, and trying to carry to the calvary of oblivion the cross of simply existing. A vain endeavour in men whose consciousness, unlike that of the original carrier of the Cross, lacks any spark of the divine.

Others, busily engaged outside their soul, gave themselves over to the cult of confusion and noise, thinking they were alive because they could be heard, thinking they loved when they merely stumbled against love's outer walls. Life hurt us because we knew that we were alive; death held no terror for us because we had lost all normal notions of death.

But others, the People of the End, the spiritual boundary of the Dead Hour, did not even have the courage to give it all up and seek asylum in themselves. They lived in negation, discontent and desolation. But we lived it all inside ourselves, making not even a single gesture, shut up for as long as we lived within the four walls of our room and within the four walls of our inability to act.

210 [401]

Pride is the emotional certainty of our own greatness. Vanity is the emotional certainty that others perceive it in us, or at least attribute it to us. The two feelings do not necessarily go together nor are they by their nature opposed. They are different yet compatible.

Pride, when it exists alone, without vanity, manifests itself as timidity. A man who believes he is great but is unsure as to whether others will recognize him as such, fears comparing the opinion he holds of himself with the opinion others might have of him.

Vanity, when it exists alone, without pride (something which, though rare, is quite possible) manifests itself as boldness. A man who is sure that others acknowledge his value and courage need fear nothing from them. Physical and moral courage can exist without vanity, boldness cannot. By boldness I mean the confidence to take the initiative. Boldness can exist without any accompanying courage, physical or moral, for these personal qualities are of a different order altogether and not to be compared with boldness.

211 [402]   *23.3.1933*

For most people life is a bore that is over before they realize it, a sad business interspersed by a few happy interludes, rather like the anecdotes told by people watching over the dead in order to pass the still night and complete their vigil. I always found it futile to think of life as a vale of tears: it is a vale of tears but one where people rarely cry. Heine said that every great tragedy was followed by a general blowing of noses. As a Jew, he saw all too clearly the universal nature of humanity.

Life would be unbearable if we were truly conscious of it. Fortunately we are not. We live as unconsciously as animals, in just the same futile, useless way, and if we think about our own death, as one supposes animals do not (though one cannot be sure of that), we do so in such an absent-minded, distracted and round-about way that we can barely be said to think about it at all.

Since that is how we live, there is really no justification for our thinking ourselves superior to animals. We differ from them only in purely external details, in the fact of our speaking and writing, in having an abstract intelligence to distract us from our concrete intelligence, and in our ability to imagine the impossible. All these things, however, are just the chance attributes of our organism. Speaking and writing make no difference to our basic instinct to survive, which is quite unconscious. All our abstract intelligence is good for is constructing systems, or semi-systematic ideas, which for animals is a simple matter of lying in the sun. Even our ability to imagine the impossible may not be a unique talent, for I've seen cats staring at the moon and for all I know they may be wishing for it.

The whole world, the whole of life, is a vast system of unconscious minds operating through individual consciousnesses. Just as an electric current passing through two gases creates a liquid, so if you pass life and the world through two conscious-nesses – that of our concrete being and that of our abstract being – you create a superior unconscious.

Happy the man, then, who does not think, for he grasps through instinct and his own organic destiny what we only grasp via the most circuitous routes and our inorganic, social destiny. Happy the man most like the brute beasts because he effortlessly is what we all struggle to be; because he knows the way home which we find only through the byways of fiction and after much retracing of steps; because, rooted like a tree, he is part of the landscape and therefore part of its beauty and not, like us, a transient myth, a mannequin wearing the bright costumes of vanity and oblivion.

212 [406]

The instinctive persistence of life over and above any intelligence is something that provides matter for some of my most intimate and most constant reflections. The unreal disguise of consciousness serves only to emphasize to me the existence of the undisguised unconscious.

From birth to death man lives enslaved by the same external concept of self as do the animals. He does not live his life, he merely vegetates on a higher, more complex level. He follows norms he neither knows exist nor knows himself to be guided by, and his ideas, his feelings, his actions are all unconscious – not because they lack consciousness but because they lack any consciousness of being conscious.

Occasional hints that they might be deluding themselves – that and only that is what most men experience.

I pursue with my desultory thoughts the ordinary story of ordinary lives. I see how in everything men are slaves to their unconscious temperament, to external circumstances, to impulses to be with people or to be alone that collide in and with that temperament as if it were nothing.

How often I've heard them come out with the one phrase that symbolizes the absurdity, the nothingness, the utter ignorance of their lives. It's the phrase they use to talk of any material pleasure: 'You have to grab it while you can.' Grab it and take it where? what for? why? It would be sad to rouse them from the shadows they inhabit by asking them such questions . . . For there speaks a materialist, because any man who talks like that is, even if only subconsciously, a materialist. What is it he expects to wrench from life and how? Where will he take the pork chops, the red wine and the girlfriend of the moment? To a heaven in which he doesn't even believe? To what earth other than this one which leads inevitably to the slow putrefaction his life has always been? I know of no other phrase more tragically, more utterly revealing of human nature. It's what plants would say if they were conscious of enjoying the sun. It's what animals inferior to man in their ability to express themselves would say of their somnambulant pleasures. And who knows but that I, now, in writing these words with the illusory idea that they might endure, do not also think that the memory of having written them is what I 'grab from life'. Like the useless corpse of the average man being lowered into the common ground, the equally useless corpse of my prose, written while I wait, is lowered into a general oblivion. What right have I to make fun of another man's pork chops, red wine and girlfriend?

Brothers in our ignorance, different vessels for the same blood, different forms of the same inheritance – which of us can deny the other? Deny your wife but not your mother, your father, or your brother.

213 [409]

Reading the newspapers, always painful from an aesthetic point of view, is often morally painful too, even for one with little time for morality.

When one reads of wars and revolutions – there's always one or the other going on – one feels not horror but boredom. It isn't the cruel fate of all those dead and wounded, the sacrifice of those who die as warriors or onlookers, that weighs so heavy on the heart; it's the stupidity that sacrifices lives and possessions to anything so unutterably vain. All ideals and ambitions are just the ravings of gossiping men. No empire merits even the smashing of a child's doll. No ideal merits even the sacrifice of one toy train. What empire is really useful, what ideal really profitable? Everything comes from humanity and humanity is always the same – changeable but incapable of perfection, vacillating but incapable of progress. Given this irredeemable state of affairs, given a life we were given we know not how and will lose we know not when, given the ten thousand chess games that make up the struggles of life lived in society, given the tedium of vainly contemplating what will never be achieved [...] – what can the wise man do but beg for rest, for a respite from having to think about living (as if having to live were not enough), for a small space in the sun and the open air and at least the dream that somewhere beyond the mountains there is peace.

214 [410]

History rejects certainty. There are orderly times when everything is wretched, and disorderly times when everything is sublime. Decadent times can be intellectually fertile, and authoritarian times fertile only in feeblemindedness. Everything intermingles and intersects, and the only truth that exists is in one's imagination.

So many noble ideas fallen onto the dungheap, so many authentic desires lost in the mire!

As far as I can see, in the prolix confusion of uncertain fate all gods and all men are equal. In the obscure fourth floor room where I live, they file past me in a succession of dreams, and they are no more to me than they were to those who believed in them. The fetishes of negroes with frightened, bewildered eyes, the animal-gods of savages from tangled wildernesses, the figures the Egyptians made into symbols, the bright divinities of the Greeks, the upright gods of the Romans, Mithras, lord of the Sun and of all emotion, Jesus lord of consistency and charity, various inter-pretations of that same Christ, new saints, the gods of the new towns, all file past to the slow march (is it a pilgrimage or a funeral?) of error and illusion. On they all march, and behind them come the empty shadows of dreams, which the more inept dreamers believe must have come down to live on earth, simply because they cast shadows. Pathetic concepts with neither soul nor face – Freedom, Humanity, Happiness, a Better Future, Social Science – they trail through the solitude of the dark like leaves dragged along beneath the train of a regal cloak stolen by beggars.

215 [412]

Everything unpleasant that happens to us in life – for example, when we appear ridiculous in the eyes of others, behave badly or lapse from virtue – should be considered merely external events without the power to touch the depths of our soul. We should think of them as the toothache or the corns of life, things that give us some discomfort but which, although ours, are outside us, as things that it is up to our organic existence to deal with, things that only our biology need concern itself with.

Once we fully adopt this attitude which is, in a way, that of the mystics, we are defended not only against the world but also against ourselves, because we have conquered what is other, what is external and contrary to us and therefore our enemy.

That's what Horace meant when he spoke of the just man who remained unmoved even as the world crashed about his ears. The image may be absurd, but the truth of its meaning is indisputable. Even if what we pretend to be – because the real we and the pretended we coexist – collapses around us, we must remain unmoved, not because we are just, but because we are ourselves and being ourselves means having nothing to do with those external things collapsing about us even if in falling they destroy what we are for them.

For the best of us, life should be a dream that eschews all comparisons.

216 [413]

Direct experience is the subterfuge, the hiding place of those devoid of imagination.

Reading about the risks taken by a hunter of tigers I experience all the risks worth taking, except the risk itself, which was worth so little that it has passed out of existence.

Men of action are the unwitting slaves of men of the intellect. Things only acquire value once they are interpreted. Some men, then, create things in order that others, by giving them meaning, make them live. To narrate is to create, whilst to live is merely to be lived.

217 [414]

To subordinate oneself to nothing – be it another human being, someone we love, or an idea – to maintain that aloof independence that consists in not believing in the truth nor, were such a thing to exist, in the usefulness of knowing it: that, it seems to me, is the proper condition of the intellectual life of thinkers. To belong to something – that's banal. Creed, ideal, wife or profession: nothing but prison cells and shackles. To be is to be free. Even ambition is a burden if it is based only on futile pride and passion; we would not feel so proud of it if we realized that it is just the string we're tugged along by. No, no ties, even to ourselves! As free from ourselves as we are from others, contemplatives without ecstasy, thinkers without conclusions, the liberated slaves of God, we will live out the brief interlude that the absentmindedness of our executioners commutes into a temporary stay of execution. Tomorrow we face the guillotine or, if not tomorrow, then the day after. Let us spend this respite before the end walking in the sun, wilfully disregarding all aims and pursuits. The sun will burnish our smooth brows and the breeze bring coolness to he who abandons all hope.

I throw the pen down and, without my picking it up again, it rolls back down the slope of the desk on which I write.

All this came to me in a rush and my happiness manifests itself in this gesture of an anger I do not feel.

218 [416]   *25.7.1930*

We never love anyone. We love only our idea of what someone is like. We love an idea of our own; in short, it is ourselves that we love.

This is true of every kind of love. In sexual love we seek our own pleasure through the intermediary of another's body. In non-sexual love, we seek our own pleasure through the intermediary of an idea we have. The onanist may be an abject creature but in truth he is the logical expression of the lover. He is the only one who neither disguises nor deludes himself.

Relations between one soul and another, expressed through such uncertain, divergent things as words exchanged and gestures made, are of a strange complexity. The very way in which we come to know each other is a form of unknowing. When two people say 'I love you' (or perhaps think or reciprocate the feeling), each one means by that something different, a different life, even, perhaps, a different colour and aroma in the abstract sum of impressions that constitute the activity of the soul.

I am as lucid today as if I had altogether ceased to exist. My thought is laid bare like a skeleton, divested of the carnal rags of the illusion of communication. And these considerations, which I first shape and then abandon, are born of nothing, of nothing at all, at least not of anything that exists in the pit of my consciousness. Perhaps the disappointment in love that our clerk experienced over the girl he was going out with, perhaps some phrase taken from an account of a love affair that newspapers here reprint from the foreign press, perhaps a vague nausea I carry within me and which I have not managed to expel physically . . .

The commentator on Virgil was wrong. It's perfectly understandable that what we feel above all else should be weariness. To live means not to think.

219 [417]

I never speak out loud of my belief in the happiness of animals, except when I want to use it as a frame to some feeling that supports that supposition. To be happy it is necessary to *know* that one is happy. The only happiness one gets out of enjoying a dreamless sleep is waking up and knowing that one has slept without dreaming. Happiness exists outside itself.

There is no happiness without knowledge. But the knowledge of happiness brings unhappiness, because to know one is happy is to know that one is passing through happiness and is, therefore, soon obliged to leave it behind. In happiness as in everything, knowledge kills. Not to know, however, is not to exist.

Only Hegel's absolute managed, over several pages, to be two things at once. In the feelings or motivating forces of life, not-being and being never become fused or confused; through some process of inverse synthesis the two things remain mutually exclusive.

So what should one do? Isolate the moment as if it were a physical object and be happy now, in the moment in which one feels happiness, without even thinking about what one feels, simply shutting out everything else. Cage up thought in feeling [...]

[...] the bright maternal smile of the bounteous earth, the dense splendour of the dark above [...]

That is what I believe, this afternoon. Tomorrow morning it will be different, because tomorrow morning I will be different. What kind of believer will I be tomorrow? I don't know, because to know that I would need to have been there already. Tomorrow or today not even the eternal God I believe in now will know, because today I'm me and tomorrow he may perhaps never have existed.

220 [419]   *21.6.1934*

Once we believe this world to be merely an illusion and a phantasm, we are then free to consider everything that happens to us as a dream, something that only pretended to exist because we were asleep. And then a subtle and profound indifference towards all life's vexations and disasters is born in us. Those who died simply turned a corner and are out of sight; those who suffer pass before our eyes like a nightmare (if we feel), like an unpleasant daydream (if we think). And our own suffering will be nothing more than that nothingness. In this world we all sleep on our left side and hear in our dreams the oppressive beating of our heart.

Nothing more . . . A little sun, a light breeze, a few trees framing the distance, the desire to be happy, our pain to feel the passing of the days, the knowledge that is never quite complete and the truth always just on the point of being revealed . . . Nothing more, nothing more . . . No, nothing more . . .

221 [420]

The further we advance in life, the more we become convinced of two contradictory truths. The first is that, confronted by the reality of life, all the fictions of literature and art pale into insignificance. Though it's true that the latter afford us a nobler pleasure than life, in fact, they are like dreams in which we experience feelings never felt in life and that conjure up shapes never seen; they are just dreams from which one awakens, not memories or nostalgic longings with which we might later live a second life.

The second is this: every noble soul wishes to live life to the full, to experience everything and every feeling, to know every corner of the earth and, given that this is impossible, life can only be lived to the full subjectively, only lived in its entirety once renounced.

These two truths are mutually irreducible. The wise man will refrain from trying to conflate them and will also refrain from repudiating one or other of them. He will, however, have to choose one and then live with his regret at not having chosen the other, or else reject both, and rise above himself to some personal nirvana.

Happy the man who demands no more from life than what life spontaneously gives him and who guides himself with the instinct of cats who seek the sun when there is sun and, when there is no sun, find what warmth they can. Happy the man who renounces his life in favour of the imagination and finds pleasure in the contemplation of other people's lives, experiencing not the impressions themselves but the external spectacle of those impressions. Happy the man, then, who renounces everything and from whom, therefore, nothing can be taken or subtracted.

The rustic, the reader of novels, the pure ascetic: these three are the truly happy men, because they have all renounced their personality – the first because he lives by instinct, which is impersonal, the second because he lives through his imagination, which is oblivion, and the third because he does not live and, not yet having died, sleeps.

Nothing satisfies me, nothing consoles me, everything – whether or not it has ever existed – satiates me. I neither want my soul nor wish to renounce it. I desire what I do not desire and renounce what I do not have. I can be neither nothing nor everything: I'm just the bridge between what I do not have and what I do not want.

222 [427]   *10.4.1930*

The whole life of the human soul is just a movement in the half-light. We live in a twilight of consciousness never sure about what we are or what we think we are. Even in the best of us there exists some feeling of vanity about something, some error whose dimensions we cannot calculate. We are something that happens in the interval of a play; sometimes, through certain doors, we glimpse what may only be the scenery. The whole world is confused, like voices in the night.

I've just re-read these pages, in which I write with a clarity that will last only as long as they last, and I ask myself: What is this, and what is it for? Who am I when I feel? What dies in me when I am?

Like someone high on a peak trying to make out the lives of those living in the valley, I look down and see myself, along with everything else, as just a blurred, confused landscape.

At times like this, when my soul is plunged into the abyss, even the tiniest detail grieves me as if it were a letter of farewell.

I feel I am always on the eve of an awakening. Beneath a suffocating welter of conclusions I struggle within an outer covering that is me. I would cry out if I thought anyone would hear. But all I feel is a terrible tiredness that shifts from one feeling to another like a succession of clouds, the sort that leave patterns of sunlight and green on the grass of long meadows lying half in shadow.

I'm like someone engaged in a random search for an object no one has yet described to him. We play hide-and-seek alone. Somewhere there is a transcendent reason for all this, some fluid divinity, heard but not seen.

Yes, I re-read these pages representative of empty hours, of minor moments of tranquillity or of illusions, great hopes turned into landscapes, griefs like rooms no one enters, a few voices, a great weariness, the gospel yet to be written.

Everyone is vain about something, and the vanity of each of us consists in our forgetting that there are others with souls like ours. My vanity consists in a few pages, a few paragraphs, certain doubts...

Did I say I re-read these pages? I lied. I daren't re-read them. I can't. What good would it do me? It's some other person there. I no longer understand any of it ...

223 [431]

I don't know why but sometimes I feel touched by a premonition of death... Maybe it's just a vague malaise which, because it does not manifest itself as pain, tends to become spiritualized, or else it's a weariness that calls for a sleep so deep that no amount of sleep could satisfy it; what is certain is that I feel as if at last, after a gradually worsening illness, I had let my feeble hands slip without violence or regret from the bedspread on which they rested.

I wonder then what is this thing we call death. I don't mean the mystery of death, which I cannot penetrate, but the physical sensation of ceasing to live. Humanity is, albeit hesitantly, afraid of death; the average man comes off lightly, for the average man, when sick or old, rarely casts a horrified glance into the abyss that he finds within the void. That is merely a lack of imagination as it is in someone who imagines death as being like sleep. How can it be if death does not in the least resemble sleep? The essential feature of sleep is that one wakes from it whereas, at least as far as we know, one never wakes from death. And if death is like sleep we should have some notion of waking from it. This is not, however, what the average man imagines: he imagines death as a sleep from which one does not wake, which is quite meaningless. What I say is that death is not like sleep, because in sleep one is alive but sleeping; I don't know how anyone can compare death to anything, because one cannot experience death or anything even remotely comparable to it.

When I see a dead person, death seems to me like a departure. The corpse looks like a suit someone has left behind. The person has departed and had no need to take with him the one suit he had put on.

224 [430]   *5.2.1932*

My head and the whole universe ache. By some spiritual reflex, physical aches and pains, more obvious than moral ones, unleash tragedies they themselves do not contain. They express an impatience with everything, everything, including the whole universe down to the very last star.

I never take communion, I never have. Neither, I suppose, will I ever be able to partake of that bastardized concept according to which we are, as souls, consequences of a material thing called the brain that exists from birth inside another material thing called the cranium. I cannot be a materialist, which is, I believe, what that concept implies, because I cannot establish a clear link – a visual link I mean – between a visible mass of grey (or any other colour) matter, and the 'I' which, from behind my eyes, sees the skies and ponders them and imagines other non-existent skies. But, even though I could never fall into the trap of supposing that one thing is the same as another simply because the two things exist in the same place, like a wall and my shadow falling on it, or of assuming that a relationship between the soul and the brain is any more logical than a relationship between me, on my journey to work, and the vehicle in which I travel, I still believe there is an intimate relationship between what is pure spirit in us and what is body and that this can give rise to disputes between them. These disputes are like those in which the more vulgar of two parties starts pestering the less vulgar one.

My head aches today, an ache originating perhaps in my stomach. But the ache, once suggested by my stomach to my head, will interrupt any meditations going on behind the fact of my having a brain. If someone covers my eyes, he may temporarily prevent me seeing but he does not blind me. And yet now, because my head aches, I find the present monotonous and absurd spectacle of the world outside me so completely lacking in value or nobility that I can scarcely conceive of it as being the world. My head aches which means that I am conscious of an offence against me on the part of the material world and because, like all offences, it upsets me, I feel predisposed to being bad-tempered with everyone, including the person nearest me even though it was not he who offended me.

My one desire is to die, at least temporarily, but this, as I said, is only because I have a headache. In this moment I suddenly think how much more nobly one of the great prose writers would put all this. Phrase by phrase, he would unwrap the anonymous pain of the world; inspired paragraphs would appear before his eyes that would conjure up all earthly human dramas and, out of the pounding of his fevered temples, he would construct a whole metaphysics of misfortune. I, however, lack all stylistic nobility. My head aches because it does. The universe hurts me because my head does. But the universe that really hurts me is not the real one, which exists because it does not know I exist, but my very own universe, which, if I run my hands through my hair, seems to make me feel that each hair on my head suffers only in order to make me suffer.

225 [432]   23.5.1932

I don't know what time is. I don't know what, if any, is the truest way of measuring it. I know that the way the clock measures time is false: it divides time spatially, from the outside. I know that the time kept by the emotions is false too: they divide not time but the sensation of time. The time of dreams is also wrong; in dreams we brush past time, sometimes slowly, sometimes fast, and what we experience is either fast or slow according to some peculiarity in the way it flows, the nature of which I do not understand.

Sometimes I think everything is false and that time is just a frame used to surround anything foreign to itself. In my memories of my past life, time is ordered on absurd planes and levels, so that I am younger in one episode of my life as a solemn fifteen-year-old than in another as a baby sitting surrounded by my toys.

If I think about these things my consciousness grows tangled. I sense an error in it all; I don't know, however, where that error lies. It's as if I were watching some kind of magic trick and, because I recognize it's a trick, I'm aware of being deceived but I can't work out the technique or mechanics of the deceit.

Then I'm invaded by thoughts which, though absurd, I can't totally reject. I wonder if a man meditating slowly inside a fast-moving car is moving fast or slowly. I wonder if a suicide hurling himself into the sea and someone merely slipping on the esplanade actually fall at the same speed. I wonder if three actions taking place at the same time – my smoking a cigarette, writing this paragraph and thinking these obscure thoughts – are truly synchronous.

One can imagine that of two wheels turning on the same axle there will always be one ahead of the other, even if only by a fraction of a millimetre. A microscope would exaggerate that dislocation to the point of making it unbelievable, impossible were it not real. And why shouldn't the microscope prove truer than our feeble eyesight? Are these just futile thoughts? Of course they are. Are they just the illusions of thought? They are. What is this thing then that measures us without measure and kills us even though it does not itself exist? It is at moments like these, when I'm not even sure that time exists, that I experience time like a person, and then I simply feel like going to sleep.

226 [231]

If some day I should happen to have a secure life and all the time and opportunity in the world to write and publish, I know that I will be nostalgic for this uncertain life in which I scarcely write at all and publish nothing. I will feel nostalgic not only because this ordinary life is over and I will never have it again, but because there is in every kind of life a particular quality and a peculiar pleasure and when we move on to another life, even if it is a better one, that peculiar pleasure is dimmed, that particular quality impoverished, they cease to exist and one feels their loss.

If one day I manage to carry the cross of my intentions to the ultimate calvary, I know that I will find another calvary within and will feel nostalgia for the days when I was futile, unpolished and imperfect. I will be in some way diminished.

I feel drowsy. I spent a boring day engaged on a particularly absurd task in an almost deserted office. Two of the staff are off sick and the others are simply not in today. I'm alone apart from the office boy who is far away at the opposite end of the room. I feel nostalgia for the possibility of one day feeling nostalgia, regardless of how absurd that nostalgia may seem.

I almost pray to the gods to let me stay here, as if locked up in a safe, defended from both life's bitterness and its joys.

227 [84] _   _31.3.34_

It's been such a long time since I last wrote anything! During those days lived centuries of hesitant renunciation. I stagnated like a deserted lake in a non-existent landscape.

During that time the diverse monotony of days, the ever varying succession of unvarying hours, in short, life, flowed over me, flowed pleasantly over me. I would have felt its flow no differently had I been asleep. I stagnated like a non-existent lake in a deserted landscape.

I often fail to recognize myself, a frequent occurrence amongst those who know themselves . . . I observe myself in the various disguises in which I live. Of the things that change I retain only what stays the same, of the things one does only what is worthless.

Far off in me, as if I were engaged on an inward journey, I remember the varied monotony of that house in the provinces . . . That's where I spent my childhood but, even if I wanted to, I couldn't say if my life was more or less happy than it is today. The person who lived there was not me but another: they are different lives, diverse, not comparable. The same monotonies that seem similar from the outside were doubtless different from within. They were not two monotonies but two lives.

But why do I remember?

Out of weariness. To remember is restful because it does not involve action. How often, to obtain a deeper sense of repose, I remember what never was . . .

So completely have I become a fiction of myself that the minute any natural feeling (should I experience such a thing) is born, it becomes at once an imagined feeling – memory becomes dream, dream a forgetting of dreams, self-knowledge a lack of self-reflection.

I have so completely divested myself of my own being that to exist is to clothe myself. Only disguised am I myself. And all around me, as they fade, unknown sunsets wash with gold landscapes I will never see.

228 [23]

Omar Khayyám

Omar had a personality whilst I, fortunately or unfortunately, have none. What I am one moment, I cease to be the next; whatever I was one day, I've forgotten by the following day. Someone, like Omar, who is who he is, lives in one world only, which is the external world; someone, like me, who is not who he is, lives not only in the external world but in a continually evolving and diverse inner world. Even if he wanted to, he could not have the same philosophy as Omar. Thus, without really wanting to, I carry within me, as if they were souls, the very philosophies I criticize; Omar could reject them all, for they were external to him; I cannot reject them because they are me.

229 [22]

Once, I found a passage of mine written in French some fifteen years ago. I've never been to France and never had close contact with the French, and since I never practised the language I could not, therefore, be said to have become unpractised in it. Today I read as much French as ever. I'm older, more experienced; I should have progressed. And yet that passage from my far-off past has a sureness of touch in its use of French that I do not have today; the style has a fluidity I could not now reproduce in that language; there are whole paragraphs, whole sentences and turns of phrase that demonstrate a fluency I have lost without even knowing I had it. How can one explain this? Whose place have I usurped within myself?

I know it's easy enough to come up with a theory of the fluidity of things and souls, to understand that we are an inner flow of life, to imagine that we are many, that we merely pass through ourselves, that we have been many people ... But there's something else going on here which is not the mere flowing of the personality between its own banks: there is here the absolute other, an alien being that was mine. That I should lose, as I grow older, imagination, emotion, a certain type of intelligence, a way of feeling, all that, whilst painful, would not shock me. But what is happening to me when I can read what I wrote as if it were written by a stranger? What shore can I be standing on that allows me to look down and see my own self at the bottom of the sea?

On other occasions I've found passages I can't remember having written, which is not so surprising, but to be unable to remember even having been capable of writing something, that terrifies me. Certain phrases belong to another way of thinking altogether. It's as if I had found an old portrait, clearly of myself, yet showing someone of a different stature, with unrecognizable features that are still indisputably, frighteningly mine.

230 [21]

Everything about me is fading away. My whole life, my memories, my imagination and its contents, my personality, it's all fading away. I continually feel that I was someone else, that I felt and thought as another. I am present at a play with different scenery and the drama I watch is me.

Sometimes amidst the accumulated banality of my literary work stored randomly in various desk drawers, I come across things I wrote ten or even fifteen or more years ago. And many of them seem to me to have been written by a stranger; I don't recognize myself in them. Someone wrote them and it was me. It was me who felt them, but in another life from which I have now awoken as if from another's dream.

I often find things written by me when I was still very young, passages I wrote when I was seventeen or twenty years old. And some of them have a power of expression that I do not remember having at that age. Certain phrases, certain sentences written when I was barely out of adolescence, seem the product of who I am now, educated by the passing years and by experience. I realize that I am the same as I was. And, having often thought that to get to where I am now I must have progressed a lot from what I was, I wonder in what that progress consists if I was the same then as I am now.

There's a mystery in this that undermines and oppresses me.

Only a few days ago I came across a short text written years ago, which really shook me. I know perfectly well that my (relative) scrupulousness about language dates from only a few years back, yet I found in a drawer a piece I had written long before, which was remarkable for this same linguistic scrupulousness. I genuinely could not understand that past self. How is it that I have advanced only to become what I already was? How could I know myself today when I did not yesterday? And everything becomes lost in a labyrinth in which I lose myself.

I let my thoughts drift and feel convinced that what I'm writing now I have already written. I remember and I ask the part of me that pretends to be me if there is not in the Platonic view of the senses, another more oblique recollection, another memory of a previous life that is in fact this life ...

Dear God, who is this person I attend on? How many people am I? Who is me? What is this gap that exists between me and myself?

231 [19]   *25.4.1930*

Today, in a break from feeling, I was meditating on the form of prose I use, in short, on how I write. Like many other people, I had the perverse desire to establish a system and a norm, even though up till now I've always written without the need for any such norm or system; in that, too, I'm no different from anyone else.

However, when I was analysing myself this afternoon, I discovered that my stylistic system rests on two principles and, following in the footsteps of the classical authors, I at once made of those two principles the general foundations of all style: first, to say what one feels exactly as one feels it – clearly, if it is clear; obscurely, if it is obscure; and confusedly, if it is confused; secondly, to understand that grammar is a tool not a law.

Let's suppose that I see before me a rather boyish young girl. An ordinary person would say of her: 'That girl looks like a boy.' Another ordinary person, more conscious of the difference between speaking and saying, would put it differently: 'That girl is a boy.' Another, equally aware of the rules of expression, but more informed by a love of brevity, would say: 'He's a boy.' I, on the other hand, would say: 'She's a boy,' thus violating the most elementary of grammatical rules that demands agreement of gender between personal pronoun and noun. And I would be right; I would have spoken absolutely, photographically, stepping outside of all vulgar norms and beyond the commonplace. I will not merely have uttered words: I will have spoken.

Grammar, in defining usage, makes divisions which are sometimes legitimate, sometimes false. For example, it divides verbs into transitive and intransitive; however, someone who understands what is involved in speaking, often has to make a transitive verb intransitive, or vice versa, if he is to convey exactly what he feels, and not, like most human animals, merely to glimpse it obscurely. If I wanted to talk about my simple existence, I would say: 'I exist.' If I wanted to talk about my existence as a separate soul, I would say: 'I am me.' But if I wanted to talk about my existence as an entity that both directs and forms itself, that exercises within itself the divine function of self-creation, I would have to invent a transitive form and say, triumphantly and ungrammatically supreme, 'I exist me.' I would have expressed a whole philosophy in three small words. Isn't that preferable to taking forty sentences to say nothing? What more can one ask of philosophy and language?

Only those who are unable to think what they feel obey grammatical rules. Someone who knows how to express himself can use those rules as he pleases. There's a story they tell of

Sigismund*, King of Rome, who, having made a grammatical mistake in a public speech, said to the person who pointed this out to him: 'I am King of Rome and therefore above grammar.' And history tells that he was known thereafter as Sigismund 'supra-grammaticam'. What a marvellous symbol! Anyone who knows how to say what he wants to say is, in his own way, King of Rome. Not a bad title and the only way to achieve it is to 'exist oneself'.

232 [15]

I enjoy using words. Or rather: I enjoy making words work. For me words are tangible bodies, visible sirens, sensualities made flesh. Perhaps because real sensuality has no interest for me whatsoever – not even in thoughts or dreams – desire has become transmuted into the part of me that creates verbal rhythms or hears them in other people's speech. I tremble if I hear someone speak well. Certain pages in Fialho† or in Chateaubriand make life tingle in my veins, make me quietly, tremulously mad with an unattainable pleasure already mine. Moreover, some pages by Vieira, in all the cold perfection of his syntactic engineering, make me shiver like a branch in the wind, in the passive delirium of something set in motion.

Like all great lovers, I enjoy the pleasure of losing myself, that pleasure in which one suffers wholeheartedly the delights of surrender. And that's why I often write without even wanting to think, in an externalized daydream, letting the words caress me as if I were a little girl sitting on their lap. They're just meaningless sentences, flowing languidly with the fluidity of water that forgets itself as a stream does in the waves that mingle and fade, constantly

---

*Presumably a reference to Sigismund, Holy Roman Emperor (1411–1437).

†José Valentim Fialho de Almeida (1857–1911) was a Portuguese writer of short stories, much influenced by naturalism and the progressive ideas of his time.

reborn, following endlessly one on the other. That's how ideas and images, tremulous with expression, pass through me like a rustling procession of faded silks amongst which a sliver of an idea flickers, mottled and indistinct in the moonlight.

Though I weep for nothing that life might bring or take away from me, certain pages of prose can reduce me to tears. I remember, as if it were yesterday, the night on which I picked up an anthology and read for the first time Vieira's famous passage on King Solomon. 'Solomon built a palace . . .' I read on to the end, trembling and confused, then burst into joyful tears that no real happiness could have provoked, tears that no sadness in my life will ever provoke. The hieratic rhythm of our clear, majestic language, the expression of ideas in words that flowed as inevitably as water down a hillside, that vocalic thrill by which every sound takes on its ideal colour: all this intoxicated me as instinctively as some great political passion. And, as I said, I wept; I still cry when I remember it today. It isn't nostalgia for my childhood, for which I feel no nostalgia: it's nostalgia for the emotion of that moment, it's the pain of never again being able to read for the first time that great symphonic certainty.

I have no political or social sense. In a way, though, I do have a highly developed patriotic sense. My fatherland is the Portuguese language. It wouldn't grieve me if someone invaded and took over Portugal as long as they didn't bother me personally. What I hate, with all the hatred I can muster, is not the person who writes bad Portuguese, or who does not know his grammar, or who writes using the new simplified orthography; what I hate, as if it were an actual person, is the poorly written page of Portuguese itself; what I hate, as if it were someone who deserved a beating, is the bad grammar itself; what I hate, as I hate a gob of spit independently of its perpetrator, is modern orthography with its preference for 'i' over 'y'.*

---

*Pessoa respected the etymological orthography of Portuguese and would thus write 'rhythmos', 'mystico', etc., rather than 'ritmo' and 'místico', as recommended by the orthographical reforms made in his lifetime.

For orthography is just as much a living thing as we are. A word is complete when seen and heard. And the pomp of the Graeco-Roman transliteration clothes it for me in the true royal mantle that makes it our lady and our queen.

233 [52]

Random diary

Every day the material world mistreats me. My sensibility is like a flame in the wind. I walk down a road and I see in the faces of the passers-by, not their real expressions, but the expressions they would wear if they knew about my life and how I am, if the ridiculous, timid abnormality of my soul were made transparent in my gestures and in my face. In the eyes that avoid mine I suspect a mockery I find only natural, aimed at the inelegant exception I represent in a world that takes pleasure in things and in activity and, in the depths of these passing physiognomies, I imagine and interpose an awareness of the timid nature of my life that sparks off guffaws of laughter. After thinking this, I try in vain to convince myself that I alone am the source of this idea of other people's mockery and mild opprobrium. But once objectified in others, I can no longer reclaim the image of myself as a figure of fun. I feel myself grow suddenly vague and hesitant in a hothouse rife with ridicule and animosity. From the depths of their soul, everyone points a finger at me. Everyone who passes stones me with merry insolence. I walk amongst enemy ghosts that my sick imagination has conjured up and planted inside real people. Everything jabs and jeers at me. And sometimes, in the middle of the road – unobserved, after all – I stop and hesitate, seeking a sudden new dimension, a door onto the interior of space, onto the other side of space, where without delay I might flee my awareness of other people, my too objective intuition of the reality of other people's living souls.

Is it that my habit of placing myself in the souls of other people

makes me see myself as others see or would see me if they noticed .
my presence there? It is. And once I've perceived what they would
feel about me if they knew me, it is as if they were feeling and
expressing it at that very moment. It is a torture to me to live with
other people. Then there are those who live inside me. Even when
removed from life, I'm forced to live with them. Alone, I am
hemmed in by multitudes. I have nowhere to flee to, unless I were
to flee myself.

Ah, tall twilight mountains, narrow moonlit streets, if only I
enjoyed your lack of awareness of the [. . .] your spiritual vision of
the material world, free of preconceptions, devoid of sensibility,
with no room for feelings or thoughts or disquiet! Trees, never
anything more than trees, with your green leaves so pleasant to the
eyes, you are so indifferent to my cares and griefs, so consoling to
my anguish because you lack eyes to see it and a soul to look
through those eyes to misunderstand and mock! Stones on the
road, broken tree stumps, the mere anonymous soil of the earth,
your insensitivity to my soul is like a sisterly caress, a balm to me . . .
[. . .] beneath the sun or beneath the moon of the Earth, my
mother, so much more tenderly maternal than my own human
mother, because you cannot criticize me, because you do not have a
soul with which unwittingly to analyse me, nor can you throw me
rapid glances that provoke thoughts about me you would not
confess even to yourself. Vast sea, my clamorous childhood
companion, you bring me peace and cradle me because you have no
human voice and will not one day whisper into other human ears of
my weaknesses and imperfections. Great sky, blue sky, so close to
the mystery of the angels [. . .] you do not look at me with envious
eyes, and when you pin the sun on your breast you do not do so to
attract me nor [. . .] nor don a mask of stars in order to make fun of
me . . . Immense peace of nature, so maternal in your utter
ignorance of me; distant quiet [. . .] so fraternal in your utter
inability ever to know me . . . I would like to pray to your oneness
and your calm, as an expression of the joy that comes with being
able to love without suspicion or doubt; I would like to give ears to
your not-hearing, eyes to your sublime [. . .] and to be seen and

heard by you through those imagined eyes and ears, glad to be present at your Nothingness, attentive to what is distant, as if to a definitive death, clinging to no hopes of any other life beyond a God, beyond the possibility of growing voluptuously old and beyond the spiritual nature of all matter.

234 [492]

The outside world exists like an actor on a stage: it's there but it's pretending to be something else.

235 [438]   29.11.1931

If there is one thing life gives us, apart from life itself, and for which we must thank the gods, it is the gift of not knowing ourselves: of not knowing ourselves and of not knowing one another. The human soul is an abyss of viscous darkness, a well whose depths are rarely plumbed from the surface of the world. No one would love themselves if they really knew themselves and thus, without vanity, which is the life blood of the spirit, our soul would die of anaemia. No one knows anyone else and it's just as well, for if we did, be they mother, wife or son, we would find lurking in each of them our deep, metaphysical enemy.

The only reason we get on together is that we know nothing about one another. What would happen to all those happy couples if they could see into each other's soul, if they could understand each other, as the romantics say, unaware of the danger (albeit futile) in their words? Every married couple in the world is a mismatch because each person harbours, in the secret part of the soul that belongs to the Devil, the subtle image of the man they desire but who is not their husband, the nubile figure of the sublime woman their wife never was. The happiest are unaware of these frustrated inner longings; the less happy are neither aware nor entirely unaware of them, and only the occasional clumsy impulse, a roughness in the way they treat the other, evokes, on the casual surface of gestures and words, the hidden Demon, the old Eve, the Knight or the Sylph.

The life one lives is one long misunderstanding, a happy medium between a greatness that does not exist and a happiness that cannot exist. We are content because, even when thinking or feeling, we are capable of not believing in the existence of the soul. In the masked ball that is our life, we're content to put on the lovely clothes that are, after all, what matters in the dance. We are the slaves of lights and colours, we launch ourselves into the dance as if it were truth itself, and – unless we are left alone and do not dance – we have no knowledge of the vast and lofty cold of the night outside, of the mortal body beneath the rags that outlive it, of everything which, when alone, we believe to be essentially us, but in the end is just a personal parody of the truth of what we imagine ourselves to be.

Everything we do or say, everything we think or feel, wears the same mask and the same fancy dress. However many layers of clothing we take off, we are never left naked, for nakedness is a phenomenon of the soul and has nothing to do with taking off one's clothes. Thus, dressed in body and soul, with our multiple outfits clinging to us as sleek as feathers, we live out the brief time the gods give us to enjoy ourselves happily or unhappily (or ignorant of quite what our feelings are), like children playing earnest games.

Someone, more free or accursed than the rest of us, suddenly sees (though even he only sees it rarely) that everything we are is what we are not, that we deceive ourselves about what is certain and are wrong about what we judge to be right. And this individual, who for one brief moment sees the universe naked, creates a philosophy or dreams a religion, and the philosophy spreads and the religion grows and those who believe in the philosophy wear it like an invisible garment, and those who believe in the religion put it on like a mask they then forget they are wearing.

And so, ignorant of ourselves and of everyone else, and therefore happily able to get along with one another, we are caught up in the folds of the dance or the conversations in the intervals, human, serious and futile, dancing to the sound of the great orchestra of the stars, beneath the scornful, distant gaze of the organizers of the show.

Only they know that we are the prisoners of the illusion they created for us. But what is the reason for this illusion, and why does this or any illusion exist and why is it that they, as deluded as we are, chose this illusion to give to us? That, of course, even they do not know.

236 [439]

The path up the hill leads to the windmill, but the effort expended in climbing it leads nowhere.

It was one afternoon in autumn when the sky had a cold, dead warmth and clouds smothered the light in blankets of slowness.

Fate gave me only two things: some account books and the gift of dreaming.

237 [444]

Man should not be able to see his own face. Nothing is more terrible than that. Nature gave him the gift of being unable to see either his face or into his own eyes.

He could only see his own face in the waters of rivers and lakes. Even the posture he had to adopt to do so was symbolic. He had to bend down, to lower himself, in order to suffer the ignominy of seeing his own face.

The creator of the mirror poisoned the human soul.

238 [450]

The basest of all human needs is the need to confide, to confess. It is the soul's need to go outside itself.

All right, confess, but confess only what you do not feel. Free your soul from the weight of all your secrets by speaking them out loud; but how much better if you had never uttered the secret you revealed. Lie to yourself rather than utter that truth. To express oneself is always a mistake. Be aware of this and in yourself make self-expression the twin of lying.

239 [452]

Inaction is our consolation for everything, not acting our one great provider. The ability to imagine is all, as long as it does not lead to action. No one can be king of the world except in dreams. And, if we are honest, each of us wants to be king of the world.

Not to be, but to think, that is the true throne. Not to want, but to desire, that is the crown. Whatever we renounce we preserve intact in our dreams.

240 [453]

Maxims

The possession of definite, firm opinions, instincts, passions and a fixed, recognizable character, all this contributes to the horror of making of our soul a fact, of making it material and external. Living is a sweet, fluid state of ignorance about all things and about oneself (it is the only way of life guaranteed to suit and bring comfort to the sage).

The ability constantly to interpose oneself between self and other things shows the highest degree of knowledge and prudence.

Our personality should be impenetrable even to ourselves: that's why our duty should be always to dream and to include ourselves in our dreams so that it is impossible for us to hold any opinions about ourselves.

And we should especially avoid the invasion of our personality by others. Any interest others take in us is an unparalleled indelicacy. The only thing that prevents the everyday greeting of 'How are you?' from being an unforgivable insult is the fact that in general it is utterly empty and insincere.

To love is merely to grow tired of being alone: it is therefore both cowardice and a betrayal of ourselves (it is vitally important that we should not love).

To give someone good advice is to show a complete lack of respect for that person's God-given ability to make mistakes. Furthermore, other people's actions should retain the advantage of not being ours. The only possible reason for asking other people's advice is to know, when we subsequently do exactly the contrary of what they told us to do, that we really are ourselves, acting in complete disaccord with all that is other.

241 [455]

The countryside is wherever we are not. There and only there do real shadows and real trees exist.

Life is the hesitation between an exclamation mark and a question mark. After doubt there is a full stop.

The miracle is a sign of God's laziness or rather the laziness we attribute to Him by inventing the miracle.

The Gods are the incarnation of what we can never be.

The weariness of all hypotheses . . .

242 [462]

To think, yes, even to think, is to act. Only in absolute daydreams, where no activity intervenes, where all consciousness of ourselves gets terminally stuck in the mud – only there in that warm, damp state of non-being can one truly abandon all action.

Not wanting to understand, not analysing . . . To observe oneself as one observes nature; to gaze on one's impressions as one would on a field – that is true wisdom.

243 [472]

Omar Khayyám

Khayyám's tedium is not that of someone who is ignorant of what he does, because the truth is that he can do nothing. That is the tedium of those who were born dead and of those who quite legitimately turn to morphine and cocaine. The wise Persian's tedium is deeper and nobler than that. It is the tedium of someone who has clearly thought things through and seen that everything is obscure. It is the tedium of someone who has weighed up all religions and all philosophies and then said with Solomon: 'I saw that everything was vanity and vexation of the spirit' or in the words of another king, or rather emperor, Septimus Severus*, as he bade farewell to power and to the world: 'Omnia fui, nihil expedit . . .' 'I was all things; all was worthless.'

Life, said Tarde†, is the search for the impossible via the useless; that's exactly what Omar Khayyám would have said.

That's where the Persian's reliance on wine comes in. Drink up! Drink up! encapsulates the whole of his practical philosophy. It is

---

*Presumably Lucius Septimus Severus (146–211), Roman emperor 193–211.

†Gabriel Tarde (1843–1904), French philosopher and sociologist.

not joyful drinking in order to feel happier and more oneself. It is not desperate drinking in order to forget and be less oneself. Joy adds to wine both love and action and it is notable that there is not one mention in Omar Khayyám of energy nor a single word about love. Saki, whose graceful figure we only glimpse in the Rubaiyat (and that rarely), is only the 'girl who serves the wine'. The poet is grateful for her slender form but only in the same degree as he is grateful for the slender form of the amphora containing the wine.

Joy speaks out of wine according to Dean Aldrich:*...

Khayyám's philosophy can be reduced then to a gentle epicurism, honed down to contain only a minimal desire for pleasure. It is enough for him to gaze on roses and to drink wine. A light breeze, an aimless, purposeless conversation, a jug of wine and some flowers: it is in that and only that the wise Persian places his greatest desire. Love disturbs and wearies, action dissipates and disappoints, no one truly knows how to know and thinking confuses everything. Better then to put a stop to all our desires and hopes, to our futile attempts to explain the world, or to any foolish ambitions to change or govern it. Everything is nothing, or as a Greek rationalist put it, 'everything has its source in the unreason.'

244 [475]

More than once, whilst out strolling in the evening, the strange presence of things and the way they are organized in the world has often struck my soul with sudden, surprising violence. It's not so much the natural things that affect me, that communicate that feeling so powerfully, it's rather the arrangement of the streets, shop signs, the people talking to one another, their clothes, jobs, newspapers, the intelligence underlying everything. Or rather it's the fact of the very existence of streets, shop signs, jobs, men and

*English humanist and Vice-Chancellor at Oxford University in the seventeenth century.

society, all getting on together, following familiar routes and setting out along new ones.

I look hard at man and I see that he is as unconscious as a cat or a dog; the unconsciousness out of which he speaks and orders his life in society is utterly inferior to that employed by ants and bees in their social life. But then, beyond the existence of organisms, beyond the existence of rigid, intellectual and physical laws, what is revealed to me in a blaze of light is the intelligence that creates and impregnates the world.

Whenever I feel that, the old phrase of a Scholastic, whose name I've forgotten, immediately springs to mind: *Deus est anima brutorum*. God is the soul of the beasts. That was how the author of this marvellous sentence tried to explain the certainty with which instinct guides the lower animals in whom one sees no sign – or at best only a glimmer – of intelligence. But we are all lower animals; speaking and thinking are just new instincts, less accurate than the others because they are so new. And the Scholastic's words, so apt in their beauty, can be expanded to read: God is the soul of everything.

I have never understood how anyone, having once intuited the great fact of this universal timepiece, could deny the watchmaker in whom not even Voltaire could disbelieve. I understand that when one looks at certain apparently mistaken facets of a plan (and it would be necessary to know what the plan was in order to know that these were indeed mistakes) one could attribute to that supreme intelligence some element of imperfection. I understand that, though I don't accept it. I understand too that, seeing the evil that exists in the world, one might feel unable to accept the idea of the infinite goodness of that all-creating intelligence. That too I understand, though again without accepting it. But to deny the existence of that intelligence, of God, strikes me as just one of those foolish whims that so often afflict one part of the intelligence of men who, in every other respect, are quite superior; such as those who can't add up or even (throwing into the arena the intelligence implicit in artistic sensibility) those who have no feeling for music or painting or poetry.

I accept neither the theory of the imperfect watchmaker nor thetheory of the cruel watchmaker. I reject the former because, without knowing the whole plan, we cannot say whether the details of the way in which the world is governed and arranged are the lapses or mistakes that they seem to be. We clearly see a plan in everything; we see some things that seem wrong but we must consider that if there is a reason for everything, there must also be a reason for the things that are apparently wrong. We see the reason but not the plan; if we do not know what the plan is, how can we say that certain things fall outside it? Just as a poet, say, a master of subtle rhythms, may introduce a dissonant line into a poem for reasons of rhythm, that is, for a reason that seems entirely contrary to its nature (and which a more prosaic critic would denounce as wrong), so the Creator may interpose in the majestic flow of his metaphysical rhythms things that our narrow reasoning perceives as mistakes.

Neither, as I said, do I accept the theory of the cruel watchmaker. I agree it's a more difficult argument to answer but only apparently so. We can say that we don't really know what 'bad' means, and cannot therefore state categorically that a thing is good or bad. What is certain is that pain, even if it is for our own good, is in itself bad and is in itself sufficient proof of the existence of evil in the world. One toothache is enough for us to disbelieve in the benevolence of the Creator. Now the essential defect of this argument would seem to lie in our complete ignorance of God's plan, and our equal ignorance of what, as an intelligent being, the Intellectual Infinite might be like. The existence of evil is one thing, the reason for its existence quite another. The distinction is perhaps subtle to the point of sophistry, but it is accurate. We cannot deny the existence of evil, but we can reject the idea that the existence of evil is in itself evil. I recognize that the problem remains, but only because of our own continuing imperfection.

245 [476]

The distinction that revolutionaries draw between the bourgeoisie and the people, between the nobility and the people, or between governors and governed is a crass and grievous error. The only true distinction one can make is between those who adapt or conform to society and those who do not; the rest is literature and bad literature at that. The beggar, were he to adapt to society, could be king tomorrow, but would thereby lose his standing as a beggar. He would have crossed the frontier and lost his nationality.

This thought consoles me here in this pokey office, whose grimy windows look out onto a joyless street. It consoles me to think that I have as brothers the creators of the consciousness of the world – the unruly playwright William Shakespeare, the schoolmaster John Milton, the vagabond Dante Alighieri [. . .] and even, if I'm permitted to mention him, Jesus Christ himself who was so little in this world that some even doubt his historical existence. The others are a different breed altogether – Councillor of State Johann Wolfgang von Goethe, Senator Victor Hugo, heads of state Lenin and Mussolini.

It is we in the shadows, amongst the errand boys and barbers, who constitute humanity.

On one side sit the kings with their prestige, the emperors with their glory, the geniuses with their aura, the saints with their haloes, the leaders of peoples with their power, the prostitutes, the prophets and the rich . . . On the other side sit we – the errand boy from around the corner, the unruly playwright William Shakespeare, the barber who tells stories, the schoolmaster John Milton, the shop assistant, the vagabond Dante Alighieri, those whom death either forgets or consecrates and whom life forgot and never consecrated.

246 [477]   *6.4.1930*

Atmosphere constitutes the soul of things. Each thing has its own mode of expression and that expression comes from without.

Each thing is the intersection of three lines which, together, shape that thing: a quantity of material, the way in which we interpret it and the atmosphere in which it exists. This table at which I'm writing is a piece of wood, it is a table and one of the pieces of furniture in this room. My impression of this table, if I wanted to transcribe it, would have to be made up of various notions: that it is made of wood, that I call it a table and attribute to it certain uses and purposes, and that in it are reflected or inserted the objects in whose presence it acquires its external soul, the things that are imposed on it and that transform it. And the colour it was given, the way that colour has faded, the knots and splits it contains, all of this, you will notice, comes from without and, more than its innate woodenness, these are what give it soul. And the inner kernel of that soul, the being a table, that is, its personality, also comes from without.

I think, therefore, that it is not just a human or a literary mistake to attribute a soul to the things we call inanimate. To be a thing is to be the object of an attribution. It might be wrong to say that a tree feels, that a river runs, that a sunset is poignant or that the calm sea (as blue as the sky it does not contain) smiles (because of the sun above it). But it is equally wrong to attribute beauty to an object, to attribute colour, form, perhaps even being to an object. This sea is salt water. This sunset is just the fading of the sun's light from this particular longitude and latitude. This child playing before me is an intellectual bundle of cells, but he is also a timepiece made up of sub-atomic movements, a strange electrical conglomeration of millions of solar systems in microscopic miniature.

Everything comes from without and even the human soul is perhaps no more than the ray of sunlight shining in and picking out on the floor the dungheap that is the body.

These considerations might contain the seeds of a whole philosophy for anyone strong enough to draw conclusions from them. I'm not that person. Intent but vague thoughts about logical possibilities surface in me and everything fades in the vision of a single golden ray of sun shining on a dungheap like dark, damp, crushed straw on the almost black earth by a stone wall.

That's how I am. When I want to think, I see. When I want to step out of my soul, I stop suddenly, absentmindedly, on the first step of the steep spiral staircase, looking out of this top floor window at the fading sun lighting in tawny gold the diffuse jumble of rooftops.

247 [478]   *6.5.1930*

I always thought of metaphysics as a prolonged form of latent madness. If we knew the truth, we would see it; everything else is just empty systems and vain trappings. We should be content with the incomprehensibility of the universe; the desire to understand makes us less than human, for to be human is to know that one does not understand.

They bring me faith wrapped up like a parcel and borne on someone else's tray. They want me to accept it but not open it. They bring me science, like a knife on a plate, with which I will cut the pages of a book of blank pages. They bring me doubt, like dust inside a box; but why do they bring me the box if all it contains is dust?

I write because I lack knowledge; and I use other people's rotund phrases about Truth depending on the demands of a particular emotion. If it is a clear, irrevocable emotion, I speak of the Gods, and thus frame it in a consciousness of the multiple world. If it is a deep emotion, I speak, naturally, of God and thus fix it in a consciousness of the singleness of the world. If the emotion is a thought, I speak, again naturally, of Fate and thus let it flow by like a river, the slave of its own riverbed.

Sometimes the actual rhythm of the phrase will demand 'the Gods', not 'God'; at others the two syllables of 'the Gods' will simply impose themselves on a phrase and then I verbally change universes; at still other times, in contrast, the needs of an internal rhyme, a shift in rhythm or an emotional shock, will tip the balance and then either polytheism or monotheism will fit itself to the moment and be preferred. The Gods are simply a function of style.

248 [479]   *15.9.1931*

Many people have come up with definitions of man and, generally, they define him by contrast with the animals. That's why in such definitions they often make use of the phrase 'man is a ... animal,' and add the appropriate adjective, or 'man is an animal that ...' followed by an explanation of the kind of animal man is. 'Man is a sick animal,' said Rousseau and in part it's true. 'Man is a rational animal,' says the Church and in part that's true. 'Man is a tool-using animal,' says Carlyle and in part that's true too. But these definitions, and others like them, are always imperfect and onesided. And the reason is very simple: it's not easy to distinguish man from the animals; there's no foolproof criterion by which to do so. Human lives pass by in the same profound unconsciousness as the lives of animals. The same deeprooted laws that rule from without the instincts of the animals rule the intelligence of man, which seems to be nothing more than an instinct in the making, as unconscious as any instinct, and less perfect because as yet unformed.

According to the Greek rationalists: 'Everything has its source in the unreason'. And everything does come from the unreason. Apart from mathematics which has nothing to do with anything except dead numbers and empty formulae and can therefore be perfectly logical, science is nothing but a game played by children in the twilight, a desire to catch hold of the shadows of birds, to fix the shadows of grasses swaying in the wind.

And it's very strange that, though it's by no means easy to find words that truly distinguish man from animals, it's easy to find a way of differentiating the superior man from the common man.

I have never forgotten that phrase of the biologist, Haeckel*, whom I read in the infancy of my intelligence, at that age when one reads scientific publications and arguments against religion. The phrase goes more or less like this: the superior man (a Kant or a Goethe, I think he says) is farther removed from the common man than the common man is from the monkey. I've never forgotten the phrase because it's true. Between myself, of little significance amongst the ranks of thinkers, and a peasant in Loures† there is a greater distance than between that peasant and, I won't say a monkey, but a cat or a dog. None of us, from the cat up, actually leads the life imposed on us or the fate given to us; we all derive from equally obscure origins, we are all shadows of gestures made by someone else, effects made flesh, consequences with feelings. But between me and the peasant there is a qualitative difference, deriving from the existence in me of abstract thought and disinterested emotion; whereas between him and the cat, at the level of the spirit, there is only a difference of degree.

What distinguishes the superior man from the inferior man and from the latter's animal brothers is the simple quality of irony. Irony is the first indication that consciousness has become conscious and it passes through two stages: the stage reached by Socrates when he said 'I only know that I know nothing,' and the stage reached by Sanches‡ when he said 'I do not even know that I know nothing.' The first stage is that point at which we dogmatically doubt ourselves and it's a point that every superior man will reach. The second stage is the point at which we doubt both ourselves and our doubt and, in the brief yet long curve of

---

*Ernst Heinrich Haeckel (1834–1919) was a German biologist and philosopher, and an early proponent of the theory of evolution.

†A small provincial town near Lisbon.

‡Francisco Sanches (1551–1623), Portuguese humanist and philosopher and forerunner of Descartes. His major work was the *Tractatus de multum nobili et prima universali scientia quod nihil scitur*, 1581.

time during which we, as humans, have watched the sun rise and the night fall over the varied surface of the earth, that is a stage very few men have reached.

To know oneself is to err, and the oracle who said 'Know thyself' proposed a task greater than all of Hercules' labours and an enigma even more obscure than that of the Sphinx. To consciously unknow oneself, that is the right path to follow. And to consciously unknow oneself is the active task of irony. I know no greater nor more proper task for the truly great man than the patient, expressive analysis of ways of unknowing ourselves, the conscious registering of the unconsciousness of our consciousnesses, the metaphysics of the autonomous shadows, the poetry of the twilight of disillusion.

But something always eludes us, there is always some analysis that slips our grasp; the truth, albeit false, is always just around the corner. That's what tires one more than life when life grows wearisome, and more than any knowledge of or meditation on life, which are never less than exhausting.

I get up from the chair where, leaning distractedly on the table, I've been amusing myself setting down these rough and ready impressions. I get up, I make my body get up, and go over to the window, high above the rooftops, from where I can see the city settling to sleep in the slow beginnings of silence. The big, bright white moon sadly points out the ragged line of the terraced roofs and its icy light seems to illuminate all the mystery of the world. It seems to reveal everything and that everything is just shadows intermingled with dim light, false intervals, erratically absurd, the incoherent mutterings of the visible world. The absence of any breeze only seems to increase the mystery. I'm sick of abstract thoughts. I will never write a single page that will reveal myself or anything else. The lightest of clouds hovers vaguely above the moon as if it were the moon's hiding place. Like these rooftops, I know nothing. Like all of nature, I have failed.

249 [482]   *18.6.1931*

If I look closely at the lives men lead I can find nothing that differentiates them from the lives of animals. Both men and animals are launched unconsciously into the midst of objects and into the world; both intermittently enjoy themselves; they daily follow the same physical path; neither group ever thinks beyond the thoughts that naturally occur to them nor experiences anything beyond what their lives happen to offer them. A cat lolls about in the sun and goes to sleep. Likewise a man lolls about in life with all its complexities and goes to sleep. Neither of them can free himself from the fate of being exactly what he is. Neither of them tries to escape from beneath the weight of being. The greatest among men love glory but they love it, not as if it meant immortality for themselves, but as an abstract immortality in which they may not even participate.

These thoughts, which I often have, arouse in me a sudden admiration for the kind of individual I instinctively reject. I mean the mystics and ascetics, all those solitary men living in Tibets all over the world, all those Simon Stylites standing on pillars. These men, though admittedly in the most absurd ways, do at least try to free themselves from the law of animals. In fact, however mad their methods, they do go against the law of life that tells them to loll around in the sun and wait unthinkingly for death. Even when they're stuck on top of a pillar, they are seeking something; even when they're locked in a windowless cell, they long for something; even if it means martyrdom and pain, they want what they do not know.

The rest of us, who live animal lives of greater or lesser complexity, cross the stage like extras with no lines to say, content with the vain solemnity of the journey. Dogs and men, cats and heroes, fleas and geniuses, we all play at existence, without even thinking about it (the best of us think only about thinking) beneath the great comforting quiet of the stars. The others – the mystics with all their suffering and sacrifice – feel the magical presence of the mystery in their own body and in their daily lives. They are free because they deny the visible sun; they are made full because they have emptied themselves of the vacuousness of the world.

Even I feel almost mystical when I speak of them but I would be incapable of being more than these words written under the influence of a chance mood. Like all of humanity, I will always belong to a Rua dos Douradores. In verse or prose, I will always be just another employee at his desk. With or without mysticism, I will always be parochial and submissive, the slave of my feelings and of the moment in which I feel them. Beneath the great blue canopy of the silent sky, I will always be a page caught up in some incomprehensible ritual, clothed in life in order to take part in it, and blindly going through the different gestures and steps, poses and mannerisms, until the party or my role in it ends and I can go and eat the fancy food from the great stalls they tell me are set out at the bottom of the garden.

250 [487]   *17.1.1932*

The world belongs to the unfeeling. The essential condition for being a practical man is the absence of any sensitivity. The most important quality in everyday life is that which leads to action, that is, a strong will. Now there are two things that get in the way of action – sensitivity and analytical thought, which is, after all, nothing more than thought plus sensitivity. By its very nature, all action is the projection of the personality onto the external world and since the external world is very largely made up of other human beings, it follows that any such projection of the personality will involve crossing someone else's path and bothering, hurting or trampling on others, depending on how one acts.

An inability to imagine other people's personalities, their pains and joys is, therefore, essential if one is to act. He who sympathizes is lost. The man of action considers the external world as being made up exclusively of inert matter, either inert in itself, like a stone that one either steps over or kicks to the side of the road, or like a human being who, unable to resist the man of action, might just as well be a stone since he too will be stepped over or kicked to one side.

The epitome of the practical man is the strategist, because he combines extreme concentration of action with a sense of self-importance. All life is war, and battle is, therefore, the very synthesis of life. The strategist is a man who plays with life the way a chessplayer plays with chesspieces. What would happen to the strategist if, with each move made, he thought of the darkness he cast on a thousand homes and the pain he caused in three thousand hearts? What would become of the world if we were human? If man really felt, there would be no civilization. Art serves as an outlet for the sensitivity action had to leave behind. Art is the Cinderella who stayed at home because that's how it had to be.

Every man of action is essentially positive and optimistic because those who don't feel are happy. You can tell a man of action because he's never in a bad mood. The man who works despite his bad mood is a subsidiary of action; in life, in life as a whole, he might well be a book-keeper as in my particular case. What he won't be is a ruler of things or men. Leadership requires insensitivity. Only the happy govern because to be sad it is necessary to feel.

My boss Vasques made a deal today which ruined a sick man and his family. Whilst making the deal, he completely forgot the existence of that individual except as a commercial rival. Once the deal was done, his sensitivity flooded back. Afterwards, of course, because had it happened before, the deal would never have been done. 'I feel really sorry for the chap,' he said to me. 'He'll be destitute.' Then, lighting up a cigar, he added: 'Well, if he needs anything from me' – meaning some kind of handout – 'I won't forget that thanks to him I've made a good deal and a few thousand escudos.'

Vasques is not a bandit; he's a man of action. The man who lost the move in this particular game could, in fact, rely on him for help in the future, because Vasques is a generous man.

Vasques is the same as all men of action: captains of industry and commerce, politicians, men of war, religious and social idealists, great poets and artists, beautiful women, spoilt children. The person who feels nothing has the whiphand. The winner is the one who thinks only those thoughts that will bring him victory. The rest, the vague world of humanity in general, amorphous, sensitive, imaginative and fragile, are nothing but the backdrop before which these actors strut until the puppet show is over, the chequered board on which the chesspieces stand until they're put away by the one Great Player, who, deluding himself that he has a partner, never plays against anyone but himself.

251 [493]

The more I contemplate the spectacle of the world and the ebb and flow of change in things, the more deeply am I convinced of the innately fictitious nature of it all, of the false prestige given to the pomp of reality. And in this contemplation, which any reflective person will have experienced at some time or other, the motley parade of costumes and fashions, the complex path of progress and civilizations, the magnificent tangle of empires and cultures, all seem to me like a myth and a fiction, dreamed up amidst shadows and oblivion. But I do not know if the supreme summation of all these aims, vain even when achieved, lies in the joyful renunciation of the Buddha, who, on comprehending the emptiness of it all, woke from his ecstasy saying: 'Now I know everything,' or in the world-weary indifference of the Emperor Severus: 'omnia fui, nihil expedit' – I was all things; all was worthless.

252 [495]

(Chapter on indifference or something like that)*

Any soul worthy of the name wants to live life to the Extreme. To

*The title is in English in the original.

be content with what one is given shows an attitude fit for slaves; only children ask for more; only madmen want to seize more, for every conquest is [. . .]

To live life to the Extreme means to live it to the limit but there are three ways of doing that and it falls to every superior soul to choose one of these ways. Life lived to the Extreme means taking full possession of it, making a Ulyssean journey through every human feeling, through every manifestation of externalized energy. However, at any time in the history of the world, there have never been more than a few who can close their eyes with a weariness that is the sum of all weariness, who have possessed everything in every possible way.

Only a few can make such demands on life and by so doing force her to surrender herself to them body and soul, knowing that they need feel no jealousy because they know they have all her love. But this should doubtless be the desire of every strong and lofty soul. When that soul, however, realizes that what he wants is impossible, that he does not have the strength to conquer every part of Everything, there are two other routes to follow. The first is that of total renunciation, formal and complete abstention, relegating to the sphere of sensibility what cannot be possessed fully in the arena of activity and energy. It is far better not to act at all than to act in vain, fragmentarily, inadequately, like the countless, superfluous and inane majority of men. The second is the path of perfect balance, the search for the Limits of Absolute Proportion, in which the longing for the Extreme passes from the will and the emotions to the intelligence, one's whole ambition becoming not to live life to the full, not to feel life to the full but to impose order on life, to live it in Harmony and intelligent Coordination.

The longing to understand, which, in so many noble souls, takes the place of action, belongs to the sphere of sensibility. Replacing energy with intelligence, breaking the link between will and emotion, stripping of self-interest every manifestation of material life, that, if one can achieve it, is what is worth more than life, so difficult to possess completely and so sad if possessed only partially.

The argonauts said that it was the journey that mattered, not life. We, the argonauts of an ailing sensibility, say that it is not living that matters, but feeling.

253 [497]

Every gesture, however simple, represents a violation of a spiritual secret. Every gesture is a revolutionary act; (an exile perhaps from the true [...] of our aims).

Action is a disease of thought, a cancer of the imagination. To act is to exile oneself. Every action is incomplete and imperfect. The poem that I dream is faultless until I try to write it down. (This is written in the myth of Jesus, for God, when he becomes man, can end only in martyrdom. The supreme dreamer has as his son the supreme sacrifice.)

The broken shadows of leaves, the tremulous song of birds, the outstretched arms of rivers, their cool light trembling in the sun, the greenness, the poppies, and the simplicity of sensation – when I feel all this, I experience a nostalgia for it as if I were not at that moment really feeling it.

Like a cart passing by in the evening, the hours return creaking home through the shadows of my thoughts. If I look up from those thoughts, the spectacle of the world burns my eyes.

To realize a dream it is necessary to forget it, to distract one's attention from it. That's why to realize something is not to realize it. Life is as full of paradoxes as roses are of thorns.

What I would like to create is the apotheosis of a new incoherence that could become the negative constitution of the new anarchy of souls. I have always thought it would be useful to humanity for me to compile a digest of my dreams. That's why I have constantly striven to do so. However, the idea that something I did could prove useful hurt me, silenced me.

I own country estates on the outskirts of life. I spend my absences from the city of my Actions amongst the trees and flowers of my daydreams. Not even the faintest echo of the life led by my gestures reaches my green and pleasant retreats. I sleep my memory as if it were an endless procession marching past. From the chalices of my meditation I drink only the [...] of the palest wine; I drink it with my eyes only, then close them, and life passes me by like a distant candle.

To me sunny days savour of all I do not have. The blue sky and the white clouds, the trees, the flute that does not play there - eclogues interrupted by the trembling of branches ... All this and the silent harp whose strings I lightly brush.

254 [505]

To write is to forget. Literature is the pleasantest way of ignoring life. Music lulls us, the visual arts enliven us, the performing arts (such as dance and drama) entertain us. The first, therefore, removes itself from life in order to make of it a dream; the others, however, do not, some because they use visual and, therefore, vital formulae and others because they live from human life itself.

This is not the case with literature. Literature simulates life. A novel is a history of what never was and a play is a novel without narrative. A poem is the expression of ideas or feelings in a language no one uses since no one speaks in verse.

255 [517]   27.7.1930

Their inability to say what they see or think is a cause of suffering to most people. They say there is nothing more difficult than to define a spiral in words; it's necessary, they say, to describe it in the air, with one's illiterate hands, using gestures, spiralling slowly upwards, to show how that abstract form, peculiar to coiled springs and certain staircases, appears to the eye. But, as long as we remember that to speak means to renew language, we should have no difficulty whatsoever in describing a spiral: it is a circle that rises upwards but never closes upon itself. I know perfectly well that most people would not dare to define it thus, because they imagine that to define something one should say what other people want, and not what one needs to say in order to produce a definition. I would go further: a spiral is a virtual circle which repeats itself as it rises but never reaches fulfilment. But, no, that's still abstract. If I make it concrete all will become clear: a spiral is a snake, which is not a snake, coiled vertically around nothing.

All literature consists of an effort to make life real. As everyone knows, even when they act as if they did not, in its physical reality, life is absolutely unreal; fields, cities, ideas are all totally fictitious, the children of our complex experience of ourselves. All impressions are uncommunicable unless we make literature of them. Children are naturally literary because they say what they feel and do not speak like someone who feels according to someone else's feelings. Once I heard a child on the point of tears say not 'I feel like crying', which is what an adult, i.e. a fool, would say, but: 'I feel like tears.' And this phrase, absolutely literary, to the point where it would be considered affectation on the lips of a famous poet (were he capable of inventing it), refers resolutely to the hot presence of tears behind eyelids burning with the bitter liquid. 'I feel like tears.' That child produced a fine definition of his particular spiral.

To say things! To know how to say things! To know how to exist through the written voice and the intellectual image! That's what life is about: the rest is just men and women, imagined loves and fictitious vanities, excuses born of poor digestion and forgetting, people squirming beneath the great abstract boulder of a meaningless blue sky, the way insects do when you lift a stone.

256 [518]

Art gives us the illusion of liberation from the sordid business of being. Whilst feeling the slings and arrows of Hamlet, prince of Denmark, we do not feel our own, which are base because they are ours and because they are in themselves base.

Love, sleep, drugs and intoxicants are elementary forms of art or rather elementary forms of producing the same effect as art. But love, sleep and drugs all bring with them their own disappointments. One grows sated or disillusioned with love. We wake from sleep and whilst we slept, we did not live. The price of drugs is the ruin of the very body they were used to stimulate. But there is no disillusion in art because its illusory nature is clear from the start. One does not wake from art because, although we dream it, we are not asleep. There is no tribute or fine to pay for having enjoyed art.

Since in some way it is not ours, we do not have to pay for or repent of the pleasure it offers us.

By art I mean everything that delights us without being ours – a glimpse of a landscape, a smile bestowed on someone else, a sunset, a poem, the objective universe.

To possess something is to lose it. To feel something without possessing it is to keep it, because in that way one extracts its essence.

257 [520]

Literature, which is art married to thought and the immaculate realization of reality, seems to me the goal towards which all human effort should be directed, as long as that effort is truly human and not just a vestige of the animal in us. I believe that to say a thing is to preserve its virtue and remove any terror it may hold. Fields are greener when described than when they are merely their own green selves. If one could describe flowers in words that define them in the air of the imagination, they would have colours that would outlast anything mere cellular life could manage.

To move is to live, to express oneself is to endure. There is nothing real in life that is not more real for being beautifully described. Small-minded critics often point out that such and such a poem, for all its generous rhythms, is saying nothing more profound than: it's a nice day. But it's not easy to say it's a nice day and the nice day itself passes. Our duty, then, is to preserve that nice day in endless, flowering memory and garland with new flowers and new stars the fields and skies of the empty, transient external world.

Everything depends on what we are and, in the diversity of time, how those who come after us perceive the world will depend on how intensely we have imagined it, that is, on how intensely we, fantasy and flesh made one, have truly been it. I do not believe that history, and its great faded panorama, is any more than a constant flow of interpretations, a confused consensus of absent-minded witnesses. We are all novelists and we narrate what we see because, like everything else, seeing is a complex matter.

At this moment I have so many fundamental thoughts, so many truly metaphysical things to say that I feel suddenly tired and decide not to write anymore, not to think anymore, but to let the fever of saying lull me to sleep whilst, with closed eyes, I gently stroke as I would a cat all the things I might have said.

258 [189]

I sometimes think with sad pleasure that if, one day in a future to which I will not belong, these sentences that I write should meet with praise, I will at last have found people who 'understand' me, my own people, a real family to be born into and be loved by. But far from being born into that family, I will have been long dead by then. I will be understood only in effigy, and then affection can no longer compensate the dead person for the lack of love he felt when alive.

One day, perhaps, they will understand that I carried out, as did no other, my inborn duty as interpreter of one particular period of our century; and when they do, they will write that I was misunderstood in my own time; they will write that, sadly, I lived surrounded by coldness and indifference, and that it is a pity it should have been so. And the person writing, in whatever future epoch he or she may live, will be as mystified by my equivalent in that future time as are those around me now. Because men only learn in order to teach their great grandfathers who died long ago. We are only able to teach the real rules of life to those already dead.

On this afternoon in which I write, the rain has finally stopped. A joyfulness in the air chills the skin. The day is ending not in greyness but in pale blue. Even the cobblestones in the streets reflect that vague blueness. It hurts to be alive, but only with a distant ache. To feel is not important. One or two shopwindows light up.

One can see, high up in another window, that the people there have just finished their work. The beggar who brushes by me would be afraid if he knew me.

In the blue, growing slowly less pale and less blue, that is reflected on the buildings, this indefinable hour falls further into evening.

It falls lightly, the end of this certain day, on which those who believe and blunder are caught up in their usual work and who, in the midst of their own pain, enjoy the bliss of unconsciousness. It falls lightly, this wave of dying light, the melancholy of the spent evening, the thin mist that enters my heart. It falls lightly, gently, this indefinite lucid blue pallor of the aquatic evening; light, gentle, sad, it falls on the cold and simple earth. It falls lightly, like invisible ashes, a tortured monotony, an active tedium.

259 [187]

High up in the lonely night an unknown lamp blooms behind a window. Everything else in the city is dark except where feeble rays from the streetlamps hesitantly rise and, here and there, resemble the palest of earthly moonlight. In the black of the night the different colours and tones of the houses are barely distinguishable; only vague, one might almost say abstract, differences, point up the irregularities of the unruly whole.

I am joined by an invisible thread to the anonymous owner of the lamp. It is not often we are both awake at the same time and there is no possible reciprocity in this for, since I am standing at my window in the dark, he cannot see me. It's something else, mine alone, something to do with the feeling of isolation, that participates in the night and the silence, and chooses that lamp as something to hold on to because there is nothing else. It seems as if it is only because that lamp is lit that the night is so dark. It seems that it is only because I am awake, dreaming in the blackness, that it is there, alight.

Perhaps everything exists only because something else does. Nothing just is, everything coexists; perhaps that's right. I feel that I would not exist at this hour (or at least that I would not exist in the exact way that I exist, with my present consciousness of myself, which because it is consciousness and because it is present is, at this moment, entirely me) if that lamp were not lit over there, somewhere, a lighthouse marking nothing, erected on the false privilege lent it by its height. I feel this because I feel nothing. I think this because this is all nothing. Nothing, nothing, just part of the night and the silence and of whatever emptiness, negativity and inconstancy I share with them, the space that exists between me and me, a thing mislaid by some god . . .

Serpent's Tail

'Serpent's Tail is a consistently brave, exciting and almost deliriously diverse publisher. I salute you!' Will Self

'Nobody else has the same commitment to the young, the new, the untested and the unclassifiable' Jonathan Coe

'Serpent's Tail is one of the most unique and important voices in British publishing' Mark Billingham

'Serpent's Tail has made my life more interesting, enjoyable, exciting, easier' Niall Griffiths

'Serpent's Tail is a proper publisher — great writers, great books. If you want a favourite new author you've never heard of before, check their list' Toby Litt

'You're a good deed in a naughty world' Deborah Moggach

'Thanks, Serpent's Tail, for years of challenging reading' Hari Kunzru